Mistletoe and Murder

A Daisy Dalrymple Mystery

CAROLA DUNN

Constable • London

CONSTABLE

First published in the USA by St Martin's Press, 2002

First published in Great Britain in 2011 by Constable

Copyright © Carola Dunn 2002

The moral right of the author has been asserted.

All rights reserved.
No part of this publication may be reproduced, stored in a
retrieval system, or transmitted, in any form, or by any means,
without the prior permission in writing of the publisher, nor be
otherwise circulated in any form of binding or cover other than
that in which it is published and without a similar condition
including this condition being imposed on the subsequent
purchaser.

A CIP catalogue record for this book
is available from the British Library.

ISBN: 978-1-84901-706-0 (paperback)
ISBN: 978-1-84901-842-5 (ebook)

Typeset by TW Typesetting, Plymouth, Devon

Printed and bound in Great Britain by Clays Ltd., St Ives plc

Constable
is an imprint of
Constable & Robinson Ltd
100 Victoria Embankment
London EC4Y 0DY

An Hachette UK Company
www.hachette.co.uk

www.constablerobinson.com

5 7 9 10 8 6

ACKNOWLEDGEMENTS

Readers of my *Smugglers' Summer* (Walker, 1987) will recognize the setting of this story: Brockdene is Cotehele, now a National Trust property open to the public. I have changed the name to protect the innocent, i.e., the actual residents of the house in the 1920s and their descendants. The Norvilles are a purely imaginary family, though I have borrowed genuine family legends, as well as one or two I invented for *Smugglers' Summer*.

That being clarified, my thanks are due to Louis Eynon, National Trust Property Manager at Cotehele, for his invaluable assistance. After changing the name of the house, I felt free to change a few details, but in the main this is an accurate description. I hope it will encourage readers to visit Cotehele, a fascinating experience.

PROLOGUE

Cornwall, 1874

The sailing barge slid smoothly down the Tamar on the ebbing tide. With no need to man the oars, the crew were at leisure to watch the two young gentlemen seated in the bows.

Beyond the obvious similarities – the fair moustaches and whiskers – their faces proclaimed a close relationship. The elder was Lord Norville, heir to the sixth Earl of Westmoor. His country tweed knickerbocker suit contrasted with his companion's military gear. Albert, his youngest brother, had recently returned from India and wore the uniform of a lieutenant in the Duke of Cornwall's Own Regiment.

The brothers' faces revealed more than their shared ancestry. They were obviously quarrelling. Their voices were lowered, so that even the closest of the sailors could not guess the cause of their dispute, but it appeared to be no minor matter.

The yellowing reed beds fell away to either side. The barge began to bob as the river merged into the widening estuary. The captain shouted an order, and the crew moved to raise sail. The Norvilles argued on, oblivious.

A frigate steamed out from the naval dockyard at Devonport.

'You're a fool!' cried Lord Norville at last. 'No good can come of this idiocy. Give me that paper!'

He darted a hand inside Albert's coat and pulled out a paper from the breast pocket. Ripping it in half, he stood up, his arm back to throw it overboard. Albert sprang to his feet and grappled with him, shouting.

His words were drowned by the throb of the frigate's engines. Heedless in her power and arrogance, the ship cut across the sailing barge's path. Her bow wave caught the small boat, tossing it about like an autumn leaf on the wind. Caught off balance, both young men toppled over the side.

By the time the horrified boatmen brought the barge around, the brothers had disappeared without a trace.

CHAPTER 1

London, 1923

'Mother, you simply can't!'

'It's no good being difficult, Daisy.' The Dowager Viscountess's smugness insinuated itself between the crackles on the wire. 'Perhaps you didn't catch what I said – this is a shockingly bad line. I wrote to Lord Westmoor as soon as Violet mentioned that you were going to Brockdene just before Christmas. And I must say I do think I shouldn't have to wait to hear your news from your sister.'

'Sorry, Mother, I've been frightfully busy since Alec and I got home from America. But . . .'

'Westmoor was most obliging. It's arranged already. We shall all join you on the twenty-third.'

'All?'

'I warned Westmoor that you had married a policeman. You ought to have invited the earl to the wedding, Daisy. The Norvilles are relatives, after all.'

'Only just,' Daisy muttered rebelliously. 'Second cousins by marriage twice removed, or something.' Still, that slight connection had emboldened her to ask his lordship's permission to write about Brockdene, so she couldn't very well complain . . .

. . . As Lady Dalrymple continued to do. Daisy had missed some of what she said, but she gathered Alec had not been banished from the family gathering because of his infra dig profession.

'And I suppose one can't very well separate him from his little girl at Christmas.'

'I should hope not, Mother! Besides, Belinda is my daughter now, too.'

The telephone wafted a resigned sigh to her ear. 'Yes, dear. And Violet tells me she and Derek are thick as thieves, so perhaps they will keep each other out of mischief.'

Or egg each other on, Daisy didn't say. 'What about Mrs Fletcher?'

'Darling, do you think your mother-in-law would be quite comfortable in such company? A bank manager's widow, I gather, and merely a bank *branch* . . .'

'Mother, Bel's her only grandchild, and it's Christmas we're talking about!' An unconvinced silence forced Daisy to play her trump. 'And she plays bridge. She's out right now at her weekly bridge evening.'

'Hmmm.' There was a thoughtful pause, then the dowager snapped, 'Oh, very well, since you've never bothered to learn the game. I did mention to Westmoor that she might come, and he raised no objection. Now really, Daisy, I can't afford to go on chatting endlessly with the cost of trunk calls what it is. I'll see you on Sunday. Goodbye.'

Daisy hung the earpiece on its hook and hurried from the entrance hall back to the sitting room. It was a pleasant room, for which Daisy gave the credit to Alec's first wife. The heavy mahogany furniture had been reupholstered with cheerful prints; the walls, no doubt once covered with the sombre wallpaper beloved by the Victorians, were now painted white; while over the mantelpiece where – Daisy suspected – a stag had stood endlessly at bay, hung a colourful view of Montmartre.

Alec's mother could not blame Daisy for that transformation. She did, quite rightly, hold her responsible for the lapse from rigid formality represented by books and magazines left open on tables, a half-completed jigsaw puzzle, a silk scarf flung over the back of a chair, and such depredations.

The worst of these sprawled on the hearthrug before the cheerful fire: Nana, Belinda's multicoloured mongrel puppy, who sprang up when Daisy entered the room and pranced to greet her as if she had been gone for five months, not five minutes.

'Down, Nana!' said Bel, tossing back a ginger pigtail as she looked round from the game of chess she was playing with her father. 'Sorry, Mummy.'

'It's all right, darling, she didn't jump up. She's getting much better.'

So was Belinda. She no longer stammered when she addressed Daisy as 'Mummy', as she had at first, though she could barely remember her own mother. She was quite comfortable now with frequent hugs and other signs of affection, which her grandmother had withheld for fear of spoiling the child. She smiled and laughed much more often than when Daisy had first entered her life.

Daisy recognized her self-satisfied musing as an attempt

to postpone revealing the Dowager Viscountess's latest machinations. At least Mrs Fletcher's absence meant Daisy could let Alec break the news to her gently, later.

'Darling,' she began guiltily, just as Alec moved a bishop, looked up, and asked, 'What did your mother have to say, Daisy?'

'You don't want to know.' Daisy dropped into a chair. 'You remember Mother was complaining that her house is too small to have the whole family visit for Christmas? But she wouldn't accept Cousin Edgar's invitation for all of us to visit Fairacres. I wish she'd be reconciled to Edgar and Geraldine. It's nearly five years since Father died and the poor man inherited.'

'She might find it easier if the Dower House weren't so close to Fairacres.'

'If it wasn't that, it would be something else. When she's in her coffin, she'll complain if she's buried five feet eleven and a half inches down instead of six feet.'

'Little pitchers,' Alec warned.

'Oh dear, forget I said that, Bel!'

'Said what?' Belinda asked, raising her eyes from the chessboard. 'Daddy, I rather think you've cornered my queen.'

'Beast,' said Daisy, who hadn't the patience for chess.

'He's not! I told Daddy he mustn't let me win.'

'And *I* told you, you mustn't let him let you win. Quite right, darling. He's still a beast.'

'No, he's not,' Bel said anxiously. 'He gave me four pawns before we started.'

'Right-oh, he's absolved.'

'You're not, though, Daisy,' Alec put in, grinning. 'What has Lady Dalrymple been up to?'

'You are not going to believe this. She's somehow coerced Lord Westmoor into inviting us all to spend Christmas at Brockdene. Vi and Johnnie, too. And your mother, of course.'

'Will Derek come?' At Daisy's nod, Bel's freckled face glowed. 'Spiffing!'

'You did say Superintendent Crane is giving you Christmas off, darling?'

'Yes, I worked over both Christmas and New Year's Day last year. I've no excuse to turn down Lord Westmoor's invitation. Does he realize what he's let himself in for, do you suppose?'

'He's not going to be there, I'm pretty sure; but I bet you anything you like Mother thinks he will be. She didn't give me a chance to break the news.'

'Our host won't be present?'

'Well, when he gave me permission to write about Brockdene, he told me it was an ancient family custom to spend Christmas there, but the custom fell into abeyance ages ago. Now the house is inhabited by poor relations. I don't believe he told Mother. Perhaps he was getting his own back for being manoeuvred into issuing the invitation. She'll be furious!'

Nor would Mother be pleased to discover what the journey to Brockdene entailed, Daisy thought, stepping up on to the cobbled quay from the motorboat which had brought her up the Tamar from Plymouth. She turned to wave goodbye to the boatman.

Lord Westmoor had warned her that Brockdene was

quite isolated. Not only was the way by road tortuous in the extreme, but at this time of year the Cornish lanes were deep in mud. Motor vehicles attempting them frequently had to be rescued by carthorses. From the nearest station, at Calstock, one might walk a couple of miles to Brockdene along a miry public footpath, but the earl did not think Daisy would care for that. To hire a launch and go up the river was quicker, simpler and cheaper than any alternative.

Though Daisy's editor at *Town and Country* took some persuading that he wouldn't be paying her expenses for a pleasure jaunt, eventually she convinced him. Nonetheless, the boat trip had been a pleasure.

For a start it was a beautiful day. Daisy was quite warm enough in her heather-mixture tweed costume, without her winter coat. The soft, mild air of the West Country had little in common with the dank chill of London's atmosphere of coal smoke and petrol fumes. The sun shone through a high, shifting haze, bringing an intermittent sparkle to the blue-grey waters of Plymouth Sound. Herring gulls circled overhead. The chatty boatman, his Devonshire accent thick and rich as clotted cream, had announced the sights to Daisy as they put-putted past: Plymouth Hoe, Drake's Island, the busy Royal Navy dockyards at Devonport, the Spanish Steps.

As they continued the channel narrowed and the water turned to grey-green. The Tamar wound between yellow reed beds and wooded cliffs, with the hills of Devon and Cornwall beyond to either side, a patchwork of green, gold and brown. The boatman pointed out a tiny stone chapel right on the riverbank at Halton Quay. He told Daisy he'd heard there was another such at Brockdene, not visible from the river. Near the chapel, lime kilns belched smoke into the air, making quicklime for fertilizer.

'Doesn't it burn the plants?' Daisy asked. She had a vague memory of reading about quicklime being used to destroy plague-ridden bodies.

''Tis slaked wi' water afore it be put on the fields,' the boatman assured her. 'See them cottages? They do say in the old smuggling days a red petticoat hung on the washing line gave warning of the Preventives, and which end it hung told whereabouts they was searching.'

He spoke with a touch of nostalgia, Daisy noted with amusement, and she plied him for further tales of the smugglers. Maybe she could develop the stories into an article.

'They do say,' he finished, nosing the boat in next to the stone wharf at Brockdene Quay, 'as one o' the chief smugglers, Red Jack, were related to the family at Brockdene and they hid him from the dragoons when he were hurt bad. But that were nigh on a hundred years past, and what the truth of it might be, Oi couldn't rightly say.'

'It's an interesting story, anyway.'

'So 'tis. Now these here docks are silting up, since they put in the railway to Calstock. Few years more and you'll only be able to come in at high tide 'less they do dredge. Times surely do change. Thank 'ee kindly, miss,' he added as she tipped him. 'There, let me put your bags ashore, then Oi'll hold her steady for you.'

Daisy watched rather anxiously as he slung her baggage on to the quay, including her camera and tripod, early Christmas presents from Alec, and her portable typewriter. Then she disembarked and the boat put-putted away downriver.

No one was about. Glancing around, she saw a small public house, a few cottages, a warehouse, more of the rather sinister smoke-belching lime kilns and a lodge guarding a very steep drive. Brockdene itself, the fortified manor house, was invisible, presumably at the top of the hill.

Daisy looked at the hill, looked at her baggage, and groaned. Lord Westmoor had said he would notify the household of her coming, and she herself had written to Mrs Norville to say when she would arrive. She hoped she was not as unwelcome as present appearances – or rather non-appearances – suggested.

At that moment a door slammed as a stringy youth in a jerkin, breeches and gaiters came out of the pub and looked over to the quay. Seeing Daisy, he trudged towards her, trundling a handcart across the cobbles.

'Hello,' said Daisy. 'I hope you've come from the house to take my baggage up?'

'Aye.' The youth, a gardener probably, touched his cap and silently loaded his barrow. Without another word, he set off.

Daisy scurried to catch up. In her usual friendly way she attempted to chat, but not only was he taciturn, when he did speak his Cornish accent was nearly impenetrable. She had the greatest difficulty understanding a single word and soon gave up hope of advance information about the household she was about to encounter.

In any case, before they reached the top of the hill she had no breath to spare for talking. Reluctant to arrive panting, she paused at the top. The gardener plodded on regardless, between a row of huge sycamores and a long, low building of lichened granite. It looked pretty ancient, though in excellent repair. A barn, perhaps, or stables? A faint odour of farm animals hung in the air. Daisy wondered whether there was a horse-drawn vehicle, if not a motor, to bring her mother up from the quay. The Dowager Lady Dalrymple would not appreciate being forced to walk.

Looking ahead again, Daisy saw the house. The three-storey crenellated gatehouse with its tiny windows and narrow entrance arch looked fit to withstand a seige. It begged for a photograph.

'Stop!' cried Daisy. 'Wait, please.'

The gardener turned and gaped at her.

She hurried to the handcart and abstracted her camera and tripod. 'I want to take a photo while the light's good,' she explained. 'It may rain tomorrow.'

The youth looked vacantly up at the blue sky, from which even the slight haze had cleared. 'Aye,' he said, and went on with the cart through the open, iron-studded door under the archway.

Daisy moved back and took several shots. She was getting better at it. Her editor no longer made ominous rumblings about sending a professional photographer with her. Not that the money mattered now she was married, but she had her pride.

Folding camera and tripod, she followed the gardener under the arch. The tunnel-like passage was cobbled, narrow enough to be easily defended, with two doors in the right-hand wall. Daisy wondered whether to knock at one – or both. There was nothing to distinguish one from the other, though, so she went on and emerged into daylight in a courtyard, with more archways and doors to choose from. Boy, barrow and baggage had vanished.

It was not a frightfully auspicious beginning to her visit.

She took the path of least resistance, straight ahead, and banged with the iron knocker on the great double doors. After a few moments, one door was opened by a tall, lean man, slightly stooped, who blinked at her puzzledly through wire-rimmed glasses.

He wore a shabby tweed jacket over a green knitted waistcoat, a grey and pale blue woollen muffler around his neck and navy blue trousers. Not the butler, then.

'Hello,' said Daisy, 'I'm Mrs Fletcher. I believe I'm expected?'

His look of puzzlement deepened. 'Mrs Fletcher? I'm sorry, do I know you?'

'No, not from Adam. Lord Westmoor . . .'

'Oh, you're Lord Westmoor's guest, of course,' he said, his face clearing. 'The front door is round the other side of the house, actually, but do come in.'

Daisy stepped over the threshold into a baronial hall some forty feet long by twenty wide. The whitewashed walls were hung with banners and arms, from pikes and swords to muskets and horse pistols. A long table, black with age, ran down the centre of the room, and chairs with the uncomfortably carved backs of a more stoic age stood along the walls. Stained glass in the leaded windows depicted heraldic emblems and fleurs-de-lis. The roof, its timbers set in decorative patterns, rose high above the stone floor. A suit of armour beside the vast fireplace appeared to be warming its gauntleted hands at the stingy fire, and in fact indoors was colder than out, explaining the gentleman's woolly scarf.

Returning her attention to him, Daisy said with a smile, 'Not exactly Lord Westmoor's guest, at least not yet. The earl is letting me write an article about Brockdene for *Town and Country* magazine.'

To her surprise, his sallow face brightened. 'A wonderful subject,' he said enthusiastically. 'I've lived here all my life and I fancy I'm something of an expert on the house and its contents. The contents are quite as wonderful as the house itself, if not more so. I am engaged in creating a detailed descriptive and historical catalogue ... But I'm forgetting my manners. Allow me to introduce myself. I'm Godfrey Norville.' As if unused to the gesture, he stuck out his hand, his bony wrist protruding from his sleeve.

'Daisy Fletcher.' It was rather like shaking hands with a filleted plaice. 'How do you do.'

'Yes, yes, happy to make your acquaintance, Mrs Fletcher. I've devoted my life to studying Brockdene, you know. I shall give you a tour, and then you must ask me any questions you like. Any questions at all! This is an excellent place to start. The hall was erected in the late fifteenth century by ...'

'I should love a tour a little later,' Daisy interrupted hastily. 'But just now, if you don't mind, I ought to wash my hands and present my credentials to Mrs Norville.'

'Credentials to Mother?' He gave her a bewildered look. 'Oh, I see! Yes, yes, I daresay that will be in order. I wonder where Mrs Pardon would be at this hour?'

'Mrs Pardon?'

'The housekeeper. Lord Westmoor keeps a good staff here to preserve the house and its contents. Some of the contents are very valuable, very valuable indeed, both in monetary terms and to the scholar. The vambrace, for instance.' He started to wander off.

Though curious, Daisy did not permit the mysterious vambrace to distract her. 'Mrs Pardon?' she repeated.

'Oh, yes. I will ring the bell, but I rather doubt that it will bring anyone. They are not employed to wait on us, you see, just to take care of the house and grounds.'

What an odd arrangement, Daisy thought, wondering exactly what his relationship was to the earl. Her mother might know, but in general the dowager was more interested in her own grievances than in the details of distant family connections, at least those who had nothing to offer her.

Godfrey Norville seemed to see nothing out of the way. He tugged on a bellpull by the fireplace, then turned to frown at the suit of armour.

Through an archway beyond the fireplace came a woman in a dark grey dress with white collar and cuffs. Norville turned at the sound of her footsteps.

'Mrs Pardon, the armour needs polishing! See here, the left pouldron is beginning to tarnish.'

'I believe the armour is on my list for next week, Mr Norville,' the housekeeper told him, at once soothing and dismissive. 'I shall check. Mrs Fletcher? The boy has taken your luggage up, madam. Your room is in the east wing, as there is no modern plumbing in the rest of the house. If you would come this way, please?' She led the way through one of the doors at the end of the hall opposite where she had entered.

Daisy gathered – gratefully – that Lord Westmoor's staff was prepared to wait on his lordship's guests. The situation was not only odd but awkward. She couldn't help regarding the unknown Mrs Norville as in some sense her hostess, whether the earl had consulted her or simply presented her with a fait accompli.

'Do you have many visitors?' she asked, following Mrs Pardon through a dining room and along a corridor.

'Not many at all, madam. Now and then his lordship lets a historian or some such come down to take a look at the house. It's not like the old days when we'd have a house party in the summer and all the family for Christmas. His lordship's not been the same since the War, I'm afraid.' She sighed, as she opened a glass-panelled door into a spacious entrance hall.

'I hope my ... our visit isn't going to cause a lot of trouble,' Daisy said, glancing around. This hall was furnished in a more modern style: a rather battered pedestal table with a looking glass hanging above it; a hat-tree sprouting tweed caps and woolly hats; an umbrella stand; several lyre-back chairs; and, oddly, a faded chaise longue.

'Oh no, madam, we can manage. At least, Lady Dalrymple won't mind eating with Mrs Norville and the family, will she? It'd make my life easier, and that's a fact.'

'No, why should she?' *Curiouser and curiouser*, thought Daisy. She hoped for an answer to her question, but Mrs Pardon treated it as rhetorical.

'Would you like to leave your coat in the coat cupboard?' she asked, gesturing towards a door in the wall to the left of the front door.

'Thanks, I think I'll take it with me.'

'Very well, madam. Up here now. You'll notice the stairs have been built right across one of the old windows. This part of the house was altered in 1862 for the dowager countess of the time. My grandmother was housekeeper here then.' Mrs Pardon sighed again. 'She'd never have guessed what the family would come to. Here's your room, madam, and the bathroom and lavatory just back there. Ring if there's anything you need. My girls aren't used to waiting on ladies, but they'll do their best.'

'Thank you, I expect they'll manage very well. Where can I find Mrs Norville?'

'I'm sure it's not my place to know where she is, madam, but her sitting room's just at the top of the stairs, over the front door.'

Daisy's room was small, crammed with heavy, dark, rather shabby Victorian furniture, but it had a wash-hand basin with running hot and cold water. The window looked out over gardens and woods, with a glimpse beyond of the river, a small town which must surely be Calstock, and a railway viaduct. Daisy didn't linger over the view. Having washed her hands and face, tidied her hair and powdered her nose, she set out to find her hostess, the putative mistress of this anything but ordinary household.

CHAPTER 2

The door nearest the top of the stairs was ajar. Daisy tapped on it.

'Come in.'

The voice was high and soft, so soft that for a moment Daisy wasn't sure she had really heard it. If the door had been closed, she would have knocked again. As it was open, she went in. And then she thought she must have been mistaken after all, because she couldn't see a living person among the multicoloured images which met her startled eyes.

In the sun, slanting in through a south-facing window, spangles glittered, gilt gleamed and coloured glass glinted. Statuettes stood on every available surface, while from the walls painted figures gazed down with varying degrees of benevolence. Among six-armed gods, elephant-headed gods, blue-faced gods and meditative buddhas, Daisy picked out several madonnas, with and without child, a crucifix and a cheap print of Holman Hunt's 'The Light of the World'.

From the midst of this bizarre array came the soft, gentle voice: 'Mrs Fletcher?'

Black eyes in a lined, dark-skinned face looked

anxiously at Daisy from a chair by the fireplace, where a log fire glowed. The tiny woman was swathed in a multitude of bright shawls. She was working on a piece of embroidery, her needle darting in and out with a casual expertise.

'Yes, I'm Daisy Fletcher. You're Mrs Norville? How do you do?'

'How do you do. Won't you sit down?' She didn't have an accent, exactly, but the intonation common to Indian speakers of English gave her speech an exotic flavour entirely appropriate to her exotic surroundings.

So that explained the mystery, Daisy assumed, taking the chair opposite her hostess. The noble earls of Westmoor would not take kindly to the introduction of a 'native' into the family. For how many decades had the poor woman been shut away at Brockdene, out of sight and out of mind? No doubt her anxious look was the product of many a snub.

'It's very kind of you to put me up,' Daisy said warmly. 'I'm looking forward to writing about your home. It looks like a fascinating house.'

'It's quite old. Godfrey, my son, says the rest of Brockdene, apart from this wing, has changed remarkably little over the centuries. He knows all about it,' Mrs Norville said with obvious pride.

'Yes, Mr Norville has already offered to give me a tour. It will be frightfully helpful to have an expert on hand. Mrs Norville, I didn't know when I wrote to you that Lord Westmoor had invited all of my family to stay here for Christmas. I do hope he warned you.'

'He wrote to Mrs Pardon, and she told Dora.' She

seemed to think it quite natural that she should be passed over. In response to Daisy's enquiring look, she explained, 'Dora is my daughter-in-law.'

'Mrs Godfrey Norville? I see.' Daisy wondered how many more Norvilles were in residence.

Curiosity must wait, though. She had work to do before the rest of her own family arrived, and she wanted to go and take photographs while the weather was fine. But a few more minutes of conversation would be only courteous. Glancing about the room, she ventured, 'What an interesting collection you have in here.'

Mrs Norville smiled. 'My older boy, Victor, is a seaman, the captain of a merchant ship. He sails all over the world. He sends me these things or brings them when he manages to get home for a few days. They remind me of my childhood, before I went to the mission school.'

'In India? You must miss it.'

'I have never grown accustomed to the English winter, though I have lived at Brockdene for nearly fifty years. But my sons are Englishmen,' she added almost fiercely.

So determined a defence must be the result of past attacks. Daisy was dying to know more, but she really must get started on her article. 'Of course they are,' she said. 'I haven't met Captain Norville, but Mr Norville couldn't possibly be mistaken for anything else. And now I'd better go and find him to take up his offer to show me about.'

'I hope you will come back for tea.' Mrs Norville was shy again. 'Dora always brings up tea at half past four.'

'I'll be here,' Daisy promised, the stale cheese sandwich she had snatched for lunch at Plymouth station already a distant memory.

As she stepped out of the sitting room, a young girl came along the passage towards her. In a blue skirt and cardigan and white blouse, with her long, flaxen hair held back by an Alice band, she looked about fourteen, and large for her age. Her pudgy face was suspicious.

'What have you been saying to my gran?' she demanded.

'"How do you do."'

'How do you do,' the girl said impatiently, scowling. 'I'm Jemima Norville.'

'How do you do?' said Daisy with a quite different intonation. 'I'm Mrs Fletcher. I've just been saying "How do you do" to Mrs Norville.'

Jemima blinked at her with a bewilderment reminiscent of Godfrey Norville, who must be her father. 'Why?' she asked.

'Because I've come to stay at Brockdene, and she is my hostess. One always says "How do you do" to one's hostess as soon as one is presentable after the journey. And now I'm going to look for Mr Norville, who is going to show me over the old house.'

'Daddy'll like that,' the girl said, with grudging approval. 'He's crazy about the house. I think he's in the drawing room.'

'Will you show me the way?'

'It's in the Tower. Oh, all right.'

'Just let me fetch my camera.'

Jemima led her back to the weapon-hung hall, where Daisy left her camera and tripod. They went on through a door at the far end and up a steep oak staircase, polished to a slippery shine. A second flight of stairs, beneath ornate granite arches, led to a door carved with roses. This opened on to a sort of interior porch built of linen-fold panels, which in turn opened to a pleasant room with windows on three sides, its walls covered with tapestries.

'Daddy, here's Mrs Fletcher.'

'Just a minute. I'll be with you in a minute.' Godfrey Norville was measuring an ornate writing cabinet. He made a couple of notations on a block of paper on the open drop-front.

Daisy went over to look at the desk. It was carved in high relief with cupids and human figures, all unclothed. She stepped back, willing herself not to blush in the horrid Victorian way she despised.

'Mummy says I'm not to look at it,' said Jemima.

'Splendid, isn't it?' Norville enthused. 'Italian, about 1600. I have had an enquiry about it from a professor in Italy. I carry on a voluminous correspondence, you know, with historians and antiquarians all over the world. I flatter myself that in a modest way my detailed descriptions further the pursuit of knowledge.'

'I'm sure they must be most helpful,' Daisy murmured.

'Take this piece, for instance. Anyone can see it's both antique and handsome, but I am able to particularize its hidden attributes. Now would you have guessed, my dear Mrs Fletcher, that it contains a multitude – yes, I think I may say a veritable multitude – of secret compartments? I doubt that even I know them all, but I shall be happy to demonstrate one or two.'

'Tell her about the treasure chest, Daddy,' Jemima urged.

'I'd love to hear about the treasure chest,' said Daisy, 'and to see some of the secret drawers; but if you don't mind, just now I want to take some photographs of the exterior while it's fine. I thought perhaps you wouldn't mind coming out, Mr Norville, to tell me what I'm photographing.'

'While it's fine?' Mr Norville cast a doubtful glance at the window. Reassured by the flood of sunshine, he went on, 'Certainly, certainly. Jemima, run and fetch my galoshes and overcoat to the hall, and my hat and gloves, there's a good girl.'

Jemima pouted but obeyed.

As they followed her, Norville told Daisy about the treasure chest. It had supposedly been hidden or buried somewhere about the house or grounds by a Dutch merchant who had fled the Spanish Inquisition in the sixteenth century and been given shelter at Brockdene. 'A mysterious figure,' Norville admitted, 'about whom I have discovered little. He may have been responsible for building the tower, which was completed in 1627.'

'And no one ever found his treasure?'

'Generations have searched in vain.'

'He didn't leave a map? Too careless!'

'No, nor have I ever come across a map of the secret passage which, legend has it, was used for centuries by smugglers.'

They reached the hall, and Daisy took out her notebook to scribble down the story in her idiosyncratic version of Pitman's shorthand. Then she was ready to go, but Norville could not be budged without his coat and galoshes.

'Damp climate,' he muttered, 'wet feet, absolutely fatal.'

So while they waited for Jemima, Daisy asked him about the 'vambrace' he had mentioned earlier. It turned out to be a piece of armour to protect the forearm. This particular example was special because it had been designed for a man who had lost his hand. The fingers and thumb could be locked into place to grip reins or even a sword.

'This is simply spiffing,' said Daisy, as he hung the gleaming vambrace carefully in its place on the wall. 'Just the sort of titbits to interest my readers.' And Derek would be fascinated, she thought. The lost treasure alone should be enough to keep him and Belinda occupied for hours.

Along with her father's galoshes and overcoat, Jemima brought mittens and a woollen hat with a pompon which matched the scarf he already had on. Fussily he put everything on, though he didn't seem concerned when his daughter accompanied them outside without coat or hat or galoshes. Since it was quite warm, and dry underfoot as long as they stayed off the grass, Daisy didn't worry either.

While she took shots of the hall court, the retainers' court, the Dutchman's tower, the kitchen court and the rebuilt east front – which blended with the old buildings in an unusually tasteful manner – Norville expatiated upon their history. He had every fact at his fingertips, and his keenness to impart his knowledge was rather endearing.

Jemima hovered around them. Once she interrupted: 'Daddy, tell her about the ghost.'

'Piffle!' he exclaimed, waving a hand in a striped mitten. 'Ghost indeed! Sheer piffle. Mrs Fletcher wants the facts.'

Jemima scowled.

'I'd like you to tell me about the ghost, Jemima,' Daisy assured her. 'But later.'

'I might,' the girl said sulkily, turning away.

Norville frowned. To distract him, Daisy asked, 'What's that great tall tower on the hill behind the house?'

His frown remained. 'The Prospect Tower. I haven't found any reliable information about it, but it's probably a late-eighteenth-century folly. Do you want to photograph it?'

Daisy considered. She rather doubted that her photographic skills were up to what looked like a difficult shot. 'No, I think not. But what about the chapel by the river? The boatman was telling me about it.'

'The Chapel of Saints George and Thomas à Becket. It was built in the fifteenth century by the first baronet, Sir Richard Norville – before the Norvilles were ennobled – at the spot where he escaped his enemies by a clever trick. He threw his cap into the river and hid in the bushes. They saw it floating and thought him drowned.'

'That's a good story,' said Daisy, scribbling madly. 'Will you show me the chapel?'

'My dear Mrs Fletcher, the damp! Nothing is so damp as the woods in winter. I never walk in the woods in winter, and I strongly advise you not to do so.'

Daisy laughed. 'Oh, I'm as healthy as a horse, I'm afraid. I'd like to see the chapel in the woods. Is it far? Is it hard to find? If you'll direct me, I'll find it myself.'

'No, not far,' he admitted vaguely. 'Not far at all. But you'd do better to come inside and see the chapel in the house. I pointed out its windows, you may recall.'

'Later,' said Daisy. 'Would you mind awfully taking my tripod indoors for me? I'd rather not carry it.'

Following his reluctant directions, she went down by the terraced gardens to a short but dark tunnel under a farm track. A good place to hide the end of a secret passage, she thought.

It was in this gloomy spot that she became aware that Jemima was not so much going with her as trailing sullenly along after her. Emerging into the valley garden, Daisy paused to admire a fish pond overlooked by a charming thatched summerhouse, and to let the girl catch up.

Jemima lingered behind, apparently entranced by a flowering hellebore. Fed up with her, Daisy went on, past a domed stone dovecote, ancient-looking and a-flutter with white fantails. She stopped to take a couple of snapshots. Jemima still hung back.

Godfrey had said to bear right, towards the gate on to the public footpath from Brockdene Quay to Calstock. The gravel paths were confusing, sometimes doubling back, here and there interrupted by a stone step or two. Daisy followed a tumbling stream down the valley towards the river, glimpsed through trees, and hoped she was going in the right direction.

She had to admit it was damp underfoot here, slippery in places, and when she passed through the gate into the woods, the trees, even leafless, created a chilly shade. Though she hadn't the least expectation of ill consequences, she could understand why someone susceptible to catching cold would avoid the place.

Noticing several holly bushes laden with bright berries, she hoped the peculiarities of the household would not prevent Christmas decorations. Belinda and Derek were of an age to be well and truly pipped at any deficiency in the festivities.

Daisy came to the chapel, a tiny, very plain stone

building half hidden by laurels and rhododendrons. A sign over the door told of Sir Richard's clever escape. Inside, she found only two pairs of pews facing each other and a small wooden altar, simply carved.

She walked around the chapel to the edge of the cliff and looked down on the river where the first baronet had thrown his cap. His enemies must have been close behind him; otherwise the cap would have sunk or been carried away by the current and Sir Richard's clever trick would have been wasted.

A rustle in the bushes behind her startled Daisy. Instinctively she jumped backwards, away from the edge.

She wasn't dressed for swimming. Besides, it was a long way down. One would hit the water hard enough to hurt if one fell over – or was pushed.

Pushed? What put that possibility into her head? It was only Jemima in the bushes, walking away now up the track. The child was surly, but Daisy had no reason to suppose her malicious, let alone murderous.

Daisy returned to the house. Godfrey Norville was waiting to give her a tour of the interior.

'Just a quick look now, if you don't mind,' she said. 'I left London awfully early this morning and I'm getting a bit tired, and Mrs Norville invited me to join her for tea at half-past four. Perhaps you could point out the most interesting items. I'll make a list; then I can investigate further tomorrow.'

With some chivvying, she got him through the main part of the old house. He wanted to tell her the story of every weapon, every coat of arms, every piece of furniture, every tapestry – and practically every wall was hung with tapestries. Her list was much too long, as she had to placate him by writing down everything he considered particularly noteworthy, but she could easily cut it down to a manageable length. By half-past four they were back in the hall.

Jemima met them there. 'Mummy says we're having tea in the library, not Granny's room, because you're Lord Westmoor's guest,' she announced scornfully.

'The library?' Daisy couldn't remember seeing a library.

'In the east wing. I've got to show you the way.'

'Thank you.' Ignoring the girl's ungraciousness, Daisy thought gratefully of her stepdaughter's excellent manners and eagerness to please. Perhaps the contrast would reconcile the Dowager Viscountess to Belinda.

On the other hand, perhaps Daisy could stop her mother coming in the first place. A carefully worded cable about the difficulties of the journey and the earl's not being expected might do the trick. Following Jemima into the entrance hall of the east wing, she glanced around for a telephone.

Even as she looked, she realized that while photographing the exterior, she hadn't noticed any wires. Brockdene had no electricity, as was to be expected in this rural fastness, but now she came to notice it, there was no gas either. Like the old house, the east wing was lit by oil lamps and candles. Her hope of finding a telephone faded. The nearest telegraph office was no doubt in Calstock, two miles away by a muddy footpath.

Lady Dalrymple would just have to come and make the best of it, not a character trait for which she was noted.

Suppressing a sigh, Daisy entered the room her guide pointed out. Library was a misnomer, for only the far wall had bookshelves, and only halfway up, on either side of a curious little door no more than four feet high. The room was furnished as a sitting room.

Jemima had vanished, but a scrawny woman with fading fair hair jumped up from one of the massive Victorian sofas, dropping a stocking she was darning. She came to greet Daisy.

'Mrs Fletcher, how do you do!' She spoke with a sort of impetuous eagerness which had something slightly artificial about it. Her front teeth brought to mind a pet rabbit Daisy had once owned. 'I'm Dora Norville, Mrs Godfrey Norville. How delightful to have you come to stay.'

'Yes,' drawled a girl of perhaps nineteen or twenty, coming up behind her, 'the Pardon has actually offered to bring our tea! I'm Felicity Norville, Mrs Fletcher. How do you do?'

Felicity was the epitome of the modish 'bright young thing'. Her blonde hair was bobbed, lips scarlet, eyebrows and lashes darkened. Her boyish figure was emphasized by a wide sash around her hips, such as Daisy would never have dared to wear. Her mauve frock had beaded embroidery all down one side, rather overdoing it for afternoon tea in the country. Mrs Godfrey wore a much more appropriate tweed skirt, with a hand-knitted cardigan and a modest string of pearls.

Their greetings answered, Daisy went on, 'I'm thrilled to be able to write about Brockdene. In fact there's so much to write about I don't know where to begin. What a marvellous place!'

'You wouldn't think so if you had to live here,' Felicity muttered.

Daisy flashed her a smile of sympathy. The isolation must be hard on a young girl dying to try her wings, though presumably whatever local society existed was more accessible in the summer. Still, perhaps Felicity longed for the bright lights of London. From what Daisy had observed, she was unlikely to get there. The 'poor' in 'poor relations' seemed pretty accurate, while Westmoor apparently had little regard for the relationship, beyond giving the family a home.

'It's a privilege to live at Brockdene,' said Dora Norville brightly. 'I've always admired it, since I was a girl.'

'You grew up in this district?'

'In Calstock, just up the river. Ah, here's Mother. You've met my mother-in-law, haven't you, Mrs Fletcher?'

Mrs Norville trotted in, spry as a sparrow, followed by Jemima bearing shawls. Mrs Godfrey jumped up and went to fuss over the old lady. She settled her by the stone fireplace, where a cheerful fire burned beneath a fanciful wooden mantelpiece carved with lions, dragons, cherubs and musicians.

'Are you warm enough, Mother?' Mrs Godfrey enquired anxiously, swathing her mother-in-law in shawls.

'Quite warm, dear. Where is my crochet work, Felicity? That's it. Thank you, dear. I shall have it finished for you in time for Christmas.'

'Thanks, Gran darling.' Felicity handed over something lacy in lilac artificial silk, and kissed her grandmother's dark-skinned cheek.

'Has my son shown you the old house, Mrs Fletcher?'

They talked for a few minutes about the house. Dora Norville grew more and more anxious, and at last said,

'Perhaps Jemima and I had better fetch the tea after all.' She jumped up, but the door opened before she reached it and Mrs Pardon and a maid came in. Daisy was pleased to see bread and butter and a good selection of cakes and biscuits as well as the tea things. She was ravenous.

'Golly!' exclaimed Jemima.

Mrs Pardon pursed her lips. No one else spoke, except Mrs Norville to thank her, until the servants left.

'What a spread,' Felicity drawled. 'All in your honour, Mrs Fletcher. Not that we're starved, but the menu tends to be spartan.'

'That's enough, Felicity,' snapped her mother. 'Milk and sugar, Mrs Fletcher? Jemima, pass the bread and butter.'

Tea and conversation proceeded on more conventional lines. Being well brought up, Daisy did not utter the myriad questions which assailed her, but she vowed to herself to try and get Felicity on her own and pump her. She looked like the best bet to provide a few answers.

And answers Daisy must have, or she was going to die of curiosity.

CHAPTER 3

Outside, the short winter day had ended by the time they finished tea. Inside, too, it was pretty dark, in spite of oil lamps and candles.

Daisy's candle flame flickered in the draughts as she found her way back to the hall. Shadows danced about her, and she recalled Jemima's mention of a ghost. She wished she had brought an electric torch. These days the arrival of electricity tended to banish ghosts, but here the shadowy centuries pressed close. Her footsteps echoed from the stone walls. She caught herself glancing nervously over her shoulder.

She had intended to take a look at the other chapel, the one in the house, but that struck her as altogether too spooky for comfort. By the feeble light of her candle, she wouldn't be able to see much anyway, in any of the rooms. She needed a torch or a good lantern.

Eyeing the bellpull, she wondered whether anyone would come if she rang. It was worth a try.

As she raised her hand to the cord, light footsteps sounded behind her. She swung round with a gasp.

'It's only me.' Felicity's smile had a touch of mockery. She set on the table her candle and the unlit lantern she was carrying. 'I thought you might need this. Sorry, did I make you jump?'

'Yes,' Daisy confessed. 'I'd just remembered that your sister mentioned a ghost. Do you know the story?'

'Do you want it for your article? I can tell you, but it's not frightfully interesting. No one bricked up in a wall to die or discovered with a lover and thrown from the tower. It's not even very ancient.'

'What happened?'

'Actually, it was rather like *Mansfield Park*. In the late eighteenth century, a poor young cousin was brought to Brockdene to be companion to a dowager countess. She got used to living comparatively well, and when the old lady died, she didn't want to go home. I don't think she actually killed herself, but she didn't live long after being sent away. She came back to haunt the place where she was happy, you see.'

'Spiffing!' said Daisy, scribbling madly. 'At least, I'm sorry for her of course, but it'll add a bit of spice to my article. Presumably she doesn't go around rattling chains?'

'No, she's just a young girl, about my age, I suppose, dressed in white, wandering from room to room. Not that I've ever seen her,' Felicity disclaimed hurriedly. 'I don't believe in ghosts.'

'Nor do I,' Daisy said, with more vehemence because a few minutes ago she almost had believed. 'Thanks for bringing the lantern, Miss Norville. I was just going to ring for one.'

'I daresay someone might have answered the bell, knowing you're staying. But please, call me Felicity, won't you?'

'And I'm Daisy. I also wanted to ask Mrs Pardon whether there's a vehicle available for my mother when she arrives on Sunday. My sister, too – she's expecting an addition to the family and it's quite a hill up from Brockdene Quay.'

'There are farm carts.' Felicity's lips quirked at Daisy's dismay. 'Or the pony-trap. It's not used much in winter because of the state of the roads, but I expect they'd bring the pony in from pasture for a dowager viscountess. That's what your mother is, isn't she?'

Daisy laughed. 'Yes, and my sister Violet is Lady John.'

'Let me tell the Pardon,' Felicity begged. 'It would be too frightfully amusing to give her an order she couldn't refuse.'

'Oh, right-oh.'

'You must think we're all mad. You see, we're poor relations, like the girl in white, only here on suffrance. Except Gran, that is. The sixth earl's will gives her the right to live at Brockdene all her life. When she dies, the rest of us get booted out.'

'What a beastly position to be in.'

'Oh well,' Felicity said with indifference, real or assumed, Daisy wasn't sure, 'I expect I'll be married by then, and Miles will be qualified. Gran may be tiny but she's healthy as a horse, good for years yet. My parents take very good care of her, I can tell you, though otherwise they bury their heads in the sand. Miles is really the only sane one among us.'

'Miles?'

'My brother. He'll be home to dinner. He's an articled clerk in my grandfather's office in Calstock. Grandpapa is a solicitor. I suppose he and Miles will have to support the

parents and Jemima sooner or later. He put Miles through
school, and we couldn't get by without the dress allowance
he gives Mother. The annuity the sixth earl left Gran
doesn't go far these days. Not much of the so-called
"dress" allowance gets spent on clothes, I can tell you.'

'What beautiful work your grandmother does, though,'
Daisy said diplomatically.

Felicity looked down at her dress. 'Yes, too clever, isn't
it? Her knitting, too. She tried to teach me, but I haven't
the patience for it. Which doesn't get me out of my share
of the mending. Jemima's not bad at knitting, for a kid. At
least, Daddy will wear what she produces.'

'The green waistcoat,' Daisy guessed.

'Most of its sins are hidden by his jacket,' Felicity said
with a grin. 'I'm so glad you came to stay, Daisy. Most of
the people Westmoor drops into our midst are musty old
historians. Sometimes I think I'd do absolutely anything to
get away from this place! Just having someone to talk to
. . . I'm actually looking forward to Christmas!'

'So am I,' said Daisy, with partial truth. Derek and Bel
and Derek's little brother would be fun; her mother and
Alec's would just have to be borne. 'But I've got to get
some work done before the others arrive. Are there spills
to light the lantern?'

Felicity found spills by the fireplace. The lantern
improved visibility no end, and Felicity had learnt enough
from her father to give Daisy quite as much information as
she needed. They went around the hall examining cross-
bows and wheel-lock pistols, breastplates and lobster-tail
helmets, Indian sabres and a Zulu shield, a whale's
jawbones and the head of an albatross.

'And there's the squint,' said Felicity, holding the lantern high when they reached the west wall.

'Squint?'

'Never tell me Daddy didn't show you his pride and joy!' She pointed at a hole in the wall above their heads.

'I did rather rush him around. What is it?'

'A peephole. It's in a niche behind the arras in the south room, which used to be part of the solar – the medieval family's living quarters. The lord of the manor could look down on his retainers and make sure they were behaving themselves. There's another one looking into the chapel, so that the lady of the manor could attend services without having to mix with the men.'

'Positively medieval!' said Daisy, and they both laughed. 'That's interesting. I'll have a look from up there tomorrow. I think I'd better go and type out my notes now. What with the rotten light and all, I probably shan't be able to read them tomorrow. Thanks for your help.'

She found the fire made up in her bedroom, and an oil lamp already lit. By its light, she managed to do her typing, but she was glad she didn't have to hunt and peck. Her secretarial training certainly came in handy, however much she had hated her brief stint as a stenographer.

Felicity Norville ought to be preparing to earn her own living, Daisy thought. It was all very well hoping to be married before her grandmother died, but with so many young men killed in the war ... Although perhaps in Felicity's case it wasn't just wishful thinking. Perhaps she was already engaged. Odd that she hadn't mentioned it, though, if she was. Most engaged girls could talk of nothing else.

Daisy washed – at least the plumbing was Victorian rather than medieval – and changed for dinner. When she went down to the library, she found a slender young man in a dinner jacket leaning against the mantelpiece, staring into the fire.

'Hello,' she said, advancing. 'You must be Miles Norville.'

He turned his head towards her. He looked older than she had expected, several years older than Felicity. Then he turned completely, and she saw the empty sleeve pinned across his chest. Old enough to have gone to war.

'Hello.' He had a charming smile. 'Yes, I'm Miles. You're Mrs Fletcher, of course. How do you do? May I get you a drink?' He gestured at the little door between the bookshelves which had intrigued Daisy. 'The cellar doesn't run to much, I'm afraid, but there's some quite decent sherry.'

He coped admirably with the bottle and glass. Daisy restrained herself from helping. When she was working in that hospital office the last years of the war, she had learnt the importance of letting injured men do things for themselves.

'Is that a wine cellar?' she asked.

'We keep our few bottles there. No one seems to know what it used to be used for, not even my father. It's just a small, windowless room with a small but very solid door.'

'A dungeon?'

'Right next door to the library?' Miles queried. 'My ancestors may not have been great readers, but still . . . !'

'No, perhaps not.' Glass in hand, Daisy scanned the shelves. 'These all seem to be fairly light reading. You must keep your books elsewhere – I hear you're going into the law? My husband's in another branch. He's a policeman.'

'Mr Fletcher? But I thought your mother was . . . Oh, I beg your pardon!'

'Yes, my mother's the Dowager Lady Dalrymple,' Daisy said ruefully, 'but I married a Scotland Yard detective. Lord Westmoor didn't mention it? If the others don't know, please don't tell them. Alec much prefers to be incognito when he's on holiday.'

'Of course. He's at Scotland Yard, is he? There's not much criminal law in our practice.'

They talked about different aspects of the law until Godfrey and Dora Norville and Jemima came in. Old Mrs Norville and Felicity soon followed, and they all went along to the dining room.

A maid waited on them, with Mrs Pardon hovering in the background to direct her. It was obvious the maid was not accustomed to waiting at table. It was equally obvious that the Norvilles were not accustomed to being waited on. Jemima even got as far as stacking several empty soup plates before Felicity noticed and said, 'Don't do that, you little ass!'

'I'm not an ass! I'm not, I'm not! Mummy, tell her not to call me an ass.'

'That was uncalled for, Felicity. Jemima was just being helpful. Now that's enough from both of you. What will Mrs Fletcher think of your manners?'

Mrs Fletcher studiously ignored the fracas, turning to Godfrey Norville with a question about the variety of swords, sabres and rapiers hanging in the hall. With excursions into halberds, pikes, spears, partisans and still more exotic pole-arms, these kept her busy throughout the meal. He gave her far more information than she could possibly use about the various implements chosen by different eras and nations intent upon slaughter. She was glad she hadn't brought her notebook, or she wouldn't have managed a single mouthful.

The meal was 'good plain cooking'. Presumably Lord Westmoor employed the cook to feed his servants, not the relatives for whom he showed so little regard. The ingredients were all fresh, though, produced on the Brockdene farm, a treat in themselves compared to the limp offerings of London shops. In any case, after living on eggs, cheese, tinned soup and sardines during her years of independence, Daisy was not inclined to be fussy.

After the meal, Jemima was sent to bed and the others returned to the library for their coffee. Daisy asked about the Brockdene farms and the lime kilns down at Brockdene Quay. Mr Norville knew nothing about them and obviously wasn't interested.

'I can explain the workings of the kilns,' said Miles. 'They used to fascinate me when I was a boy. As I'd never seen a factory, they were my idea of "dark, Satanic mills".'

'They are rather dark and Satanic, aren't they?' Daisy agreed.

'And I used to help on the home farm in the summer, but that was before the war, so I'm afraid my information's a bit rusty.'

'I expect things haven't changed much. What do they grow, or is it mostly animals?'

'I remember bottle-feeding lambs in the spring,' said Felicity.

They talked for a while; then Miles excused himself to study some papers he had brought home. Mrs Norville took up her crochet-work. Mrs Godfrey suggested bridge.

That should please the Dowager Viscountess, Daisy thought. Before she had to confess that she did not play (she had, in fact, carefully avoided learning), Felicity said, 'Oh no, Mother, I think I'll go for a bit of a stroll. I could do with some fresh air.'

'It's December; you'll catch your death.'

'Bosh! It's a beautiful night and I'll change into something warm.' Without further ado she went off.

Mrs Godfrey watched her with a frown. 'Girls!' she said to Daisy. 'Always moody. I'm sure I never had such trouble with Miles.'

Overhearing, Miles said with a grin, 'I was away at school, Mother, and then in the army. I was deprived of the opportunity to trouble you. What Flick wants is something to keep her occupied.'

'What Felicity wants is to go up to London to do the social season, and there's no chance of that!'

'I expect she's happier in the summer,' Daisy said tactfully, 'when it's easier to see other local young people.'

'Oh yes, there are always plenty of tennis parties, and picnics and drives to the seaside, with friends and friends of friends. She was hardly home a single day last summer. But that makes one anxious, too. I never knew just whom she was meeting.'

Daisy had no consolation to offer. She was relieved when Mr Norville called her over to examine the plans of the fifteenth-century, pre-pendulum clock in the chapel. Not that she understood his explanation of its mechanism;

her school had not considered science a suitable subject for young ladies.

She retired early, intending to get up early so as not to waste daylight. If it was sunny again, she might even try a few indoor photographs. She had brought magnesium powder for flashes, but she hated using it. In her experience, it tended to either fizzle or explode in clouds of smoke. A long exposure was much easier to cope with, though she still often ended up with over- or under-exposed pictures.

When she went down in the morning, she found Miles already at breakfast.

'A hot breakfast,' he said cheerfully, waving at the row of spirit-lamp-warmed dishes on the sideboard, 'in your honour. I wish you'd come and stay more often! Try the sausages, they're homemade.'

'Mmm, they smell delicious.'

Halfway through her meal, Miles had to leave her to walk into Calstock to the office. 'It's Saturday, so I'll be back at midday,' he told her, 'and then four days free! We've been given a holiday on Monday, Tuesday is Christmas, of course, and Boxing Day is a Bank Holiday. Your people arrive tomorrow?'

'Yes, in the afternoon.'

'It'll be fun having children around for Christmas. I'm off. Cheerio, Mrs Fletcher.'

Daisy finished her breakfast without seeing any of the others and went through to the old house. Taking notes and noting questions to be asked, she moved from the old dining room, into the chapel, then back to the punch room with its miniature wine bins, now empty. Thence stone stairs, steep and narrow, led to the white room in the Dutchman's tower.

Above the white room was the drawing room. With windows on three sides, it was flooded with light. The most prized items here were the two cushions sat upon by King George III and Queen Charlotte when they came to breakfast in 1789, but they weren't exactly picturesque. The most photographable piece was the Italian writing cabinet with the secret drawers. Daisy contemplated trying a shot, but if the naked figures came out well enough to distinguish, her editor would probably balk at printing it.

A quick foray up to the two small bedrooms in the top of the tower showed each so full of a four-poster bed as to make photography impossible. The hall and dining room must be sunny by now, though, and both were worth a photo or two. Daisy went back down.

The rest of the morning she spent taking photos in the hall and the old dining room. At lunch, she asked the questions she had noted down, which the ever-helpful Godfrey Norville answered with his usual flood of information. He was winding down when the tramp of boots was heard in the corridor.

'Not too late for lunch, I hope, Mr Calloway,' cried a hearty voice. 'Come in, come in, my dear fellow. You must be as sharp-set as I am.'

'Uncle Vic!' Felicity sprang to her feet.

The door swung open. A big, weather-bronzed, bearded man in a gold-braided jacket filled the doorway. 'Mother, here's your wandering son come home again. How are you, my dear?' He strode in and bent to kiss his mother, then stood with his hands on the back of her chair, looking around with evident satisfaction. 'Your servant, Dora. Felicity, my word, but you're a young lady now and no mistake! Jemima, come kiss your old uncle. Well, Godfrey, how do you go on, old man? And Miles, my dear fellow, it's good to see you again.'

A babble of greetings answered him. As far as Daisy could see, everyone was pleased to see him, but no one seemed to notice the man who had taken his place in the doorway.

The man Victor Norville had addressed as Calloway was an elderly clergyman, a tall, thin figure in black with a dog collar. His yellowish face, set in stern lines, bore an expression of resigned weariness. He seemed an odd companion for the genial captain.

Victor Norville's voice, accustomed to battling gales and crashing waves, cut through the babble. 'Dora, I've brought a guest. He won't upset your housekeeping too much, I daresay.'

'We already have a guest, Victor,' Mrs Godfrey pointed out. 'Mrs Fletcher, as you will have gathered, this is my brother-in-law, Captain Norville.'

The captain engulfed Daisy's hand in his own. 'Happy to make your acquaintance, ma'am. My sister-in-law's guest is a sight prettier than mine! No offence meant, Calloway – you can't deny it! Mother, Dora, Godfrey, this is the Reverend Calloway, who's come all the way from India with me.'

By then, Felicity and Jemima had set two more places at the table. Daisy liked the look of Captain Norville, but she excused herself to go back to work, not wanting to cramp the family reunion.

As she left, Miles stopped her to say he had brought a couple of letters for her from the Calstock post office. She picked them up from the cluttered hall table: an oil lamp; a pair of leather gloves; several candlesticks with remains of candles of various heights; a man's handkerchief, clean and neatly folded; two library books; a jar of spills and another of pencils; a week-old *Times*.

One of Daisy's letters was from Violet, forwarded from St John's Wood in Belinda's careful handwriting. The other was from Alec. He must have written it very shortly after Daisy had caught that ghastly early morning train to Plymouth.

Tearing it open on her way up to her room, she prayed that no rash of murders had called him to the other end of the country, putting paid to his holiday after all.

She scanned his clear, firm writing, and as she dropped into a chair by the window she actually laughed aloud in relief. His mother had decided to spend Christmas with her sister in Bournemouth! Daisy would have only her own mother to cope with.

But what had Vi written for when they would see each other tomorrow?

A moment later she put down her sister's letter with a sigh. Johnnie didn't think Violet was well enough to travel. Derek was devastated. Well, Belinda would be equally devastated, and Daisy was going to have to cope with Mother without the able assistance of the 'good' daughter Violet had always been.

'Blast!' she said. She moved to the writing table to pen a

reply to her sister. Having finished it, she realized that it probably wouldn't be posted till the day after Boxing Day, unless she walked into Calstock herself. 'Oh, blast! Oh, well, back to work.' Turning to the typewriter, she made notes of Godfrey Norville's answers to her questions.

The housekeeper had better be told that the Frobishers and Mrs Fletcher senior were no longer expected. Daisy went to find Mrs Pardon, running her to earth in the kitchen court.

'Well, I don't mind saying, madam, it's a great relief. I was going to have to put someone in the old house, which isn't at all convenient, there's no denying.'

Daisy took the opportunity to investigate the complex of kitchens, store rooms, sculleries and laundry rooms around the court, still in use though coeval with the old house. Then she made her way to the 'red room'.

Above the punch room, the red room had been part of the solar in medieval times. Its huge four-poster was hung with crimson drapery, hence the name. The tapestries on the walls were particularly spectacular, especially a more-than-lifesize battle scene, but there were also three charming panels of children at play. Reluctantly, Daisy decided the light was too dim for photography, but the south room, the other part of the partitioned solar, would be brighter with its big windows on to the hall court.

Daisy went through. Here hung more splendid tapestries, and well lit now, but to Daisy the most interesting feature of the room was what they hid – the squints Felicity had described.

The far-right corner must overlook the chapel. Pulling back the arras, Daisy was delighted to find a closet big enough for two or three people at a pinch, and the promised opening through the wall. The worshippers above would be visible to the priest, but not to the congregation, thus preserving the ladies' modesty, Daisy supposed.

She crossed the room to find the peephole on to the hall. As she pulled aside the tapestry, she saw that someone was there before her, an obscure figure in the shadows.

And from the hall beyond came the voices of two angry men, raised in a shouting match.

CHAPTER 4

Alone, Daisy might have succumbed to temptation, against every precept of ladylike behaviour drummed into her at an early age. With someone else already present, eavesdropping was out of the question, alas, especially as that person was turning towards her.

She backed out, with a word of apology. Jemima followed, into the room's brightness. She looked upset.

Daisy wasn't surprised. Though she hadn't heard what they were shouting, she had recognized the disputants' voices. With Godfrey Norville's she was by now familiar, and the stentorian second could only be his brother's. The amity of the captain's return had not lasted long.

'Are you all right, Jemima?' she asked. 'I heard your father and uncle arguing, but I don't suppose for a minute it had anything to do with you, did it?'

Jemima gave her a sullen glare. 'I don't know. I didn't hear what they said.' She ran from the room.

Daisy was pretty sure the girl was lying, but after all it was none of her business. With a shrug, she decided to take a proper look at the hall squint later. She turned to consideration of the south room's furnishings, including a walnut escritoire with – according to Godfrey – secret drawers, like the one in the drawing room. Frustratingly, she failed to find a single one.

By the time she finished, the light was fading fast and she was in need of a cup of tea. She returned to her bedroom for a wash and brush up. Then she went along to old Mrs Norville's sitting room to find out whether the tea ceremony had returned to its accustomed place.

Mrs Norville was just setting the final stitches in her piece of embroidery. 'Tea in the library again,' she said in answer to Daisy's enquiry.

'I hope buzzing up and down those stairs isn't too much for you?'

'Not at all, my dear.' The old lady gave her the sweetest smile. 'On the contrary, I'm sure it's good for me. Godfrey and Dora do tend to keep me wrapped in cotton wool, however often the doctor swears there's nothing wrong with me bar a few aches and pains, the tribute one pays to old age.'

'Mother?' Captain Norville blew into the room like a fresh sea breeze. 'Hello, Mrs Fletcher! What, no tea? Has the custom of the house changed since I was last at home?'

'Tea in the library today, Victor dearest, in honour of our guests. Come in, come in, Mr Calloway,' she invited the clergyman, who had come with the captain but paused on the threshold. 'I shall be with you in just a minute.' She tied a last knot, folded the cloth and started to put away her needle and silks.

But the Reverend Calloway was staring in horror at the colourful images scattered about the room. 'Pagan idols!' he exclaimed. 'My life has been spent in fighting these demons. I did not expect to find them worshipped in my own country. Madam, better you had remained a heathen all your days than to accept our Lord and then renounce Him!'

'Poppycock!' cried the captain. 'My dear sir, my mother is as Christian as you or I, or Mrs Fletcher there. I gave her these gewgaws myself, just as mementos of her homeland. Ornaments they are, nothing but ornaments, I assure you.'

'Indeed.' Calloway gave him a hard, suspicious look. 'I trust you are right, Captain. But this is most disturbing.'

Mrs Norville looked quite frightened. Daisy decided it was time to stick her oar in.

'I find the chap with the blue face particularly jolly,' she said brightly. 'It rather reminds me of Picasso's blue period.'

'Picasso?' Calloway asked, frowning.

'Pablo Picasso, the French painter. Or is he Spanish? Too, too fearfully modern, anyway. Gosh, do let's go down to tea. I'm simply parched.'

She practically forced the clergyman to accompany her, leaving the Norvilles to come together. While she went on chattering inanely about modern art – a subject with which she was not widely acquainted but hoped Calloway was less – she wondered what on earth had possessed Captain Norville to bring the grim missionary home with him.

From what she had seen of the captain, Daisy was sure he had been motivated by a kindly impulse. Perhaps he had thought Mrs Norville would like to talk to someone who had spent his life in India. More likely Calloway had nowhere to go for Christmas, and Victor Norville had not considered that he might throw a blight over the festivities. Maybe that was what Victor and Godfrey had quarrelled about.

As on the previous day, Godfrey Norville didn't come

in for tea. With no interaction between the brothers to observe, Daisy was foiled in her hope of finding out more about their squabble. She wondered whether it was responsible for the tension, almost excitement, she sensed in the rest of the family.

It was nothing she could put her finger on. They just seemed more vivid, more like oils than the pastel water-colours they had been yesterday. Perhaps the enlivening presence of Captain Norville was enough to explain the change. And, of course, Christmas was nearly upon them, with more unknown and therefore interesting guests arriving tomorrow.

Daisy hadn't yet informed either Mrs Norville or her daughter-in-law about the reduction in numbers, so she went ahead and told them now.

They were expressing their regrets when Calloway burst out, 'Travelling on Sunday! When I left England, decent people did not travel on Sunday for pleasure, only if forced by circumstances. Things are sadly changed!'

Daisy suspected his memory was at fault, but she said politely, 'When did you go abroad, Mr Calloway?'

'As soon as I had taken orders. I was called to minister to the heathen, and in that field I have laboured for over fifty years.'

He must be over seventy then, Daisy reckoned, though he didn't look it. The tropical climate must have suited him. 'Always in India?' she asked.

'Always in India,' he confirmed, throwing a significant glance at old Mrs Norville. 'Naturally I came home on leave several times, though not in recent years. I see that England has not changed for the better.'

'The war altered many things,' Daisy said, and used the excuse of refilling her teacup to exchange the Jeremiah for Miles's more cheerful company.

'Sorry about the old grouch,' he said, as she sat down beside him. 'He's a bit of a blister, isn't he?'

'Oh dear, did my face give me away?'

'No, no! Or only because I was looking. I'm afraid the Rev is here for a purpose, and he's going to be staying for Christmas. Uncle Victor told me what happened upstairs in Gran's room. He's a good egg, Uncle Vic, behind all the hail-fellow-well-met. By the way, he's hoping you won't mention that business to the rest of the family.'

'Of course not.'

'I want to thank you,' Miles said awkwardly, 'for jumping to Gran's defence.'

'The chap with the blue face . . .'

'Krishna.'

'Krishna really did remind me of Picasso. On the whole, I prefer Krishna.'

Miles laughed, and they dropped the subject.

For the rest of the day and the following morning, Daisy saw the Norvilles and their clerical guest only at meals. She was madly trying to get her article, if not written, at least planned before her own family arrived. She had a wealth of material to sort out, much of it the kind of stuff which would make for a marvellously lively piece.

By an hour after lunch on Sunday, she had her outline prepared and was ready to call it a day. The afternoon was overcast, but still mild, with no sign of impending rain. She decided to walk down to the quay to meet Alec, Belinda and the Dowager Lady Dalrymple. She couldn't tell exactly when the boat would arrive, but she knew the early Paddington–Plymouth express ran an hour later on Sundays.

In the entrance hall, she met Felicity and Miles, bound on the same errand to welcome the newcomers, and they found themselves following the pony-trap down the drive.

'We didn't like to tell you at lunch,' said Felicity, 'because the Rev was there, but you missed his service this morning. Gran invited him to preside in the chapel, and Uncle Vic herded us all in willy-nilly, servants too.'

'How very remiss of me,' Daisy said, 'though I plead that I didn't know about it. No one herded me. But perhaps my lack of piety will make Mr Calloway look more kindly on the rest of you.'

'Not a hope,' Miles scoffed. 'He took one look at Flick's lip rouge and gave us a sermon on vanity.'

'You've got the wrong kind of vanity,' his sister argued. '"Vanity of vanities, all is vanity", that's about the unimportance of worldly things.'

'My word, you must have been listening!'

'And you weren't,' Felicity retorted.

They went on teasing in a brotherly-sisterly way. Daisy thought how much she missed Gervaise, who had not returned from the trenches of Flanders, where she assumed Miles had left his arm. The loss of her brother still hurt, though she had to admit she didn't think of him as often these days, nor of her dead fiancé. Michael held a corner of her heart forever, but Alec filled the rest, Alec and Belinda, and she was going to see them any minute. She hastened her steps.

When they came in sight of the quay, a motor launch was already moored at one of the wharves. The trap and a farm wagon stood nearby, with pony and cart-horse waiting patiently. On the quay, a pile of luggage was growing, handed up from the launch by the boatman to the hands of two farm labourers. Alec was already ashore, directing the operation. The heap of bags concealed the passengers still aboard.

Looking down into the boat, Alec said in his firmest voice, 'I wouldn't do that if I were you, old fellow. If you don't both land in the water, you'll land in the mud.'

Old fellow? The only thing less likely than that he should so address his daughter was that he should so address his mother-in-law. Whom had they brought with them?

Alec reached down and helped Belinda up on to the wharf. She saw Daisy at once and came running, pigtails flying.

'Mummy, Mummy!' She flung herself into Daisy's open arms. 'Mummy, Derek's come too! He rang up and said couldn't we invite him without telling Aunt Violet or Uncle John he'd asked, so Daddy rang back right away and I talked on the phone to Aunt Violet and told her I'd be *frightfully* sad if Derek couldn't come and she said yes!'

Before she finished, Derek had disembarked and was tearing along after her, hauled at top speed by Nana, the breeze ruffling his blond hair.

'Nana!' Daisy exclaimed.

'Hello, Aunt Daisy,' called Derek. 'Did Bel tell you about me coming?'

Fending off the puppy, Daisy listened with half an ear to her nephew's rhapsodies on their journey up the Tamar. Meanwhile Belinda had turned to Felicity and Miles.

'Hello, I'm Belinda Fletcher,' she said. 'I'm most awfully sorry about bringing Nana. My friend she was going to stay with couldn't have her, right at the last minute. Daddy says she'll have to stay tied up outside.' Doubtfully she added, 'He says she won't be too awfully miserable.'

Felicity glanced at Miles. Her eyes full of mischief, she said, 'Nana might pine. We can't have that. No one will mind if she comes into the house.'

'The east wing,' Miles qualified. 'Father would have forty fits if she were let loose in the old house.'

Belinda and Derek promised faithfully that the puppy should not put so much as her nose over the threshold, and Daisy performed belated introductions. By then her mother was ashore, moving towards the trap, leaning heavily on Alec's arm.

'Grandmama is in a fearful bate about Nana,' Derek observed, 'and about having to come by boat, and because Uncle Alec told her in the train he thought Lord Westmoor wasn't going to be here for Christmas, and because Mummy and Daddy didn't come. She's mad as a whole hive of hornets.'

'Don't speak of your grandmother like that, you horrid little brat,' said Daisy, quailing. 'Felicity, I think it would be a good idea if you and Miles took the children up to the house while I see if I can smooth a few ruffled feathers.'

'Right-oh,' Miles said promptly. 'We'll go the back way, through the woods, and give the dog a run. Come on, you two.'

Felicity looked down at her rather smart shoes. 'Not me. I'll stick with Daisy.'

'Mummy?' Belinda clung.

'Go along with Mr Norville and Derek, darling. Nana's your puppy. You're in charge of her, even if you let Derek hold the lead.'

'You can have her now, Bel,' said Derek magnanimously. His dog, Tinker Bell, was a country dog and hardly ever had to go on a lead.

Belinda felt better holding Nana's lead. She had been worrying about coming to Brockdene. Gran had warned her that going to stay in a grand house with a grand lord would be very different from staying with Uncle John and Aunt Violet, who were practically part of her family. If Belinda's manners were not perfect, they would look down on her as ill-bred! And then there was Grandmama Dalrymple, who was as grand as a grandmother could be and rather frightened Bel, and maybe already considered her ill-bred.

Bel was awfully glad Derek had been allowed to come. Nothing bothered Derek, not even turning up with a dog who wasn't invited. Belinda was in two minds about Nana. On the one hand, Nana would go on loving Belinda even if all the rest of the world thought she was ill-bred; on the other hand, she was an uninvited guest, and just turning up with her might make people think her mistress was ill-bred.

'Mr Norville,' she said, as they reached a path through the woods by the river, 'do you really, really truly not mind Nana?'

'Not at all. Why is she called Nana?'

'After *Peter Pan*, because Derek's dog is called Tinker Bell, only he usually just calls her Tinker. 'Specially now he knows me, 'cause he calls me Bel, you see.'

'I see. May I call you Bel? You'd better call me Uncle Miles, I should think. Mr Norville is my father. And he won't mind Nana as long as you keep her out of the old house.'

'Why?' asked Derek. 'I mean, I should have thought he'd care more about new stuff than old.'

'He's a historian,' Miles explained. 'The old house is full of valuable antiques – tapestries and four-poster beds and cabinets with secret drawers and all that sort of thing.'

'Secret drawers! Gosh!'

'And a secret passage, and lost treasure, and a ghost.'

'Crikey!' breathed Derek. 'Ripping!'

Belinda wasn't so sure a ghost was 'ripping', but she saw a twinkle in Uncle Miles's eyes and guessed he was teasing Derek. 'Have you ever seen the ghost, Uncle Miles?' she asked.

'Not I, but I live in hope. Aren't you going to let Nana off to chase squirrels, Bel? Won't she come when she's called?'

'Mostly.'

'She always comes when I whistle,' said Derek.

'It's not fair. Girls aren't supposed to whistle.'

'Who said that? Your gran or Aunt Daisy?'

'Gran,' said Bel, grasping Derek's point at once. Her new mother had very different ideas from her grandmother about what was proper for girls to do. 'But I don't know how.'

'Let Nana off and we'll teach you,' Uncle Miles promised.

By the time they reached the house, Nana was exhausted and muddy, while Uncle Miles and Derek were wheezing from laughing at Belinda's efforts, but she could almost whistle. Whenever she tried, Nana cocked her head, so it was worth persevering.

'Better not whistle indoors,' suggested Uncle Miles, 'and we'd better take Nana to one of the gardeners to be washed before she comes in. This way.'

With the puppy clean and as dry as a couple of sacks could make her, they went into the house. Nana went straight to the fireplace, lay down on the hearthrug, and fell asleep. No one seemed very interested in her. They were busy fussing around Lady Dalrymple with cushions and tea.

There was a girl not much older than Belinda and Derek, but she wasn't a bit friendly. There was a cross-looking clergyman, not at all like chubby, cheerful Mr Preston at home. Derek started to talk to a man who was a sailor, a captain. Belinda went politely to sit with an old lady who smiled at her. Her name was Mrs Norville. She said she came from India, a long, long time ago, so Bel told her about her schoolfriend Deva, who was Indian. Mrs Norville was very nice.

After tea, Uncle Miles took Belinda and Derek on a tour of the old house. He warned them to be very careful because of everything being so valuable. They had to take a lantern because it was getting dark and there was no electricity, not even gas.

'I've got an electric torch,' Derek announced. 'Daddy gave it to me for an early Christmas present. I'll go and get it.'

'Save the battery for when you need it,' Uncle Miles advised, lighting his lantern.

The old house was full of interesting things, but it was a bit eerie by lantern-light. There were shadows everywhere, and the people in the tapestries seemed to jump out at you when you went into a room. They kept moving, too, because it was windy outside now and the draughts made the tapestries ripple and rustle.

'It's sort of like being in a house full of ghosts,' Belinda said.

'Real ghosts moan and rattle their chains,' Derek objected. 'I say, Bel, let's come back tomorrow when it's light and look for the treasure map in the secret drawers.'

'May we, Uncle Miles?'

'I don't see why not, as long as you're careful not to break anything. Right-oh, we'd better get back now. It's your suppertime, and I have to dress for dinner.'

Jemima had supper with Derek and Belinda. She was simply furious because she usually had dinner with the grown-ups. The silly thing was she was angry with Bel and Derek, though it wasn't their fault at all. She scowled and muttered, and after pudding (delicious apple pie with very thick cream the maid called 'clotted'), she said loudly, 'It's going to be a rotten Christmas,' and went off without another word.

'She can have a rotten Christmas if she wants,' said Derek, 'we're going to have a ripping Christmas. Nanny packed a big box of crackers and gummed paper for making paper chains. And Captain Norville said there'll be a Christmas tree and carols and mince pies, and plum pudding with sixpences in if he has to put them there himself. And if we hang up stockings tomorrow night, Father Christmas will come, only he'll have a grizzledy grey beard instead of white.'

Belinda giggled. 'What a nice man! I hope you didn't tell him we're too old for Father Christmas.'

'Gosh, no! I said could we borrow a pair of his socks 'cause they're probably the biggest stockings in the house, and he said yes. He's a brick. Maybe I'll be a sailor when I grow up.'

'Right now what you've got to be is a gentleman. I have to take Nana out. Please, may I borrow your electric torch?'

Derek hesitated, then came up with a compromise. 'Tell you what, I'll come with you.'

Even with the torch, it was very dark outside, very different from London with its street lamps and lights in people's houses. The wind was blowing in great gusts which hurried them along in one direction and held them back when they turned around. Some of the gusts showered them with raindrops. Derek thought it was very jolly, and Belinda could see what he meant, but she was glad to go back inside.

They took Nana to the scullery where they had been told she was to sleep, then found their bedroom candles and lit them. They both thought it was very funny to be carrying lit candles up to bed with them, and Derek laughed so hard he blew his out halfway up the stairs. There were two lots of stairs, the second one very steep and narrow and sort of twisty, with a tiny landing at the top.

The bedrooms were very small, with sloping ceilings because they were up under the roof. Derek's was next to Belinda's, with a connecting door. There was a door on the other side, too, which a maid had told her was to the Reverend Calloway's room, and her parents were just at the bottom of the twisty stairs.

She and Derek got ready for bed, then sat cross-legged

on Belinda's bed planning tomorrow's treasure hunt. Derek was sure the map must have been hidden in the desk with the naked people on it. Bel voted for the other desk Uncle Miles had shown them, in the south room, mostly because she didn't think they ought to be looking at the naked people.

'We won't *look* at them,' Derek argued. 'We'll be too busy searching for the secret drawers no one else has found. I bet that's why they didn't find them, because they were squeamish about the naked people. You're not squeamish, are you?'

'No!' Bel denied hotly, though she wasn't at all sure what squeamish meant. It was a good word, though. Derek probably learnt it at his boarding school.

'Right-oh, that's settled then. Oh, hello, Aunt Daisy. Is it bedtime already?'

'Yes, darling, off you go. I'll pop in when I've tucked Bel in. I've brought you a night-light, Bel, because you're in a strange place and there's no switch to turn on a light if you need one.' She lit a little, fat candle and set it on the chest-of-drawers. 'All right, darling?'

Belinda was asleep almost before Daisy had kissed her good night.

She woke with a start some hours later. The wind was howling around the eaves and down the chimney, making the night-light flicker. When the howling paused moment-arily, something scratched at the windowpane. Just the creeper growing up the wall, Belinda assured herself stoutly. That wouldn't have wakened her – so what did?

She lay straining her ears. Was that a footstep? Some-thing moaned softly. Bel sat bolt upright.

A white figure drifted towards her from the direction of Derek's room. It had a head, but no face. When she sat up, the moaning grew louder. The figure floated on across the room, and then came a rattling noise.

Belinda screamed.

CHAPTER 5

Daisy and Alec had retired early, though a considerable time passed before they settled to sleep. Daisy lay in bed, curled up against Alec, with his arm around her waist. He was already asleep. She mused on how wonderful life was. Before she was married, she hadn't realized that one could miss a person physically as well as emotionally, and after just a couple of days apart.

She was glad they had a double bed. No modern nonsense about separate singles in this old-fashioned house, she was thinking drowsily, when she heard Belinda scream.

'Daddy!'

Alec stirred. Daisy sprang out of bed. Not wasting time hunting for her abandoned nightie, she grabbed her dressing-gown, pulling it on as she felt her way through the pitch-darkness, barefooted on the chilly polished floor-boards. Where was the door? Oh for the flip of a switch!

A narrow line of light from a lamp left burning in the passage showed her the way. Flinging open the door, she stumbled up the awkward stairs to Belinda's room. The child's voice was a wail now: 'Daddy!'

'Darling, I'm here. Everything's all right. Did you have

a bad dream?' As she spoke, Daisy gathered the sobbing girl in her arms and glanced around the dimly lit room.

A paler rectangle – the door to the clergyman's bedroom was open. Daisy's upbringing had not been so sheltered that she hadn't heard tales of clergymen who . . .

'A ghost! It was a ghost, Mummy, all white, moaning and rattling its chains.'

'Did it touch you, darling?' Even as she spoke, Daisy became aware of voices in the next room. 'Wait here, Belinda, I'm going to see just what's going on.'

Mr Calloway, fully dressed, had the ghost by its thoroughly corporeal wrist. It had on an ankle-length white garment, with a lacy white shawl completely covering its head.

'. . . dabbling in the occult,' the clergyman was saying sternly, 'a highly dangerous pastime. You put your immortal soul in danger for the sake of a silly prank.'

'Let me go! It was just in fun.'

'Jemima,' whispered Belinda, slipping her hand into Daisy's. 'She doesn't like Derek and me.'

'The supernatural is not "fun". From playing the ghost, you may easily come to the deadly sin of attempting to raise ghosts and spirits.'

'I hardly think so,' said Daisy, walking in. 'A stupid bit of mischief, that's all, isn't it, Jemima? I have a word to say to you, young lady, but we don't want to keep Mr Calloway from his devotions.' She had noticed a pillow on the floor by the bed, indented by two knees.

'I am sorry to hear you make light of this, Mrs Fletcher. However, this is not the time for serious remonstrances. I shall speak to her parents in the morning and ask their permission to see if I cannot make her see the evil of her tricks. This is a troubled house. I shall pray for all within its walls.'

Daisy was tempted to say, 'Not for me, thank you,' but that would be a very bad example for the girls; and anyway, she was far too well brought up. 'Good night,' she said instead, and beckoned imperiously to the ghost. She was her mother's daughter in that, she thought ruefully.

Even with bare feet and no nightdress under her dressing-gown, she could make a gesture imperious enough to bring Jemima slouching after her into Belinda's room.

Shutting the door, she moved to stand on the bedside rug, saying, 'Belinda, get back into bed before you catch cold. Jemima, take your grandmother's shawl off your head, if you please. Now tell me, why did you play such an unkind trick on a younger child who is a guest in your house? Why did you want to frighten Belinda?'

'I didn't care about frightening Belinda,' Jemima said sulkily. 'I just wanted to make Mr Calloway go away.'

'Mr Calloway? Why on earth . . . ?'

'He's upset everyone. He's going to absolutely ruin Christmas! I suppose you'll tell everyone what I did,' she snarled at Belinda.

'No, I shan't. I don't carry tales.'

'Mr Calloway's going to tell your parents,' Daisy pointed out. 'You'll have to explain to them what it was all about. Now you'd better get to bed. Off you go.'

Jemima left through the door to the landing, which Daisy had left open. As she closed it behind her, the handle rattled slightly.

'That's what it was,' said Belinda. 'That's the noise I thought was chains. It must have been Mr Calloway's door handle, and I should think what woke me up was when she came in through Derek's door.'

'She came through Derek's room?'

'I think so. When I saw her, she was coming from that direction. Do you think he's all right?' Bel started climbing out of bed.

'You just stay put, young lady, and do your best to go back to sleep. I'll see to Derek.'

Daisy wondered if she'd find her intrepid nephew cowering under the bedclothes. She should have known better. He was fast asleep, sprawled on his back, the bedclothes around his waist. She pulled them up around his neck, tucked them in, and went back to her own room.

Alec was as fast asleep as Derek. Of course, he'd worked hard all week and had had the exhausting task of bringing her mother plus children and puppy from London to Brockdene. Yet before their marriage he would have awakened at the slightest sound of distress from his precious daughter. Daisy sighed. She supposed it was flattering that, even dead to the world, he relied on her to take care of Bel.

Icy feet against his thighs brought only an indistinct mutter as his arm closed around her again. Feeling wide awake she started to try to puzzle out what Jemima had really been up to, and what it had to do with whatever was going on with the rest of the Norvilles. But in spite of the subject's fascination, within a couple of minutes she drifted off.

When Daisy and Alec went down to breakfast on Christmas Eve, only Miles was in the dining room.

'Your two are off somewhere doing something deadly secret,' he reported, as they helped themselves from the sideboard.

'Not outside, I hope,' said Daisy, looking at the rain beating against the window.

'I think not. They took the pup out for a quick dash earlier, then apologized profusely to her for shutting her up again, so I suspect they're in the old house. I suppose they're to be trusted not to do any damage?'

'Oh yes, they're good children.' Daisy sat down opposite the young man.

'On the whole,' Alec qualified. 'You did warn them to be especially careful, I trust?'

'I told them Father would beat them within an inch of their lives if anything was broken. I remember the time I . . . Ah well, that's water under the bridge. It's about the only thing that really gets his goat. The Rev was fulminating against Jemima this morning, but Father didn't seem to care a hoot. I don't suppose you know what that was all about?'

Daisy exchanged a glance with Alec, whom she'd told about the night's adventures.

'I see you know all and are not going to tell me,' said Miles. 'Ah well, I'll worm it out of Mother. *She* was pretty annoyed about Jemima's shenanigans. Jemima's been sent up to wind wool for Gran. I was asked to present Mother's excuses for not being here when you came down. She's gone to consult Mrs Pardon about Christmas frolics, the Pardon being expected to cooperate for once because there's a "Lady" in the house, with a capital L. Said Lady is breakfasting in bed, I understand.'

'Said Lady always does,' Daisy affirmed. 'I hope Mrs Pardon has assigned a maid to her full time. I'm surprised she didn't bring her own woman.'

'Lady Dalrymple gave her maid Christmas off,' said Alec, 'assuming that Lord Westwood's house would have plenty of well-trained servants.'

'Plenty of housemaids.' Miles looked at Daisy. 'Am I out of line, Mrs Fletcher, if I say we've all been wondering why Lady Dalrymple chose to come to Brockdene for Christmas?'

'I never attempt to explain anything Mother does,' Daisy said lightly. 'Where is everyone else?'

'The Rev's in the chapel, praying to be preserved from Gran's idols. You haven't seen them yet, have you, sir? I'll take you up after breakfast, if you like. They're rather magnificent.'

'So Daisy tells me.'

'Uncle Victor's dragged a couple of gardeners out to cut a Christmas tree and some greenery. Flick . . . Oh, good morning, sir.' Miles jumped up as an elderly gentleman in a decidedly damp tweed suit came into the room.

'Sit down, sit down, my boy, and finish your breakfast.'

'Just a last cup of coffee. Will you have one? Mrs Fletcher, may I present my grandfather, James Tremayne? Mr and Mrs Fletcher, sir.'

So this was the solicitor, Dora Norville's father, who had paid for Miles's schooling and now employed him. 'How do you do, Mr Tremayne,' Daisy said with a smile. 'Don't tell me you walked over from Calstock in this weather?'

'Pooh, pooh, a bit of a breeze and a drop of rain, nothing to a countryman, Mrs Fletcher, I assure you.' He stood on the hearth, his back to the fire, his steaming clothes releasing an odour of cigars into the room. 'Now, the weather forecast is something different. I listened to it this morning on my wireless receiver. I have an excellent wireless set. They say this wind will grow to gale force in the course of the morning. That's why I came over early.'

'We're quite sheltered at Brockdene,' said Miles, taking his grandfather a cup of coffee. 'I daresay it won't amount to much except for those at sea. But you'd better reckon to spend the night, sir.'

'Perhaps so, perhaps so. I wouldn't wish to put out Lord Westmoor's guests.'

'You won't do that, Mr Tremayne,' Daisy assured him. Her mother could not possibly have any greater objection to a country solicitor than she already did to a dark-skinned poor relation, and her host's absence. 'The more the merrier, especially at Christmas.'

He beamed at her. 'Just what I think, dear lady! And that reminds me, I brought the post with me, and there was a letter for Lady Dalrymple, as well as one or two for your father, Miles. And the newspapers. They are on the hall table. Godfrey doesn't take a newspaper, so I generally bring a couple when I come over. I expect you'd like to see the *Times*, Mr Fletcher.'

Alec agreed, though his usual paper was the *Daily Chronicle*, a shockingly liberal choice for a policeman. They chatted about the news of the day for a few minutes, until a maid came in and said to Daisy, 'Please, madam, her ladyship wants to see you.'

'Right-oh, I'll go up in a minute. Thank you . . . ?'

'Jenny, madam. Right away, madam, her ladyship said.

Her ladyship's in a proper state, madam, and I'm sure I hope 'tis not something I've done; but I weren't trained up for a lady's maid and that's the plain truth of it.'

'She'd have left you in no doubt if it were your fault, Jenny.' Regretfully Daisy abandoned what little remained of her sausage and toast. 'Oh dear, what now, I wonder?'

'I reckon it's that letter, madam,' Jenny said, as they left the dining room. 'Knowing Mr Tremayne were come, and him sometimes bringing the post, I looked and saw it on the table when I were going up to get her ladyship's breakfast things, so I took it up to her ladyship. She sent me to run her bath, and she were opening it when I left, and when I come back she were in a state.'

'I'm sure it must have been the letter. Thank you, Jenny, you can go now. I'll ring if you're needed.'

Hurrying up the stairs, Daisy wondered whom the letter was from and what on earth it said that was so upsetting it required her immediate presence. Surely not Violet! If anything had happened to her or the baby, she or Johnnie would have written to Daisy first and let her break it to their mother.

'Mother, what . . . ?'

'Daisy, how could you be so remiss, so utterly lacking in duty to your only parent, as to leave me to learn the truth from a stranger?'

'Mother, I've already explained that Westmoor didn't tell me he wasn't going to be here for Christmas, though I gather he's spent Christmas at Tavy Bridge for years. And I didn't know Mrs Norville was Indian, either.'

'Indian!' Lady Dalrymple snorted and waved the offending letter. Sitting up in bed in a powder-blue quilted satin bed jacket, she was a study in outrage. 'That is the least of it!'

'Whom is it from?'

'Eva Devenish. An utterly reliable source.'

'Blast!' Daisy muttered. Lady Eva never invented gossip; she didn't need to. She had at her fingertips every scrap of scandal which had shaken the aristocracy in the past five or six decades. No use Daisy trying to cast doubt on whatever she had raked up this time. 'Lady Eva's not exactly a stranger, Mother, even if she isn't family. But how did she know you were here?'

'I happened to run into her at Claridge's, where I spent Saturday night, since your husband's house is not suitable for inviting your mother to stay when she is in town. We spoke briefly, as she was rushing off somewhere – and how she manages it at her age I cannot imagine. There's really something quite indecent about it – but I mentioned that I was to be Westmoor's guest at Brockdene. If only she had had the common courtesy to enlighten me there and then!'

'Enlighten you about what, Mother?'

'I suppose you believe the Indian person is the widow of the sixth earl's youngest son.'

'Honestly, I never thought twice about whose widow she is.'

'She's not.'

'If you want me to understand, you'll have to be less oracular,' Daisy said, patience wearing thin.

Momentarily, the dowager looked flummoxed, as if she wondered what 'oracular' meant. She knew when Daisy was being unfilial, though. 'I'm afraid being married to a policeman has not improved your manners, Daisy. Eva says it was all well known at the time. I was much too young to hear about it, of course.'

'Of course, Mother,' said Daisy, less to redeem herself than in the hope of speeding the awaited revelation.

'It was in the seventies. Albert Norville was a subaltern in India. His commanding officer wrote to Westmoor, the sixth earl, that Albert was involved with a native woman and had even had a child by her. Naturally Westmoor summoned Albert home.' Lady Dalrymple scanned the letter to refresh her memory of the misdeeds of the unfortunate Albert. 'His ship arrived in Plymouth some months later.'

'He came?'

'Naturally. In *those* days one did not lightly disobey one's parents. According to Westmoor's man of business in Plymouth, Albert called on him and learnt that his parents were in London, but his eldest brother, Lord Norville, was here at Brockdene. He announced his intention of sailing up the Tamar to win Norville's support before he faced Westmoor.'

'How on earth did all this become known?' Daisy demanded.

'According to Eva, the sixth countess was a thoroughly indiscreet woman, even a trifle underbred. Of course, the shock must excuse a certain lack of self-control,' Lady Dalrymple said with conscious tolerance, 'though I should never allow myself such latitude.'

'What shock, Mother?'

'They were both drowned.'

'What! Who?'

'Albert and his brother. The servants here reported that

they quarrelled bitterly, and the sailors who took them down the river said they actually came to fisticuffs on the boat. They fell overboard and could not be saved.'

'How dreadful!'

'The middle brother became the seventh earl, and the present Lord Westmoor is his son. I shall write him a stiff letter, a very stiff letter indeed. I consider his conduct towards me unconscionable.'

'He does seem to have gone a bit too far,' Daisy conceded.

'He's become downright eccentric since the war!'

'But how did Mrs Norville end up living here at Brockdene, Mother? Surely Lady Eva hasn't left you in suspense.'

'"Mrs" Norville turned up in England some months later with two children, claiming to be married to Albert. She offered no proof, and the sixth earl didn't believe her for a moment; but to keep her quiet he gave her an allowance and a home here as long as she made no claims. Can you imagine the scandal if the newspapers had got hold of the story?'

'They would have had a field day,' said Daisy, trying to imagine the feelings of the unhappy girl, arriving in England with two little boys to find her husband dead and his family refusing to acknowledge her – always supposing Albert had actually been her legal husband. Surely she would have had some sort of proof, though. Perhaps he had just gone through some sort of Hindu ceremony with her.

'I presume the earl left provision for her in his will,' her mother continued, 'to save his heirs from any unpleasantness. But what possessed Westmoor to suppose I would consider the woman an acceptable hostess is beyond me! I have a very good mind to leave immediately.'

'What an excellent idea, Mother. I'm sure you could spend a very comfortable Christmas at Claridge's ...' Daisy's voice trailed off. She swallowed a sigh. 'Only even if we could summon a boat to take you to Plymouth, the weather's already foul and there are gale warnings on the wireless. I'm afraid you'll have to stay.'

CHAPTER 6

Everyone helped with the Christmas decorations. Even Lady Dalrymple.

Once she accepted the impossibility of leaving in a huff, she had descended to the hall. In her best grande dame manner she thoroughly enjoyed supervising the decking of it, as far as Daisy could see. Captain Norville was the moving spirit, nominally in charge, but the dowager sent him and Alec, his able assistant, rushing back and forth with ladders: this paper chain (turned out by the dozen by Derek and Belinda, with Miles sorting the rainbow colours for them) hung not quite symmetrically; that bunch of mistletoe was not perfectly centred over the doorway. The captain accepted her ladyship's corrections with unfailing good humour. She seemed to have forgotten, however temporarily, that he was the illegitimate offspring of a native.

Meekly accepting her ladyship's occasional condescending remarks, the native herself sat by the wide hearth. A noble fire burned there today, though its warmth was vitiated by the gale howling down the chimney. Mrs Norville was turning scraps of wool into little dollies which Jemima hung on the Christmas tree. Daisy and Felicity tied ribbons and sweets on its branches and draped tinsel. Mr Tremayne fixed the Christmas tree candles firmly in their little metal holders, while Dora Norville fussed over clipping them on safely.

Her husband had fastened the silver paper star to the top of the tree. Thereafter he hurried about the hall uttering cries of distress every time a nail holding some ancient weapon was required to do double duty for a paper chain or bunch of holly. Whether his presence counted as helping was questionable, but at least he was present.

Everyone was present, except the clergyman.

'Mistletoe!' The Reverend Calloway stalked through the door from the east wing, his eyes on the green leaves and pearly berries dangling above him. 'Do Druids worship here? And an evergreen tree? I scarcely believe my eyes! Why do you celebrate the holy birthday of our Lord with these pagan symbols?'

'A Christmas tree is a pagan symbol, Mr Calloway?' asked the captain, doubtful and anxious. 'I'd never have guessed, I promise you.'

'Stuff and nonsense!' exclaimed Lady Dalrymple. 'My good man, my uncle the bishop saw no harm in Christmas trees. Your dogmatism is preposterous. And as for mistletoe . . .' A touch of pink tinted her cheeks, to Daisy's astonishment. Mother blushing? 'My late husband always insisted on mistletoe at Christmas.'

'I'm sure if Lady Dalrymple has no objection, there is nothing more to be said.' Godfrey Norville cast a defiant glance not at the clergyman but at his brother, as Daisy was interested to note.

'It's all for the children, Reverend,' said Captain Norville, placatory now.

'For our guests,' Mrs Godfrey put in with determined brightness. 'The old traditions are such fun, aren't they?'

'There's another tradition which will be more to your taste, Padre,' said Miles. 'We're going to sing carols in the chapel this evening.'

Calloway seemed mollified. 'I shall be pleased to join in hymns appropriate to the church calendar.'

'Mr Calloway.' At the unexpected sound of old Mrs Norville's gentle voice, everyone turned to stare at her. 'I hope you will be so kind as to take a Christmas service for us in the chapel tomorrow morning?'

'Gladly, ma'am.' He didn't go so far as to smile, but the look he bent upon her was definitely softened. 'I am happy to see that so much proper feeling remains.'

Daisy saw the captain surreptitiously wipe his forehead. What on earth could make it so important to him to keep on the clergyman's right side?

The gong in the east wing rang out, interrupting her thoughts. Captain Norville gallantly offered his arm to Lady Dalrymple, and she, after a moment's hesitation, deigned to accept it. The rest followed them through to lunch.

'At last!' said Derek. 'I thought we'd never get away.'

'I don't mind,' said Belinda. 'It was fun making decorations, and I like having lunch with the grown-ups. Anyway, Mummy wouldn't have let us go out while the wind was so strong even though it stopped raining.'

'The gale's blown away the clouds. It's a good thing it didn't last long. Come on, let's get Nana.'

Belinda hung back. 'I still think we ought to tell someone where we're going. So Daddy can find us if . . .'

'Oh, all right. We prob'ly ought to ask Mr Norville if it's all right to go there anyway, but *don't breathe a word* about what we found.' His hand touched his pocket. 'I've got my torch.'

She envied his pockets. Why were boys allowed to have great big pockets you could fit everything in, while girls could only fit a hankie in theirs?

They found Godfrey Norville. 'You ask,' Derek whispered. 'People always think boys are planning mischief.'

'Please, sir,' said Belinda, hoping what they were planning didn't count as mischief, 'may we go to that tower on the hill?'

'The prospect tower? Yes, certainly. I don't believe it's locked. There's nothing in there you can damage. The sixth earl had the rotten old stairs removed, so you can't come to any harm.'

With a rapturous Nana bouncing around them, they set off up the grassy hill. As they approached the tall stone tower, they saw that it was a triangle with concave sides, though from a distance it looked as square and solid as anything.

'No wonder it's called a folly,' Derek said scornfully, 'but I bet you could see a long, long way from the top. I bet the smugglers used to signal to each other from the top. Then when it was safe, they used the secret passage to hide their loot.'

'Contraband,' Belinda corrected him. 'Pirates have loot.'

'Never mind, it's all treasure. I hope the mechanism hasn't gone all rusty. It'll be jolly mouldy if we can't get in.'

The door pushed open easily enough. Inside, Belinda looked up and saw a triangle of sky, for the tower had no roof.

'Everything's bound to be rusty with the rain coming in,' she said, half disappointed, half relieved.

'Not if it's all inside the walls. Let's look at the map.'

Derek took from his pocket a piece of paper yellowed with age and not much improved by its latest resting place. He knelt on the damp, rough floorboards and unfolded it with the greatest care, fending off the puppy's inquisitive nose. Bel knelt beside him. Together they pored over the spindly, faded writing and diagrams.

'It's right opposite the door,' said Belinda.

'Two feet up. People wouldn't notice because it's below eye-level.' Derek jumped up. 'Come on.'

Belinda folded the map and brought it with her. She didn't want to enter any secret passage without instructions on how to get out again. Derek had already found the loose stone. He pried it out, and there was the promised lever.

It moved with surprising ease. In the darkest corner of the tTower, a square of floor swung downward.

'Gosh!' Derek exclaimed, running over to the black hole.

'Derek, what if it's not a secret after all?'

'What do you mean?'

'I was just thinking. If the floor was really really old, wouldn't it be rotten, like Mr Norville said the stairs were? I think the sixth earl must've put in a new floor, and he couldn't do that without everyone finding out about the room underneath.'

'Oh. Well, maybe, but maybe they didn't find the secret tunnel on the map. That'll be where the treasure's hidden.' He sat on the edge of the hole with his feet dangling and turned on his torch. 'I'm going down anyway. Look, there's steps.'

Abandoning whatever she had been sniffing in the far corner, Nana beat him to it. She trotted down the steps and disappeared into the blackness below. Derek hurried after her, and Belinda didn't want to be left behind.

'Is there anything there?' she called, feeling her way cautiously as Derek wasn't shining the torch towards the stairs.

'Treasure chests!'

Belinda was low enough now to see the torch beam playing over a stack of wooden boxes. They didn't look anything like the treasure chests in the pictures in *Treasure Island* or *The Arabian Nights*. 'Are they locked? Can you open them?'

Derek was raising a lid, shining the light inside. 'Nothing.' He dropped that lid, raised another.

'They say "Darjeeling" on the outside,' said Belinda, coming close enough to read the large, painted letters. '"Darjeeling, Calcutta, London." I bet they had tea in them. They used to smuggle tea as well as brandy, didn't they? "Brandy for the parson, 'baccy for the clerk . . . laces for my lady . . ."'

'Laces? They smuggled shoelaces?'

'No, silly, French lace for dresses and things. The song doesn't say tea, though.'

'Never mind, they're all empty anyway. Let's find the tunnel.'

'It said we have to close the trapdoor. I don't think . . .'

'Don't be such a *girl*, Bel! Come and help.'

It took all their united strength to lift the trapdoor into place. Derek had to lay down the torch, so that was no help, nor was Nana, who kept getting in the way. At last it clicked into place above them. The sound gave Belinda a sort of horrid hollow feeling inside.

Derek retrieved his torch. He flashed it around the stone-walled room.

'I can't see anything,' he said, bitterly disappointed. 'Let's look at the map again.' As he turned towards Belinda, the beam swung across the area which had been hidden by the trapdoor.

'No, look!' she cried, pointing. 'A latch! It'd be jolly hard to see with just candles.'

It was a large but perfectly ordinary latch, of grey-painted metal without a speck of rust. They raised it and pulled with all their might on the handle. With much creaking and groaning, a wooden door faced with very thin stone slabs swung open. An earthy smell wafted out.

'Let's go!' shouted Derek, and plunged into the narrow tunnel revealed by his torch. Nana frisked after him.

'*Wait*!' Belinda wanted to say, '*What if there's a skeleton*?' but that would only make him call her a *girl* in that horrid way. 'Remember, I haven't got a torch. And shouldn't we put something to block the door, so it doesn't close?'

'Good idea. We'll use one of those chests.'

Bel breathed a silent sigh of relief. At least she knew they could get out again.

The tunnel was perfectly beastly. She couldn't see much

because Derek went ahead, but at least he was the one who got cobwebs in his face, not that he minded. First there was a slope going down, then a long flight of stone steps. On the plan it looked as if there was a room at the end.

'Derek, if we find the treasure, we can't keep it, can we?'

'Blast!' He stopped dead, turned and shone the torch into her eyes. She covered them with one hand and flapped at him with the other. He lowered the beam to her feet, which wasn't much help. 'I suppose we can't. But who do you think it belongs to? Mr Norville?'

'I don't think so. I don't think any of the stuff is his; he's just frightfully keen on it. I think everything belongs to Lord Westmoor. I wish we could give it to Mrs Norville.'

'The old lady?'

'Yes, she's nice. Couldn't we give it to her secretly?'

'We have to find it first. Come on.'

Nana added a 'hurry up' bark. They went on, and suddenly the passage ended and they stepped into a sort of half cave, half room. It was quite small, square, with three walls of rock and packed earth shored up with wood and one of neat stonework.

'No skeleton,' said Belinda, relieved.

'No treasure chest,' said Derek gloomily. 'What a washout.'

'Maybe there's another map,' she consoled him. 'We haven't tried the other desk yet, the one in the south room. But look, Nana's got something!'

'Nana, drop it!'

Nana didn't want to give up her find, but Belinda made her sit and Derek prised it from her jaws. She barked as he examined it, with Belinda allowed to hold the torch.

'What is it, Derek?'

'It looks like a dagger in a sheath. Gosh, it's almost as good as treasure.' Holding one end, he pulled on the other. A blade slid out. It wasn't rusty, but it had rusty-brown stains on it. 'Blood!' said Derek, with ghoulish glee. 'I bet someone was murdered with it.'

'It doesn't look much like a dagger, though, just a knife.'

'D'you think Lord Westmoor would want it, Bel? Maybe he'd let me keep it.'

'He might; but if it's historical, Mr Norville will want it. He'd prob'ly get to keep it.'

'But I found it!'

'Nana found it – and she's got something else. Quick, get it away from her!'

How ragged and dirty the dirty rag had been before the puppy got hold of it and Derek wrested it from her would remain a mystery. He swore it was a bloodstained handkerchief. Bel was not so sure, but no doubt that would also remain a mystery.

'At least no one else will want it,' she said.

'I'm going to keep it forever,' Derek vowed. 'Let's see if we missed anything else.'

In examining every inch of the cave-room, they discovered a door in the woodwork. 'See if it opens,' said Belinda. 'I don't want to go back through that horrid tunnel if I don't have to.'

'It might be difficult,' Derek admitted, his voice suddenly shaky. 'I think my battery's dying.'

He laid the torch on the floor. By its now wavery light, they shoved frantically on the door.

At last it opened an inch or two, just enough to let in a streak of greenish light. There it stuck.

'It's going to get dark outside soon, too.' Belinda felt her eyes fill with tears. She didn't want to be buried alive, not now, when she had a puppy and a brand-new mummy. And poor Daddy would be most awfully sad!

CHAPTER 7

Blinking away her tears, Belinda put her eye to the crack. Outside was a green gloom, a curtain of ivy. She heard birds singing and water running and muffled voices.

'Someone's there. Let's shout for help.'

'No! That'd be a pretty wet end to a real adventure. Come on, push harder.'

'They might go away,' said Belinda, but she pushed with all her strength.

The door creaked open a few more inches. Nana pricked up her ears, slipped through the gap, and dashed off.

'Nana! Oh no, I'll never find her,' Belinda cried.

'I bet we can get out that way. Take your coat off.'

It was a squeeze, but they made it. Behind the ivy was a tree trunk, and they had to squeeze past that, too. They came out into the valley garden, face to face with Daisy, Alec and the captain.

Captain Norville took his pipe from his mouth and roared with laughter.

'Where did you two spring from?' Alec enquired around his pipe, grinning.

'You're filthy!' said Daisy. 'What have you been up to?'

The story poured out.

The captain laughed again. 'An enterprising pair. I knew about the room under the prospect tower. God and I . . .' He cast a quick uneasy glance over his shoulder. 'Godfrey and I, I should say, used to play at smugglers down there, and prisoners in dungeons, and all manner of games.'

'We asked Mr Norville if it was all right to go to the tower,' Derek said.

'Good for you! But I didn't know about the tunnel and the room at this end. Without a map we didn't think to close the trap, so we never noticed the latch. Of course we didn't have electric torches, just stubs of candles usually, or an oil lantern. I wonder if Godfrey discovered it later?'

'He wouldn't have left this there, would he?' Derek brandished the knife. 'Uncle Alec, don't you think this is a bloodstain?'

'It could be,' Alec agreed, inspecting the blade. 'It's hard to tell, though. My guess is the knife's been there a long, long time.'

'I wonder if it's connected with the story the boatman told me,' Daisy said. 'I expect you know the tale, Captain. About a hundred years ago there was a smuggler chief called Red Jack who was related to the Norvilles. The family hid him when he was badly injured by the dragoons.'

'I bet that's it,' said Derek excitedly. 'I bet they hid him in the secret room, the *really* secret one, and this is the knife he fought the dragoons with.'

'Could be,' said the captain. 'The haft is teak, nicely carved. Dolphins and sea serpents – typical. It looks like the sort of sheath-knife seamen still carry today, to be used for rope and 'baccy and salt pork and anything else that needs cutting or whittling. I've heard the story, Mrs Fletcher, but Godfrey would know more about it, I expect.'

'I'll ask him.' Derek slid the blade back into the sheath. 'Come on, Bel.'

'Hold on, young man!' Alec commanded. 'First you'll go and shut all the secret doors you've left open.'

'Right-oh, Uncle Alec. But I don't think we can shut the one at this end. It was frightfully hard to open'

'I'll see what I can do,' offered the captain.

'Gosh, thanks, sir. Bel and I can manage the other end, I think.'

'And then,' put in Daisy, 'before you even dream of speaking to Mr Norville, you'll both go and wash your hands and faces and change your clothes. And brush your hair.'

Bel slipped her grubby hand into Daisy's. 'Are you angry, Mummy?'

'Not a bit of it, darling. Like the captain, I think it's frightfully enterprising of the two of you. But you still need to wash your face and comb the twigs and cobwebs out of your hair. Oh, and brush Nana before you go in. Off you go.'

It was nearly teatime when Belinda and Derek came downstairs, clean and tidy, Derek carrying the precious knife. They met Mr Norville, Miss Norville and Jemima in the hall on their way to tea. ('Mince pies and Christmas cake,' the maid who took their dirty clothes had promised.)

'Please, sir, look what we found,' said Derek.

They told the story again. Jemima scowled the whole time. Bel was sure she was dying of envy.

'What an adventure,' said Miss Norville. 'Miles will be

simply wild. He used to drag me around endlessly hunting for that passage and the treasure, and we never even found the room under the prospect tower. You never told us about it, Daddy.'

'There was nothing worth seeing in it.' Mr Norville didn't seem very interested. He pulled the blade from the sheath and said, 'Yes, yes, a common seaman's knife. It could be eighteenth century, but far from rare. The carving might be worth a second look, but I haven't time for such things at present. Leave it here on the table. I'll see to it when everything's settled.'

'No one wants that dirty old thing,' Jemima sneered.

As the children followed the Norvilles to the library, Derek glanced back sadly at his slighted treasure lying abandoned on the hall table. He sighed.

'Never mind,' Belinda whispered. 'I bet there's another map, in the south room, and we'll find the *real* treasure.'

The chapel was decorated with holly, ivy and evergreens. Candles burned in silver and brass candlesticks on the altar and in the gleaming brass candelabra hanging from the barrel-vaulted ceiling. The woodwork gleamed, too: the pews, the small organ console and the beautifully carved rood-screen. Whatever their faults, Lord Westmoor's servants took good care of his possessions.

Many of them were already in the chapel, seated at the rear, when the ancient but still working clock chimed the hour and his lordship's guests and poor relations came in.

As Daisy entered down the steps from the old dining room, she recognized Mrs Pardon and two or three maids

she had met. The others, having had no business with the
guests, gazed curiously at the strangers and whispered to
each other. The whispering ceased abruptly as the Reverend
Calloway appeared. Daisy, seated in the front row between
Bel and Derek, saw the clergyman glance around at the
decorations and frown. He really was too finicky for words!

As it was not a formal service, just carol singing, he sat
down in the pew behind Daisy. Dora Norville went to the
organ, and her husband stood up at the front and
announced, 'The Wassail Song'.

'Oh good,' Belinda murmured as the organ piped out an
introduction. 'We sing this at school.'

> 'Here we come a-wassailing,
> Among the leaves so green.'

Daisy heard a snort behind her. She had no doubt from
whom it emanated. The Rev's voice was notably not raised
in song.

> 'We have got a little purse,
> Of stretching leather skin.
> We want a little of your money
> To line it well within!
> Love and joy come to you,
> And to you your wassail too . . .'

'The Wassail Song' was followed by 'O Come, All Ye
Faithful', and that by 'The First Noël'. Mr Calloway bore
a strong baritone line in each. Then Miles stood up and
moved to the front.

'I'd like to teach you a carol I learnt from a wounded German soldier . . .' A gasp from more than one throat interrupted him, but he continued steadily '. . . who was in the bed next to mine in hospital at Christmas in nineteen-eighteen. He translated it for me. It's very simple. If I sing it through once, I hope you'll join me the second time:

'Oh Christmas tree, oh Christmas tree,
How evergreen your branches!
You thrive amidst the winter's snow
And bloom with lights when cold winds blow . . .'

The repeat started uncertainly, then grew in strength, but the sound remained thin. Daisy was sure a number of people were not even attempting to sing. Her mother's penetrating soprano was missing, for one. She herself sang, thinking of Gervaise, thinking of her dead fiancé, Michael, a pacifist blown up by a mine with his Friends Ambulance Unit. His vision of peace was worth preserving. The Boches – the Germans – were human beings after all. Daisy finished with tears in her eyes.

But all the while she was conscious of the ominous silence behind her. It seemed to focus right between her shoulder blades, though she was sure it was aimed at this impious paean to a pagan symbol.

Matters were not improved by the next carol, 'Deck the Halls', or after that the 'Gloucestershire Wassail', a paean to good ale. Daisy began to wonder if the choices were a deliberate effort to affront Calloway. If so, they were succeeding. Who had decided what they were to sing? Godfrey Norville was consulting a list as he announced the songs. Had he written it himself? Was it Felicity or Miles's notion of a lark?

Miles had been deadly serious, though, when he sang the German carol. On the other hand, that was the one Daisy felt had most upset the clergyman, and not because he hated the Germans.

'Once in Royal David's City' and 'While Shepherds Watched' improved the atmosphere in Calloway's vicinity. Then Godfrey Norville announced the final carol, 'We Wish You a Merry Christmas', which could only be described as a paean to figgy pudding.

Belinda and Derek threw their hearts into this one:

'We won't go until we've got some,
We won't go until we've got some,
We won't go until we've got some,
So bring some out here.'

As the final chord died away, Derek leaned across Daisy and said, 'Bel, do you actually *like* figgy pudding?'

'Ugh,' said Belinda, 'but it's a jolly good song!'

They filed back up the narrow, curving steps into the old dining room. At once the Dowager Viscountess began to complain about the German carol.

'The Germans were our allies a hundred years ago,' Alec pointed out philosophically, 'and the French our bitter enemies. I daresay they'll change places again some day. We can't hold the whole German race to blame for Kaiser Bill forever, any more than we still hold the French responsible for Napoleon.'

Lady Dalrymple responded that she for one would never

trust the French. Daisy listened with half an ear, more interested in what was going on behind her.

'Secular songs!' Calloway exclaimed.

'Celebrating the season,' pleaded Captain Norville.

'Celebrating strong drink and heathen nature-worship.'

'Christian charity and the hope of eternal life. Joy at Christ's nativity,' the captain urged.

'Secular songs,' Calloway repeated obdurately, 'in a consecrated chapel decorated with greenery. I cannot be expected to hold a sacred service surrounded by symbols of pagan polytheism.'

'I'll go and take the holly and the ivy down myself immediately,' promised the captain, but Daisy thought she heard as much resentment in his voice as appeasement.

The children had run ahead into the hall. Following, Daisy saw that someone had lit all the candles on the tree and extinguished the lamps. Derek and Belinda stood gazing at it, the yearly miracle forever fresh. Then Bel began to sing:

'Away in a manger, no crib for a bed . . .'

Derek joined in:

'The little Lord Jesus laid down his sweet head.
The stars in the bright sky looked down where he lay,
The little Lord Jesus, asleep on the hay.'

'Isn't it beautiful, Mummy? Like the stars in the bright sky for baby Jesus.'

'It is beautiful,' said someone softly, and Daisy was

astonished to find the Reverend nearby. 'A beacon of light in a dark world, like our Lord. I cannot see my way clearly. I must pray. Mr Norville, is the chapel in the woods locked?'

'No,' said Godfrey Norville mistrustfully, 'it's kept open.'

'I shall pray there tonight. I must be alone, away from the conflict I feel in this house.'

'What, now?'

'No, later. As the hour of the birth of our Lord approaches, I shall pray for guidance.' He laid his hand on Belinda's head. 'Thank you, my child, for helping me to see the meaning.' He moved away.

'My word!' marvelled Felicity. 'Perhaps he's human after all. I wonder which way he's going to jump.'

'Jump?' Daisy queried, hoping for enlightenment.

Felicity shook her head, a touch of mockery in her smile. 'Sorry, Daisy, my lips are sealed.'

Daisy decided to be frank. 'I wish I knew what's going on. There are so many undercurrents, it's quite unsettling. The conflict Mr Calloway feels, I suppose.'

'I *said* he'd ruin Christmas,' Jemima butted in malevolently. 'I wish he'd never come. I wish Uncle Vic never found him. I wish he was *dead*!'

'Oh, stow it, Jemmie. It's you who'll be spoiling Christmas if you don't look out.'

'Buck up, Jem.' Miles joined them. 'You look like the end of a wet week. Think of presents and turkey and flaming Christmas pud.'

'I don't like Christmas pudding.'

'I'll let you in on a secret: Cook's made a trifle in honour of our distinguished guests.'

'I wish *they*'d never come, too!' said the impossible girl, and flounced off.

Her brother and sister sighed in union. 'Sorry, Daisy,' said Miles. 'She's rather too much for Mother, I'm afraid.'

'Her manners are simply dire,' Felicity agreed. 'I wonder if Uncle Vic or Grandfather could stump up for a couple of years of school for her.'

'A good idea. It's worth putting out a few feelers.' Miles paused. 'But not until this business is over. There's no knowing what may come of it. Ah, the candles are sputtering. Light a couple of lamps, Flick, while I snuff them before the tree goes up in flames.'

Her curiosity burning, with no prospect of satisfaction, Daisy went to send the children to bed.

'. . . And I don't think I've ever been so utterly clueless as to what's going on.'

'Daisy, don't talk to me of clues,' Alec groaned, tearing off his stiff collar. He hated stiff collars, but he would have hated still more to give his mother-in-law any extra ammunition to use against him. 'I was hoping for a rest from sleuthing. All that's happened is that the captain has invited a bigoted zealot to stay and the rest of the family wants – quite reasonably in my opinion – to see the last of him.'

'He's simply frightful, isn't he, darling?' She wrinkled her nose in the adorable way which always made him want to kiss her. 'But Captain Norville travelled all the way from India with him, so he knew quite well what he was like. Why invite him? And why try so hard to please him now he's here?'

'Common courtesy to a guest. And I expect the captain invited him before he found out what a pill he is.'

'There's more to it than that,' Daisy said with conviction. She was halfway out of her frock by now, and Alec didn't want to talk about the Norvilles, or even think about them. 'He'd hardly go off into the woods at midnight on his own to wrestle with his soul about whether to stay a few more days.'

'Enough, love! If I know Belinda, she'll be here at dawn to show us the contents of her stocking, even if she doesn't believe in Father Christmas anymore. No doubt bringing Derek with her. Let's get some sleep!'

'Sleep?' Daisy queried innocently, but there was a beguiling glint in her usually guileless blue eyes.

'To bed, woman! I'll be with you as soon as I've folded this damned instrument of torture.' He wrestled with the studs of his starched shirt.

'Let me help, darling,' said Daisy.

Somehow the shirt ended up on the floor, where it spent the night.

Bel and Derek appeared at first light. By the time Daisy chased them out to wash and dress, they had consumed two tuppenny bars of Fry's chocolate, two sherbet dabs and the tangerines from the toes of their stockings, and had read their own and each other's comic papers.

'I'm sticky,' said Daisy.

'I'm exhausted,' said Alec, 'but I suppose we'd better get up. It'll take a policeman to stop those two opening all the rest of the presents before breakfast.'

'Breakfast before presents and presents before church. I suppose Calloway will insist on giving a sermon even on

Christmas morning. I hope it's short and not too full of hellfire.'

After breakfast everyone gathered in the library. Daisy, having had no idea who lived at Brockdene, had provided a large box of chocolates which was well received. Trust her to get it right, Alec thought.

He was worried about the present he had bought Daisy for their first Christmas. She had admired some petrified wood they had seen somewhere in the western United States, and he had secretly bought 'wood opal' earrings and a long string of beads. Knee-length beads were fashionable, but would she rather have had real pearls, even though he could afford only a short string and not of the best?

He need not have worried. She was thrilled, and when he muttered something about pearls, she said dismissively, 'Oh, everyone has pearls. I bet no one else in England has anything like this.'

Belinda and Derek were equally pleased with their presents from America, but the big hit was something Daisy had picked up for a few pennies. When she explained that the dried maize kernels would turn into 'popcorn' when toasted, they had to try it at once. Derek ran off to the kitchens for a frying pan.

Everyone gathered around the library fireplace to watch. When the kernels started to pop, Nana howled and hid behind a chair. Some of the white puffs flew out and flared up in the fire. They were bigger than Daisy had expected and soon overflowed the frying pan, eliciting a great deal of hilarity.

Everyone tasted, including Nana, even Lady Dalrymple, but when Belinda and Derek went on crunching, she said, 'Daisy, stop them. They'll ruin their meal.'

'No, no,' said Mr Tremayne, 'they're nothing but air, my lady. And there's the service in the chapel for the kiddies to sit through before we get to Christmas dinner.'

A pall fell over the company. Alec had been aware that Calloway had not joined them at breakfast nor afterwards, but more as a lifting of spirits than a conscious noting of his absence. He was off duty. He didn't care where anyone happened to be at any particular time.

'The Rev must be sleeping in after wrestling with his demons in the wood all night,' Miles said lightly.

'Don't speak so disrespectfully of Mr Calloway,' the captain snapped.

'Especially on Christmas Day.' For once Godfrey supported his brother, though his zeal seemed to Alec less a change of heart than a rather forced and unconvincing tribute to the season of goodwill to all men. 'We'd better get along to the chapel. It's nearly eleven. He'll be upset if we're late.'

The ancient clock began to chime the hour as Alec followed Daisy down the steps into the chapel. A few servants sat at the back, though not nearly as many as had come to the carol singing. By daylight the chapel had lost some of its charm, but several beautiful old paintings were visible and sun slanting through stained glass cast patches of colour on the white walls. There was no sign of Calloway. No doubt he was hanging behind to make a grand entrance.

The congregation settled down into an expectant hush. Still no Calloway. The children began to fidget. Daisy put her arm around Belinda, and Lady Dalrymple confiscated the rubber band Derek had taken from his pocket.

Still no Calloway. Captain Norville got up and went out. A couple of minutes later he returned, without Calloway. He went to speak to the housekeeper at the back.

In the quiet, their whispered exchange was audible.

'Who took the Reverend his morning tea?' asked the captain.

'No one, sir,' the woman said unabashed. 'Mr Calloway is not a guest of his lordship.'

Captain Norville let out a gusty, exasperated sigh. Miles jumped up and joined him. 'I'll go and see if he's still asleep, sir,' he offered.

'Thank you, my boy.' The captain raised his voice. 'In the meantime, while Miles fetches Mr Calloway, I suggest that anyone who wishes should go out to the hall and make themselves comfortable.'

Daisy immediately shepherded the children out. Alec paused to let Lady Dalrymple go ahead, but she stayed behind for a moment of private prayer. When she caught up with them, she made straight for his side and started to complain about the ill-breeding of modern churchmen in general and the Reverend Calloway in particular.

Alec supposed it was better to be the recipient of her complaints than their subject.

He did not have to suffer long before Miles came into the hall from the east wing. 'Mr Calloway's bed hasn't been slept in,' he announced.

'He's hooked it,' Felicity said at once.

'Don't be vulgar, dear,' said her mother automatically, but she looked relieved.

The captain stared at Miles, seemingly silenced by shock,

while Jemima muttered, 'Good riddance!' and old Mrs Norville murmured, 'Oh dear!'

'Piffle!' cried Godfrey Norville, much perturbed. 'Why should he leave so unceremoniously? As Victor's guest, he was welcome at Brockdene. We did our poor best to make him welcome, didn't we?'

'Don't worry, Father, he hasn't gone off,' said Miles. 'At any rate, as far as I can tell only his outdoor clothes are missing. Perhaps he decided to walk into Calstock to go to the service there instead of preaching to the heathen.'

'Miles!' His mother was scandalized.

'Sorry, Mother.'

'Maybe he fell asleep in the chapel,' Daisy proposed soothingly. 'The one by the river.'

'Dashed uncomfortable.' Miles shook his head. 'No, more likely he fell on his way through the woods. The gale brought quite a few branches down, and it was dark, remember. He might have tripped and sprained his ankle.'

'I hope he broke his leg,' said Jemima viciously, 'or his neck.'

'Jemima!' Poor Dora grew more and more flustered.

'In any case,' Alec said calmly, 'we'd better go and look for him. Miles, Captain, Mr Norville, you'll come with me? I'm not certain of the way.'

'I'm coming too,' Derek whooped. 'Come on, Bel. We'll take Nana. She'll be a ripping bloodhound.'

Daisy instantly quashed that plan. 'You're staying right here, both of you.' She exchanged a look with Alec.

He seconded her. If they found Calloway injured, or if he'd managed to fall into the Tamar and drown himself, they wouldn't want the children underfoot.

When Alec came downstairs, having changed his shoes and put on his overcoat, Miles, Captain Norville and Mr Tremayne awaited him.

'Father's soothing my mother,' Miles said uncomfortably. 'I'm afraid her undutiful children are a trial to her.'

They walked down the terraces, through the tunnel under the lane, and into the valley garden. Here they spread out to cover the several winding paths, looking about them as they went. The paths, steep and slippery in places, must have been difficult to negotiate safely in darkness, but no one saw any sign of the missing clergyman.

The previous afternoon, Alec and Daisy had not gone all the way to the bottom of the garden. Now, when they reached the woods, Alec saw that Miles was right about the damage done by the gale. The broad woodland path was scattered with twigs and a few quite large branches.

'If one of those fell on the poor chap,' said Tremayne, 'he wouldn't have had a chance.'

'No,' Miles agreed, 'or he could easily have tripped over one in the dark, though I suppose he brought a lantern.'

'Let's assume he didn't veer from the track,' Alec proposed, 'unless we find he isn't in the chapel. We'll stick to the track.'

'Even with no more than a ricked ankle,' said the captain, subdued, 'which I hope is the worst of it, he might have gone to the chapel for shelter rather than try to make it back to the house.'

'Watch out for footprints though,' Alec said. 'If he strayed, we might be lucky enough to spot it.'

But the dying gale had dried the ground, leaving no muddy patches to show footprints. Last autumn's fallen leaves, spread in drifts across the path, crunched underfoot. Perhaps they left a trail an expert Red Indian tracker could have followed, but to Alec's eye no obvious trace showed where they had trodden.

The chapel came into view.

'Hello, the door's open,' said Miles. He strode ahead, pushed the half-open door and went in.

As the others approached, he suddenly came out, his face dead white. He took two steps and stopped, swaying, his eyes shut, his one hand clenched.

Alec reached him first. 'Steady, old man. Lean on me.'

'I'm . . . all right. I've seen much worse. It . . . it's just that it brings it all back.'

'What?' the captain demanded. 'What did you see?'

'Calloway. He's there all right. Dead. With a knife in his back.'

CHAPTER 8

'No!' Captain Norville rushed towards the open chapel door. When Tremayne caught his arm, the force of his charge swung him round, fists bunching. 'Let go of me!'

'Stop! You mustn't go in there, Victor. This is a matter for the police.'

'He's dead? Calloway's dead?' Fists relaxing, the captain shook his head like a bewildered bull whose chosen victim had just jumped a fence. His shoulders slumped. 'Then Mother will never be vindicated.'

'To be honest, Uncle Vic,' said Miles, still pale but with a touch of colour returning to his cheeks, 'I don't think Grandmama cares much anymore.'

'Little you know! Did you know she still sleeps with a miniature of my father under her pillow? To you she's just a wrinkled old lady, but inside she's still young and pretty and in mourning.'

Alec never would have expected such a flight of fancy from the seaman. What on earth was going on? He vaguely remembered Daisy recounting some tragic story from old Mrs Norville's past, but he hadn't paid much attention. It didn't do to ignore Daisy's apparently idle chatter, he thought. Then he reminded himself that it was Christmas

Day, and he was on holiday. He wasn't going to have anything to do with investigating Calloway's death, dammit!

All the same . . . 'I'd better make sure the poor devil's not lying there slowly bleeding to death,' he said to Tremayne. 'I won't touch anything but his wrist.'

Miles gave him a puzzled look. 'But . . .' he started, then fell silent as Alec frowned at him.

Something else Daisy had told him: she had mentioned his profession to young Miles, and sworn him to secrecy when she discovered that Lord Westmoor had not passed on the information to his poor relations.

Alec went into the dimness of the tiny chapel. In spite of himself, he kept a lookout for footprints, and though he saw none, not even Miles's, he kept to one side so as not to leave his own. The Reverend Calloway lay prone before the simple altar. He might have been performing a profound obeisance before his Lord, were it not for the knife hilt protruding between his shoulder blades.

His head was turned away from Alec. The arms were caught beneath the body, as if he had been on his knees praying when he was struck down. He was wearing his funereal black suit, his overcoat folded over the back of a pew, next to the burnt-out lantern. Mortifying the flesh, Alec thought wryly, or warmed by the fervour of his devotions.

Alec bowed his head briefly towards the crucifix, but when he knelt, he was kneeling beside the fallen man, not before the altar.

Against the black cloth, the wide patch of blood around the knife was hard to make out. The base of the haft was stained. Alec thought a fair amount of blood must have welled out immediately, but not spurted. The murderer would have blood on his hands, but probably not his clothes.

The blade had gone in high on Calloway's back, between the shoulder blades, slanting downwards but too high, Alec guessed, to hit the heart. Nevertheless, when he reached beneath the body for the wrist, he knew before he touched it that the man was dead.

No pulse. Cold, and rigor mortis well advanced. Soon after midnight, probably.

Dammit, he was not going to start detecting!

But he couldn't stop his mind working. As he started to stand up, he saw the dark pool of congealed blood by Calloway's open mouth, spreading under his cheek pillowed on the cold stone. The knife must have nicked a lung. Perhaps it had severed the spinal cord, paralysing the man. That would explain why he had not struggled in his death throes, why he was laid out so neatly.

There was something oddly familiar about that knife hilt. Alec stooped to take another look. Yes, if he was not mistaken, it was the seaman's knife Belinda and Derek had found yesterday in the secret passage.

Where had they left it?

DAMMIT, HE WAS NOT GOING TO START DETECTING!! This was one for the local police.

He hurried out of the chapel, using his handkerchief to pull the door shut behind him. 'Where's the nearest police station?' he asked.

'Calstock,' Tremayne told him. 'It's . . .'

The captain interrupted. 'Calloway's dead, then, Fletcher?

I searched half of India for that man, talked him into coming home when he was all set to retire over there, put up with his prudish ways for weeks on end . . .'

'Why?' Alec asked bluntly.

'Why? Because—'

'The less said the better, Vic,' Tremayne interrupted in his turn, and repeated, 'This is a matter for the police.'

'I'll go and fetch them,' Miles offered.

'Are you sure you feel up to it, my boy?' his grandfather asked with concern.

'Yes, perfectly. I'll be better with something to do.' He looked at Alec. 'I suppose . . . I suppose I'll have to tell them it's murder.'

'It's difficult to see how it could be accident or suicide,' Alec agreed dryly, 'or even self-defence. But just report a violent death, and make sure they bring a doctor.'

'Yes, sir.'

'I believe Dr Hennessy is away for Christmas,' said Tremayne. 'You can say I suggest they ring up county police headquarters in Bodmin for advice. Don't tell them any more than you absolutely must.'

'Yes, sir.' Again the young man glanced at Alec, who nodded. From the family's point of view, if not from that of the police, the canny old solicitor was quite right. 'Right-oh, then, I'm off.' He strode off up the path, back the way they had come.

'Wait!' Alec called. He turned to Tremayne. 'Does he go near the house?'

'No, the public footpath skirts the garden on the river side. There's a hairpin bend, then another gate into the garden, then a rather steep slope up to the top before it straightens, meets the farm track and then runs on to Calstock. Why?'

'Never mind!' Alec shouted to Miles, waved him on, watched him go past the gate, then said to Tremayne, 'Because I don't want the children hearing about this.'

'Gad, no!' Captain Norville, who had been standing in gloomy contemplation of the chapel, swung around. 'Nor the ladies, by Jove.'

'We'll have to tell them something,' Tremayne argued, 'the ladies at least. We must agree on a story before we go back to the house. Something which won't spoil Christmas for everyone.'

'They'll find out soon enough when the police arrive,' Alec pointed out. 'Better to tell them the truth in the first place. Tell the ladies Calloway's dead, anyway, and Miles has gone for a doctor. Let them assume natural causes. I don't think anyone was sufficiently fond of him for his demise to spoil their Christmas dinner.'

'It's spoilt mine!' the captain muttered.

'Very well,' said Tremayne, 'we'd best get back and break the news before they start to wonder what is going on?'

'I'll have to stay,' Alec said reluctantly, 'to make sure no one goes in and disturbs the evidence. With any luck, Miles will bring a bobby back in time for me not to miss my dinner.'

'I'll stay,' grumbled the captain. 'Can't leave a guest of Westmoor's out here.'

'Sorry, I wish I could let you, Captain. But I'm afraid it looks as though you and your family are going to be the chief suspects.'

'Me? I wanted him alive. His death has ruined everything!'

'Fletcher's right, Victor. Unaccustomed as I am to criminal practice, I can see that all of us, even I, shall be under suspicion. Come along, now, we must go and break the news of the reverend gentleman's demise. We don't want to keep the ladies in suspense.'

'Do please try to keep it from the children,' Alec begged.

'Of course,' said the captain gruffly.

'And if there's a key to the chapel, I expect the police will want to lock it up until they can examine it properly.'

'I'll send someone with the key.'

They tramped off. Alec strolled up and down in front of the chapel. He hadn't done guard duty for years, but waiting was still a not infrequent part of his duties, usually in far less pleasant surroundings. Birds sang in the trees, and a pair of rusty red squirrels chased each other, leaping from branch to branch like trapeze artists. Somewhere in the distance, a peal of bells rang out in joyful clamour: the end of the morning service in Calstock, probably.

There would be no church service at Brockdene today. The intended celebrant had bled to death or choked on his own blood – but Alec was not going to speculate on the precise medical cause of his departure to a better world, nor on who had sent him there.

He took his pipe from his pocket ... and put it back again. Much as he longed for a smoke, it would somehow be disrespectful to the dead, a feeling he had encountered before. To distract himself, from that and from the irrepressible instinct to detect, he took a turn around the chapel.

Patches of evergreen bushes, laurels and rhododendrons, grew on each side, but there was room to pass between thicket and wall. Behind the chapel, the ground fell away abruptly in quite a high cliff, fifty or sixty feet, with a mud flat at the bottom. The river was a muddy brown after the gale and heavy rains, turbulent, with quite a bit of debris racing seaward on what looked like an ebb tide. The opposite bank, bordered with yellowed reeds, was much lower, a gentle hillside dotted with red Devonshire cattle.

'Alec!' It was Daisy's apprehensive voice. 'Alec, where are you?'

'Here. Coming.' He hurried round to the front.

Daisy flung herself into his arms and hugged him tightly. 'Gosh, darling, I was afraid you'd been done in, too.'

'Too? I suppose the captain couldn't keep his mouth shut.'

'So Calloway has been murdered. How dreadful! Captain Norville and Mr Tremayne just told us he had died.'

Alec groaned. 'And I've just told you he was done in!'

'Give me credit for a little *nous*, darling. If he'd popped off from a heart seizure or something, the captain would have stayed to wait for the doctor. If you stayed, it meant there was something suspicious about his death, and you didn't trust the captain not to mess about with your clues.'

'Not *my* clues. I'm on holiday. I managed to stop Miles giving me away, so don't you breathe a word of my profession. Where are the children?'

'I caught them sneaking out right after you left. I made them promise not to come this way, and Derek said they'd go up the hill to the prospect tower. It's to be a giant wigwam, I gather. They were both wearing the Red Indian costumes we brought them. Bel's adorable in the beaded jacket and the squaw feather with her ginger braids! Poor Nana was to be a buffalo, but she likes to be chased, and they won't hurt her. How was he killed?'

'Stabbed with . . . Dash it, Daisy!'

'You might as well tell me, darling. It won't be a secret once the local bobby arrives.'

'I hope we can keep it from Belinda and Derek. And I had hoped for a peaceful, if not merry, Christmas dinner before it's generally known.'

'Well, I shan't tell anyone. Especially Mother. Oh heavens, she's going to be simply livid! Livider, I mean, if there is such a word. Let's put off telling everyone as long as possible. We'll persuade the bobby not to come up to the house till after dinner, so only – let's see – four of us will know. Besides the murderer. Who do you think stabbed him?'

'I'm trying hard not to think about it,' Alec pointed out.

'No one was exactly keen on the poor chap,' Daisy mused. 'I'm afraid no one will really mourn him. I wish I knew why Captain Norville invited him in the first place.'

'He said something odd,' Alec revealed reluctantly. 'He said, "Then Mother will never be vindicated." And then he talked about her still mourning her husband.'

'But he wasn't. Her husband, I mean. I knew you weren't listening when I told you about Mother's letter. Or was he?'

'Great Scott, Daisy, what the dickens are you talking about?'

Daisy held up her hand. 'Hush a minute. Let me think. This does rather change things. Surely "vindicated" in that context must mean . . . Darling, I rather think I know what Calloway was here for!'

'Must I beg for enlightenment?'

'No, why should you?' She wrinkled her nose at him. 'You're absolutely determined not to investigate so you have no reason to want to know. In any case, it's all hearsay and guesswork, not evidence.'

'I give you fair warning, a second murder is about to be committed,' Alec growled.

'Keep your hair on, darling, I'm rather fond of that black thatch of yours. Right-oh, I'd better start from the beginning.' She narrated Lady Eva's tale of the events leading up to the drowning of Albert and his eldest brother, Viscount Norville, the sixth earl's heir.

'A sad story. Presumably they quarrelled because the viscount wouldn't lend his support. But that leaves the native girl still in India. We're talking about the old lady known as Mrs Norville?'

'Yes. She arrived a few months later, with two babies. Can you imagine, darling? She came all that way to join him only to find him dead. Simply ghastly! She claimed to be married, though without proof I don't suppose there was the slightest chance of the earl's believing her. Or admitting to believing her, rather.'

'Not a chance, even if it were true. Yet all these years later, she's living here in his house.'

'He gave her an allowance and let her live at Brockdene to keep her quiet. He even let her use the family name, but she was never acknowledged as part of the family, and Victor and Godfrey were considered illegitimate. Assuming they're really Albert's sons, they're the present earl's first cousins. And I believe we can assume that they're not only Albert's sons, but legitimate sons.'

'Very probably,' Alec said, 'though their chance of proving it must have died with Calloway.'

'You agree then?' Daisy crowed. 'Calloway was the clergyman who married Albert to his native girl, and the captain brought him home to swear to the marriage!'

'It's a reasonable deduction. But whom does that leave with a motive for murdering the man? They should all have been as happy as larks at the prospect of being legitimized.'

'Unless Calloway changed his mind. He found a great deal to disapprove of – Mrs Norville's idols, and the carols, and the mistletoe – and I'm sure he was in two minds about the whole business. That was why ... Listen, there's the chapel clock chiming twelve. The other chapel. I hope Miles gets back in time for Christmas dinner. I'd hate to miss it.'

'Why don't you go on back to the house, love?' Alec suggested. 'It might be a good idea to check on the children's whereabouts. I wouldn't put it past them to start out in one direction and somehow end up here in the woods, without ever realizing where they were heading, of course! They could always blame it on Nana.'

'Yes, hunters must follow where the buffalo leads. Perhaps I ought to go and see what they're up to. Are you going to present the local bobby with our deductions?'

'Based on hearsay, and possibly nothing to do with Galloway's death? If he's got any gumption, he'll find out for himself, or his superiors from county headquarters will. Besides, I don't want anyone wondering why I'm so keen on making deductions – which I was absolutely determined not to do. You witch, Daisy!'

'Don't blame me, darling. Detection is not only your profession, it's in your blood. Oh, here's the key to the chapel. The captain asked me to bring it. He was very impressed by your anticipating the police wanting to lock up.' She went off, laughing, up the path.

Needless to say, before she was out of sight, Alec's mind drifted back, willy-nilly, to what she had revealed of the Norvilles' history, and to its bearing on the murder. Unlike some of her wilder theories, her guess as to Calloway's function in the scheme of things seemed pretty sound. It would have to be continued, but that shouldn't be difficult. The captain could have no reason to deny it, rather the reverse, as it would tend to exculpate himself and his family.

Unless, as Daisy suggested, Calloway had changed his mind because of the many offences against his particular puritanical dogma. In that case, might not Captain Norville have lost his temper and assaulted him?

Alec remembered the captain's fists clenching when Tremayne caught at his sleeve. Fiery temper or the automatic defensive reaction of one whose life had taken him to dangerous parts of the world? Even in a fury, the captain seemed more the sort to face his adversary and knock him down, clergyman or no, rather than stabbing him in the back.

On the other hand, those dangerous places included many where an insult to one's honour or that of one's family cried for retaliation in any possible shape or form. Perhaps in the course of the captain's travels, the code of the English gentleman had worn thin. In any case, like a policeman, a merchant marine captain hardly qualified as a gentleman, to say nothing of his being a poor relation, presumed illegitimate – and the man was also half Indian. What sort of oriental *mores* had Victor learnt at his mother's knee?

Luckily, Alec reminded himself, it was not his business to delve into Captain Norville's psyche. And here at last came Miles and not one but two policemen, pushing bicycles.

'Sergeant Tilton, sir, and Constable Redkin. This is Mr Fletcher, Sergeant. He's a guest at Brockdene.'

Tilton was a defeated-looking man not far shy of retirement age. Redkin, judging by the faint fuzz on his cheeks and his spick-and-span uniform, was a new recruit.

'A guest?' Tilton enquired suspiciously. 'Might I ask, zir, what keeps you 'anging about 'ere at the zene of the crime?'

'I stayed to make sure no one entered the chapel, Sergeant. Are you in charge of the case?'

'Aye, for now I am. The gales brung down the telephone lines all around Bodmin. 'Tis on the edge o' the moor, exposed like. Bessie at the exchange zays the lines east and downriver are all right.'

'Then what about phoning Plymouth?'

The sergeant stared at him in outrage. ''Tis not my place, zir, to go a-letting the Devon police know what's 'appening 'ereabouts. I'd zooner call in Scotland Yard, that I would.'

Alec and Miles carefully didn't look at each other. The constable's eyes widened. 'Lor, Sergeant, you going to call in the Yard?'

'It'll maybe come to that, lad. I bain't a detective, and I don't pretend to be a detective, and what with the 'olidays, no one's going to be out repairing telephone lines for a couple o' days.'

'What about a doctor?' Alec asked, professional instinct asserting itself again.

'My grandfather was right,' Miles told him. 'Dr Hennessy's gone to relatives in Exeter for Christmas. Sergeant Tilton rang up Saltash and asked them to send Dr Clay, but at best it'll be a few hours before he can get here.'

'Aye, if zo be 'e's at 'ome. Now I'll thank you, zir, and Mr Miles, to be leaving me and Redkin to take a look.'

'Willingly. Here's the key,' said Alec, wondering how much evidence they would manage to destroy between them. He and Miles set off up the path. 'Thank you for preserving my incognito, under what must have been considerable temptation.'

'It was difficult when Tilton started talking about calling in Scotland Yard. Will you really not take a hand, sir? I can't believe those two oafs have the slightest idea what they're doing. They're used to miners fighting outside the pubs on a Saturday night, and the odd tinker stealing a hen. You don't suppose it was a tinker did it, or some passing tramp?' Miles finished hopefully.

Alec wondered how good a look the young man had taken at the knife hilt protruding from Calloway's back. Considering the effect on him of finding the body, he had probably not examined the weapon closely enough to recognize it, if, indeed, he had ever been shown the children's discovery.

'I refuse to speculate,' Alec said. 'I'm on holiday. Let's try to put the whole thing out of our minds for the moment and enjoy our Christmas dinner.'

* * *

Dinner was more festive than might have been expected in the circumstances. The children, including Jemima, had not been told of Calloway's death. Bel and Derek, chattering about their Red Indian adventures, didn't seem inclined to question his absence. Jemima, caught in that awkward space between childhood and adulthood, made some gloating remark about the clergyman missing the turkey and was firmly put in her place by her mother.

For the children's sake, most of the adults tried to be bright and cheery. In this they were aided by the wine, which Godfrey, reminded by Dora, produced from behind the four-foot door in the library.

Daisy was too busy keeping an eye – between forkfuls – on Belinda and Derek to pay as much attention as she would have liked to the rest of the company. She wished she had watched everyone that morning, instead of concentrating on children and presents. Surely the murderer, awaiting discovery of his crime, must have behaved differently from normal?

Now, as far as she could see, Felicity and Miles seemed pretty much unaffected, she lively with an ironic edge, he more good-natured though equally quick-witted. Jemima was sulking, but that was nothing new.

Their mother was jolly, the doggedness behind the enthusiasm more evident than usual. Godfrey Norville could not at the best of times have been accused of conviviality. His mind appeared to be elsewhere, his thoughts of a distressing nature, natural in the circumstances. Victor Norville did a better job of hiding his chagrin at the wreck of his plans, but now and then a shadow of gloom overcame even his genial nature. Old Mrs Norville, always quiet, was perhaps a shade quieter. After so many years of ostracism, the sudden raising and then dashing of her hopes must be hard to deal with.

Mr Tremayne was preoccupied. Daisy didn't know whether he had been let in on the secret purpose behind Calloway's advent, but as a lawyer he must be well aware that the clergyman's death could mean nothing but trouble for the Norvilles.

The prospect spoiled no one's appetite. Turkey, chestnut stuffing, parsley-thyme-and-onion stuffing, sausage force-meat, bread sauce, brussels sprouts and peas, roast potatoes and gravy were followed by trifle and a Christmas pudding flickering with blue flame. The captain served the pudding. He made sure Belinda and Derek each got a sixpence in the tiny helpings they each had in the hope of just that. Nor would he let Daisy make them eat what they had taken.

'After all, it's Christmas,' he exclaimed. 'Now where's that gigantic box of crackers Master Derek brought with him?'

There were enough crackers for everyone. Captain Norville persuaded even Lady Dalrymple to pull one with him, and to put on the paper hat and blow the tiny silver whistle she found in hers. The sharp *snap* and the faint smell of gunpowder gave way to the reading of mottoes.

By the time all had been read, the children were restless. Daisy sent them out to play, reminding them to stay away from the woods. The adults retired to the library for coffee.

It was there that Sergeant Tilton found them. He sidled into the room, cap in hand, looking distinctly sorry for himself. 'Beg pardon, ladies and gents,' he said, 'for int'rupting on zuch a day as this, but I 'as to ask a few questions, zeeing this do be a case o' murder.'

'Murder?' Lady Dalrymple raised her eyebrows in displeasure. 'This is quite the most badly regulated household it has ever been my misfortune to encounter.'

'Zorry, ma'am,' said the miserable sergeant.

'Alec,' said her ladyship commandingly, 'presumably you can deal with this person. If one must have a police detective in the family, the least he can do is to make himself useful!'

CHAPTER 9

'Scotland Yard!' Tilton, otherwise rigidly at attention, turned his cap round and round in nervous fingers. His eyes flickered around the entrance hall, to which he and Alec had retreated, as if noting every escape route. 'Detective Chief Inspector! Why didn't you tell me, zir?'

'Because I had . . . have no intention of trespassing on your territory, Sergeant. If it wasn't for my mother-in-law blowing the gaff . . .'

'Ah,' said Tilton, enlightened.

'Do sit down, man. It's Christmas, I'm on holiday, and in any case the Met has no business in Cornwall unless your Chief Constable calls us in. There's nothing I can do.'

Tilton perched on the edge of a lyre-back chair. 'But the Chief Constable's away for Christmas.'

'He would be!'

'And you 'eard me, zir: I can't get ahold o' the detective branch in Bodmin to request assistance. I were already thinking o' telephoning Scotland Yard. We don't 'ave murders 'ere, zir, barring young Jackie Levitt that got stabbed outside the Boot Inn back in oh-two, and that were a fair fight. 'Zides, I bain't used to dealing wi' the gentry, 'zepting motoring offences and zuch. Won't you give us an 'and, zir?' he pleaded.

'Not without express authorization.' Alec sighed deeply. 'I suppose, in the circumstances, the least I can do is to accompany you back to Calstock. You can ring up the Yard, and should authorization be forthcoming, I'll be on the spot to send for my men.'

'Aye, zir!' The sergeant started up, eager to go.

In the meantime, the trail would be growing cold, Alec thought, but no colder than if he left Tilton to struggle on unaided. It was already more than twelve hours since Calloway was attacked, he reckoned. He sighed again. 'What a way to spend Christmas afternoon!'

'I missed me dinner,' Tilton said reproachfully, 'likewise Constable Redkin that I left guarding the chapel.'

'Great Scott, my dear chap, so you did. We'll stop by the kitchens and have them put together something you can eat as we walk, and send up something for the constable. "If it were done, when 'tis done, then 'twere well it were done quickly," but a few minutes is neither here nor there. And I'd better put on my boots.'

He left the sergeant in the kitchen and went up to change into outdoor clothes. In the bedroom he found Daisy on the same errand.

'So sorry about Mother, darling,' she said. 'Whoever would have guessed she'd practically boast about having a 'tec in the family? That really set the cat among the pigeons. Godfrey was inclined to take your "deceitfulness" amiss, but Miles pointed out you could hardly have known beforehand that there was going to be a "crime wave" at Brockdene. Mr Tremayne said it would be just as well to have a competent detective in charge. I take it you're going to Calstock to ring up the Yard?'

'Why should you take anything of the sort?' he retorted irritably.

'Miles told me about the sergeant not being able to get in touch with his superiors. I'll walk with you. I need the exercise after that dinner, and there's tea and supper to come. Miles and Felicity will keep an eye on the children.'

Alec gave in. He wasn't on duty yet, after all, and half the point of a holiday was to have time to spend with Daisy. They picked up the sergeant and set out.

It was a beautiful afternoon. At first the path led through woodland, with glimpses of the Tamar between the trees. Sergeant Tilton had turned gloomy again when he discovered Daisy was going with them. He tramped ahead, wheeling his bike with one hand, a sandwich in the other, so she and Alec were able to hold hands and talk privately.

'You were saying something,' Alec said, 'at the chapel, when we were talking about the possibility of Calloway changing his mind. You said, "That was why . . ." and then the clock chimed and your mind instantly turned to dinner.'

'I must say Mrs Pardon did us proud,' Daisy mused. 'I wonder what sort of poor excuse for a Christmas dinner the Norvilles get when Westmoor hasn't landed them with his unwanted guests.'

'What were you going to say?' Alec asked patiently. '"That was why" what?'

'Let me think back. Oh, I know. That was why Calloway went to the chapel, to pray for guidance because he couldn't make up his mind. Didn't you hear him talking about it?'

'No. Who did?'

'Felicity was there. Her father, I think. Miles? I can't remember. Jemima. But they would have talked about it later, I'm sure. They probably all knew.'

'I suppose so. So any of them could have followed to ask him if he'd made a decision and attacked when he said he wouldn't swear to the wedding. It sounds a bit berserker. The sensible thing would be to wait and see if he changed his mind again. You know, Daisy, the logical murderer would be someone who'd be done out of an inheritance if the marriage were proved. Who is Westmoor's heir?'

'His son, of course. Heir apparent rather than heir presumptive. No one could displace him.'

'He has a son? Bother!'

Daisy was suddenly uncertain. 'I think so. Of course, what with the war, I didn't have to do the social season, so I didn't get to know all those sorts of people. I'm sure I've met a daughter or two though.'

'Daughters are beside the point.'

'Don't let Bel hear you say that, darling. I bet Sergeant Tilton knows. Westmoor's a local bigwig, after all. Tavy Bridge – his principal seat, as they say – is somewhere near Tavistock.'

'Devon? Two counties involved. I haven't a hope of staying out of the business then.'

'I'll ask Tilton whether Westmoor has a son.'

'No, don't do that. The Norvilles must know. If I end up taking over, I don't want to give the local police unnecessary cause for speculation about the family.'

'That's a point,' Daisy agreed. 'Anyway, I can't see how a putative heir-presumptive-who-is-not-Westmoor's-son could have found out about Calloway. He and the captain landed in Plymouth just a couple of days ago and came straight to Brockdene.'

'That's a point,' said Alec, with a smile. 'Look, there's a heron.'

The path had descended a hill, crossed a bridge over a small stream running into the Tamar, and now bordered a marshy area along the river. They continued past a pair of the ubiquitous lime kilns and a couple of cottages, then under an arch of the spectacular railway viaduct. Calstock spread up the hillside from the Tamar, a grimy tin, copper and arsenic mining town and river port.

Walking along the narrow, winding main street, they saw a house with a gleaming brass plaque announcing:

TREMAYNE & WEDGE
SOLICITORS
Notaries Public
Commissioners for Oaths

'They look quite prosperous?' Daisy remarked interrogatively to Sergeant Tilton, who had slacked his pace to rejoin them.

'Aye, doing nicely enough. Mr Tremayne's partly retired nowadays, picks and chooses his clients, he does. Young Mr Miles'll take over the partnership when he's done wi' his articles. Copes pretty well, does young Mr Miles, considering. Here we are then.'

Leaning his bicycle against the wall of the small police station, he led the way inside. He ushered Daisy into a waiting room at the back and firmly closed the door before tackling the telephone in the front office.

Daisy was left to cool her heels for what seemed an age. She tried to put her mind to the mystery of Calloway's murder, but without further evidence she had reached a dead end. When gazing out of the window palled, she picked up a copy of the *Sporting Times* which someone had left lying on a table. Since it was a week out of date, and she had no interest in 'The Pink 'Un' at the best of times, it did not hold her long.

Her patience expired. She opened the door a few inches to hear Alec say, 'I'm sorry, Tom. My most abject apologies to Mrs Tring. And I'm afraid I'm going to spoil Piper's Christmas, too. Will you get on to him?'

So Alec had sent for his team. He was in charge of the case. Daisy was not sure whether to be sorry, because of his ruined holiday, or glad, because she had a much better chance of worming information out of Alec than Sergeant Tilton.

'Yes, the mail train to Plymouth,' he was saying. 'It leaves Paddington at some ungodly hour of the night, but I need you as soon as possible. Enough time has already been wasted. Then the local to Calstock, and someone here will show you the way to Brockdene. All right, Tom, I'll see you and Ernie in the morning. Bye.' He hung up. 'You can come out now, Daisy.'

Unabashed at being caught eavesdropping, Daisy emerged from her seclusion. 'Where's Sergeant Tilton?'

'He was called out on a domestic assault. He rang up the Yard, and they ran the Cornish CC to earth. I gather he wasn't pleased to have his jollifications interrupted. In fact, he was only too delighted to pass off the responsibility, so I'm "It". Let's get back to Brockdene.'

'You're not going to wait for Tom and Ernie before you start asking questions, are you?' Daisy asked as they set out.

'If you're fishing to be asked to take notes, it would be a help,' Alec admitted. 'As long as no one objects, of course. Is there anyone we can absolutely rule out? Not counting Lady Dalrymple and the children, of course. Old Mrs Norville, I suppose. I can't see her traipsing up to the chapel at midnight. Mr Tremayne must be about the same age, but he's a spry old fellow.'

'With even less motive than the rest. You know, I'm a bit surprised he let his daughter marry a man whose legitimacy was in doubt.'

'I daresay he despaired of getting her off his hands.'

'Don't be beastly, darling. She can't help her teeth, and I suspect her manner, which I'll admit is rather grating, is a product of years of marriage to a wet fish like Godfrey. I think she was quite keen on coming to live at Brockdene. In its way, it's a step up for a country solicitor's daughter.'

'All right, but that doesn't exactly provide Tremayne with a motive for doing away with Calloway. As far as motive is concerned, Victor Norville seems the best bet, but however hard I try I can't see him, however angry, stabbing an unarmed man in the back. He'll have to go to the top of my list, though.'

'What about opportunity?' Daisy pondered. 'Anyone could have followed Calloway up to the chapel unseen, and as we all went to bed about eleven, no one is likely to have an alibi for midnight. Except Godfrey and Dora, and it doesn't count when it's husband and wife, does it?'

'It's not quite that simple,' Alec said, 'but naturally a

wife's evidence in favour of her husband doesn't usually bear a great deal of weight. As you say,' he added gloomily, 'anyone else could have gone to the chapel unnoticed, and no one can be expected to produce an alibi for the middle of the night.'

'You don't think it was a passing tramp, I take it, who hoped Calloway had money on him?'

'Not a chance.'

'Why not, darling? Were his pockets full of money untouched?'

'I didn't check. The weapon rules out a tramp or that other popular canard, an escaped lunatic.'

'You never told me what he was stabbed with. I suppose it was one of those dire weapons hanging in the hall.'

'I'm not sure you really want to know, love.'

'It wasn't one of those? What was it, Alec? Of course I want to know!'

'I'm pretty sure it was the seaman's knife Bel and Derek found.'

'Not really? Gosh, how frightful! Don't for heaven's sake let them find out.'

'Do you know what they did with it after they showed it to us?'

'Derek said they showed it to Godfrey Norville. He wasn't very interested, but he told them to leave it on the hall table – the east wing entrance hall – so they did.'

Alec groaned. 'The hall table. Anyone could have picked it up.'

'Absolutely anyone at all,' Daisy agreed. 'And the chances are no one would have noticed it was missing, unlike the historic stuff in the hall, so it could have been taken any time.'

'Oh, for a butler with an all-seeing eye. Oh, for a parlour-maid who listens at doors and a lady's maid who knows all her mistress's secrets. It's an odd household and no mistake. I'm not at all sure where to start unravelling it.'

'If the knife isn't still lying there on the table, hadn't you better make sure the children didn't take it? If they put it somewhere else, it might be possible to work out who could have retrieved it from wherever it was, if you see what I mean.'

'I'd rather keep them out of things altogether, though they'll have to know Calloway's dead. I'm sorry young Jemima was there when Tilton announced that it was murder.'

'She wasn't upset. I'd swear I saw a gleam in her eye. She hated him. Oh, darling, you don't think . . . ?'

'Jemima? Great Scott!' Alec looked at her in horror. 'I'm afraid it can't be ruled out,' he said soberly. 'She's at an unsettled age. Adolescents do commit murder. Why did she hate him?'

'I suppose for the same reasons nobody else much liked him, topped by the wigging he gave her over the ghost business. He really was frightfully fierce about it, and at her age feelings do tend to swing to extremes. Though once or twice I have wondered whether she's slightly unbalanced. I didn't tell you how she sneaked after me when I went to look at the chapel in the woods, before you came.'

'You don't think she was just playing a childish game? Like Belinda and Derek stalking buffalo?'

'Yes, of course, very likely,' Daisy said, relieved.

'All the same,' said Alec, 'she's going to have to go on my list, with the rest of her family.'

'It does seem to be a family affair. I can't see how the servants could have got involved. And you know, darling, I rather think there is a Westmoor son, a Lord Norville who's the earl's heir. He wasn't at school with Gervaise, but I seem to remember he came to stay at Fairacres one summer, because of the distant cousinship. Nothing could affect his position as heir, so it wouldn't matter to him if he'd somehow found out about Calloway.'

'But you're not absolutely certain, are you? I'll ask first about the heir,' Alec decided. 'If nothing else, it may disarm my suspects to find out they're not the only ones. Doesn't this right branch lead to the house? I'm going to have to go on back to the chapel to tell that young constable what's going on.'

'I'd better get back to the children.' Daisy had never realized quite what a responsibility children could be in a household not provided with a nanny and nursemaids as her own childhood had been.

'Check whether the knife has gone, will you? But for heaven's sake, *don't* start asking questions. If the doctor from Saltash has turned up but hasn't inspected the body yet, send him ... No, say I request his presence at the chapel, before it gets dark.'

'Yes, Chief. I'll send someone with a lantern anyway.'

'Yes, do, please. I'm pretty sure Calloway's lantern burnt out and needs refilling.'

The sun was sinking behind the house as she turned up the right-hand fork in the path. The few small puffs of cloud were tinted with pink. Another fine day on the morrow, Daisy hoped. Bel and Derek would be able to play outside and keep out of the way of the interrogation of suspects.

Who had murdered Calloway? Entering the house, Daisy thought that perhaps, instead of going with Alec, she should have stayed to observe people as the fact of the murder sank in. The shock of her mother's divulgence of Alec's profession had superseded the shock of Sergeant Tilton's announcement, muddying the waters of their reactions.

She checked the hall table. The knife was gone.

She went to the library. Jemima lay on her stomach on the hearthrug, reading the *Boys' Own Annual* which was one of Derek's Christmas presents. Captain Norville and Miles were playing chess with the exquisite ivory Chinese set the captain had given his nephew. Felicity lounged nearby, apparently in the terminal stages of boredom. She looked up and sat up as Daisy entered. Jemima obstinately kept her head down. The men started to stand.

Daisy waved them back to their seats. 'Alec's been put in charge,' she said. 'He's gone back to the chapel. Has a doctor from Saltash turned up?'

All three shook their heads. 'Not that I know,' said Felicity. 'Have you been deputized, like in a Wild West novel?'

'Not exactly. Alec's sergeant and a detective constable will be turning up in the morning. I said I'd have someone take a lantern to the chapel. Should I ask Mrs Pardon to send someone?'

'No, I'll go,' said Miles, rising again.

The captain shook his head, lumbering to his feet. 'You've done your bit, my boy,' he said. Daisy saw that Miles was rather pale, his shoulders hunched as if his missing arm pained him. Or his conscience? Was he too eager to return to the scene of the crime? Was his Uncle Victor too eager? 'I'll go, Mrs Fletcher. I've already left my footprints all over the place.' He went out.

'Is Mr Fletcher sleuthing for footprints?' Felicity asked, with an unconvincing attempt at casualness. 'He'll find mine all over the place, too. I quite often walk up that way.'

Jemima raised her head from the book at last. 'That's because the chapel's where you meet your lover,' she said spitefully.

Felicity jumped up. 'You filthy little sneak!' she cried, advancing on her sister. 'I'll show you what happens to spies!'

Jemima abandoned Derek's annual and scampered for the door, dodging Felicity. She squealed as Felicity reached out and yanked on a hank of her hair, but escaped further retribution, at least for the present, and disappeared.

'Have you really been meeting a man secretly?' Miles asked, his face grave. 'At the chapel?'

'Oh, don't ask me questions. What business is it of yours? We haven't done anything *immoral.*' The stress on the last word was contemptuous.

'Well, I *am* your brother,' Miles responded mildly. 'But whether I ask questions is irrelevant at the moment. You can be quite sure Mr Fletcher is going to.'

CHAPTER 10

'I must speak to you, Daisy!' Felicity begged.

'Of course. I'd better go and see where Belinda and Derek have got to. Come with me.'

'It's all right,' said Miles. 'They came in a few minutes ago. Flick sent them to clean up for tea. I'll go and make sure that's what they're doing.' He started to leave, then hesitated and looked back at his sister. But apparently he decided whatever he'd been going to say was likely to do more harm than good. He shrugged and went on, closing the door behind him.

'Do you have to tell Mr Fletcher what Jemima said?' Felicity asked.

'It would be much better if you told him yourself,' Daisy temporized. 'He's bound to find out one way or another, from Miles . . .'

'Oh, Miles might disapprove, but he wouldn't tell. It's not as if . . . my friend had anything to do with Calloway's death. We hadn't planned to meet on Christmas Eve, and he's not the sort to come mooning around when I'm not going to be there. He had something else on anyway.'

'Alec's much more likely to believe you if you've told him yourself, before Jemima lets the cat out of the bag again.'

'I suppose so,' said Felicity disconsolately. 'What a little horror she is!'

'If she found out, there's a fair chance someone else has, too.'

'What a frightful bore everything is, don't you think?'

'No, actually. On the whole I find life pretty interesting. Maybe you should get a job.'

'No fear! That would be even more boring. I'm going to get married.' Felicity sighed. 'Which will probably turn out to be the biggest bore of all. Daisy, Mr Fletcher won't tell the parents, will he? I'd rather keep it quiet as long as possible.'

'Someone they will disapprove of?' An unsuitable young man madly in love might expect even more opposition if his beloved's father suddenly became a legitimate, acknowledged relative of the earl. Motive enough for murder? 'Mother was furious when I got engaged to a policeman.'

'Not exactly like that.' Felicity gave her a twisted, sardonic smile. 'Call it family complications. We're a complicated family. Here's Gran. It must be teatime.'

Bel, Derek and Miles came in right behind Mrs Norville. Daisy was kept occupied for some time listening to the children's chatter of the afternoon's adventures. Tremayne, Dora Norville and Jemima came in together. Except for Belinda and Derek, everyone was subdued, speaking in low murmurs. Looking up once or twice, Daisy caught Dora Norville's eye, which sent her a desperate appeal. When Lady Dalrymple entered a few minutes later, Daisy sent the children to talk to her and went over to join Dora.

'Jemima, go and see if your father will join us for tea.'

'Why?' the girl whined. 'He hardly ever does.'

'Because it's Christmas Day and we have guests,' her mother said sharply. 'He said he was going to the drawing room to write letters. Off you go.'

Jemima slouched out. Dora turned to Daisy. 'Mrs Fletcher, I must talk to you.'

'Be careful what you say,' Tremayne warned.

'Oh, Papa, what can I possibly say that will make things worse? I'm not going to confess because I have nothing to confess to.'

'All the same, my dear, be careful.' Excusing himself, the old lawyer went to speak to Miles.

'Mrs Fletcher, is your husband going to investigate this terrible business?'

'Yes, he's been put in charge of the case. I'm afraid it puts us in a rather awkward position as your guests.'

'Not at all, not at all. You're Westmoor's guests, but in any case, I'd rather have Mr Fletcher asking questions than the local people. So humiliating! At least, I suppose we must all be under suspicion?'

'I believe so. But a new suspect has recently come to light who may change everything.'

Her face brightened; a rabbit offered a carrot. 'I'm sure it can't possibly have anything to do with the family. We all had the best of reasons for preserving the Reverend Calloway in good health. I suppose it will all have to come out now.'

'Alec will want to know your reasons, of course, though I rather think we have a pretty good idea already. He'll be as discreet as is humanly possible.'

'I'm sure he will. Quite the gentleman. One would never have guessed ... But I'd better tell you the whole story to make sure you have it right. You see, when I was a girl, the earl – the seventh earl, the present earl's father – used to bring house parties to Brockdene in the summer and at Christmas.'

'So I gather,' murmured Daisy, with an amused glance at the Dowager Viscountess.

'It was always the best society, of course. I wouldn't have dreamt of being invited to take part. But when Lord Westmoor wasn't here, we used to come up to play badminton and for picnics and so on. The vicar's children, and the squire's, the doctor's, and my sister and I, we were all of an age with the Norville boys.' Her voice sank to a near whisper. 'We knew Mrs Norville was a ... a foreigner, of course, but that's all. Our parents certainly had no idea she *wasn't married*!'

'But she was, wasn't she?'

Dora Norville flushed. 'Yes, of course. She always told Godfrey and Victor so, and Godfrey told Papa so when he asked for my hand. But he had to explain the ... the uncertainty, so that I wouldn't expect to be included in Lord Westmoor's company when he came down. Mrs Norville and Godfrey and Victor were expected to keep to themselves at those times. So *unfair*!' she burst out aggrievedly.

'Rather hard lines,' Daisy agreed. 'When did Westmoor stop bringing parties here?'

'When the old earl died, the present earl stopped coming so often. Just occasionally, really. The war finally put the cap on it. He hasn't shown his face here since nineteen-fourteen. And then Victor turns up with the Reverend

Calloway, who could swear to my mother-in-law's marriage! Lord Westmoor would have had to accept us as part of his family. Why should any of us want Mr Calloway dead?'

'A good question,' said Daisy, but one which was not presently destined to be investigated, as Mrs Pardon came in with the tea and Dora had to pour.

Having walked to Calstock and back since midday dinner, Daisy was quite ready for Christmas cake and mince pies. Both were excellent. The former had a good thick layer of almond paste between the royal icing and the rich, dark cake. The mince pies were made with flaky pastry and thickly dusted with icing sugar. The latter, however, were not what she would have chosen to serve to children in company. Derek and Belinda both managed to get crumbs all over their clothes (and probably the floor, but Daisy didn't examine it) and icing sugar all over their faces.

'It just happens,' Belinda explained, 'when you breathe.'

'Go and wash your faces – and hands.'

'Again?' Derek protested. They both sighed heavily and departed.

Daisy was glad they had gone when Alec came in a few minutes later with Captain Norville. However hard they tried, they couldn't have kept the knowledge of the murder from the children.

'The doctor came up the river from Saltash and took the body away for autopsy,' the captain announced heavily, 'though he's pretty certain the blade nicked a lung and the poor man drowned in his own blood.'

'Really, Captain!' Lady Dalrymple objected, outraged. But he didn't hear, and she didn't leave.

'I'm sorry, Mother,' he went on, going to old Mrs Norville and enveloping one tiny brown hand in his great paws. 'It's all over. I did my best.'

She laid her other hand against his cheek as he bent over her. 'It doesn't matter, Victor love,' she said gently. 'I know, and the Lord knows, that the Reverend Calloway married me to your father.'

'Married!' exclaimed Lady Dalrymple. 'That presumptuous parson was here to testify to your marriage? Then Captain Norville is Westmoor's heir presumptive?'

'No, no, my lady, not I. Lord Westmoor's son, young Lord Norville . . .'

The dowager interrupted, stating flatly, 'George Norville was killed in the Great War.'

In the electrified silence, Daisy glanced around at the faces of the family. Victor Norville was astonished, no doubt about it. Whatever his motive for bringing Calloway to Brockdene, the expectation of succeeding to an earldom had not been part of it.

Mr Tremayne had known of George Norville's death, Daisy thought. He had not told his daughter, and now looked anxiously at her to see the effect of the news. Dora Norville was surprised, doubtful, perhaps confused. She was trying to work out just what it meant to her family. In a minute or two, she would realize that nothing was going to change, because of Calloway's untimely demise.

The clergyman's testimony could have made her a countess. Victor was childless, unmarried. By the orderly rules of aristocratic inheritance, his brother would have been his heir presumptive.

Godfrey had come in just in time to hear Lady

Dalrymple's revelation. He stood in the doorway, behind but slightly to one side of Alec, so that Daisy could see his face. He was shocked, appalled even. Daisy was surprised by the strength of his reaction. She wouldn't have expected a man of his studious habits to put so much stock in a title. Of course there would be a certain amount of wealth to go with the title, even in these days of death duties and income tax, and a love of history did not preclude a man from coveting wealth.

Miles would have been his father's heir, almost certain to become earl in the course of time. Daisy missed his immediate reaction to her mother's announcement, but when she looked at him, she had the impression that it was no surprise to him. He had been in the army, and the identical surnames would have ensured that someone brought George Norville's death to his attention.

What about Felicity? By the time Daisy glanced her way, she was looking singularly inscrutable. Daisy could see no reason why she should want to hide surprise, which suggested that she had not been surprised. Which in turn begged the question, what was she trying to hide?

Godfrey broke the silence. 'I suppose,' he said heavily, 'those upstarts the other side of the river consider themselves the earl's heirs.'

Daisy thought she saw a flash of dismay, almost alarm, in Felicity's eyes, as Alec demanded, 'Upstarts?'

'Not exactly "upstarts",' said Miles. 'The Mr Norville at Helstone is Lord Westmoor's second cousin, Mr Fletcher. I believe he's acknowledged as the heir.'

'We're the earl's *first* cousins!' cried Godfrey. 'Miles, you knew George Norville was killed in the war? Why didn't you tell me?'

'It wouldn't have changed our position, sir, or only to worsen the chagrin. And then, when Uncle Victor brought Calloway along, I didn't want to queer his pitch with a complicating factor. The balance was delicate enough already.'

'Quite right, my boy,' the captain approved. 'Goodness knows what the Reverend would have thought of our chasing worldly honours. Well, that's all done with and no skin off my nose. What do I know about lording it? The sea's good enough for me, and I've got my little bit put away for later on. Let's have another cup of tea, Dora, and I wouldn't say no to another piece of cake. There's no victuals like this at sea! Another cup, Mother? Another cup, Lady Dalrymple?'

Amid the one-man bustle he created, Daisy made for Felicity, the only one whose reaction had aroused questions in her mind. Alec apparently had the same idea, though he stopped for a word with Miles on the way.

Felicity took the offensive. 'Mr Fletcher, I have something to tell you. Shall we go to the dining room?'

'Yes, that will do very well. Do you mind if Daisy comes to take notes? She has no official standing, of course, but it would be a great help to me, until my constable arrives.'

'Notes? I haven't that much to tell.'

'Perhaps not,' said Alec, 'but I have several people to interview, and I have to keep their stories straight.'

'Oh, right-oh. Daisy already knows most of it anyway.'

'I haven't got my notebook,' said Daisy, as they left the library. 'I'll have to go upstairs and fetch it.'

'Where is Ernie Piper with his ever-sharp pencils when I need him?' Alec teased.

'There's a drawer in the hall table which should have writing paper among the gloves and odd keys,' said Felicity. 'Yes, will this do?'

Mr Tremayne had followed them out to the hall. 'Felicity, you mustn't make a statement to the police without a solicitor present. I must assume I'm under suspicion, Chief Inspector. Does that preclude my acting for the rest?'

'I'm not at all sure of the legal niceties, sir. But I'm not taking formal statements at present, so if you want to sit in . . .'

'There's no need, Grandfather, honestly. I didn't murder Mr Calloway, and I haven't anything earth-shaking to tell Mr Fletcher. Nothing about the family. Just now I think Mother's hand probably needs holding more than mine does.'

The old man shook his head. 'These modern young ladies . . . Well, as you wish, my dear. Ah, here's Miles. Perhaps you'll let him "hold your hand". Miles, my dear boy, I believe you have enough law to stop your sister incriminating herself.'

'But I haven't done anything!' Felicity insisted. With an irritable gesture, she opened the glass-paned door to the corridor. 'Oh, all right, Miles can come if Mr Fletcher doesn't mind.'

'Miles may come,' said Alec, at which Mr Tremayne returned to the library, closing the door behind him. 'I have a few questions for him on the same subject.'

Miles nodded. They followed Felicity to the dining room and all sat down at the long table.

'You first, Miss Norville, and let's start with what you have to tell me, before we go on to what I want to ask you.'

Felicity's sulky face made her look very like Jemima. 'It's just that I've been meeting someone, a man, at the chapel. But we hadn't arranged to meet on Christmas Eve. He had something else on, with his family, that he couldn't get out of.'

Alec hadn't expected anything like this revelation. It opened up all sorts of possibilities. 'His name, please.'

'I can't see what that has to do with anything. I told you, he couldn't come last night.'

'If he wasn't here, he has nothing to fear. Who is he?'

'Oh lord, Flick, it wasn't ...' Miles shut his mouth abruptly as Alec gave him one of the icy looks which made subordinates jump to attention and chilled the souls of malefactors. He turned it on Felicity.

'Well, if you must know, I suppose you'll find out somehow. He had to land at Brockdene Quay, and someone's bound to have seen him. It was Cedric Norville,' she said defiantly.

'One of the Helstone Norvilles?'

'The eldest son,' Miles confirmed, clearly shocked.

'Second in line to inherit the earldom,' said Alec. 'As long as Calloway didn't spill the beans.'

'He didn't know about Calloway; I didn't tell him.' She was lying, Alec thought. 'Anyway, he had no way of knowing Calloway was going to the chapel in the woods. We didn't know ourselves till a couple of hours before.'

Though true enough, that was irrelevant. If Cedric Norville had come to meet Felicity, or come in hope of meeting Felicity, found Calloway in the chapel and discovered who he was . . . But what about the knife? How could Cedric have obtained the seaman's knife Belinda and Derek had found in the secret passage?

'So you see,' Felicity went on, 'Cedric had nothing to do with it. What was it you wanted to ask me?'

'It was obvious from your expression, when your father and brother mentioned the Helstone Norvilles, that you knew something about them,' Alec said dryly. 'I didn't guess you were so intimately acquainted, but as they are obvious suspects, I wanted to find out what you knew.'

'Now you know,' said Felicity, rising with languid grace.

'Not so fast. I have a few more questions. First, you knew the earl's son was killed in the war. Cedric Norville told you, I assume? Why didn't you tell your family?'

'Isn't that obvious?' she drawled. 'They'd have wanted to know how I found out.'

'All right. Now, taking your word for the moment that you didn't meet Cedric Norville yesterday, I don't suppose you saw anyone, or anyone saw you, between say half past eleven last night and five this morning?'

'Jemima might have,' Felicity said indifferently, 'though she was fast asleep when I went up. She's sharing my room while "his lordship's guests" are with us. No one else, unless they crept into my room and gazed entranced upon my sleeping form.'

'Unlikely, I agree. Did you happen to hear any unusual sounds in the night – doors closing, floorboards creaking, and such.'

'Not a thing. I slept like a log. But if I had heard anything out of the way, I'd have assumed it was Jemima making her ghostly rounds. I doubt I'd have opened my eyes to check whether she was gone. I don't care.'

'I daresay,' Alec said, his dry tone bringing a slight flush to Felicity's cheeks.

'In any case, I didn't wake till morning. One way or another, I've missed quite a bit of sleep. I had some catching up to do.'

Alec changed tack. 'Are you aware of what Belinda and Derek found in the secret passage?'

'The seaman's knife? Yes, I was there when they showed it to my father. I'm afraid he wasn't very enthusiastic. But why . . . Oh gosh, is that what . . . ?'

'Mr Norville wasn't very enthusiastic? Why was that?'

'He said it wasn't at all rare.'

'I see. And come to think of it, Captain Norville said the carving of dolphins and sea serpents on the hilt was typical of a seaman's knife. So the weapon which killed Calloway may simply be similar to that one. I'd appreciate it if you'd keep that under your hat, by the way. I wouldn't want the children to find out.'

'No, of course not.'

'Have you seen it since then?'

'Not consciously,' said Felicity, frowning. 'Daddy told Derek to leave it on the hall table. I doubt I'd notice whether it was still there. There's usually quite a bit of clutter, but as we don't have the post or newspapers delivered, we don't have the usual reasons for checking the table. I suppose the children might have taken the knife to play with and dropped it in the grounds. Anyone could have picked it up, one of the gardeners, or a tramp.'

Or Cedric Norville, Alec thought. 'Are you meeting Cedric tonight?'

'No! Not till . . . till New Year's Eve.'

'Thank you, Miss Norville, that will be all. For now.'

'That's all?' Felicity seemed more confused than pleased. 'Right-oh, then. You're putting Miles through the "third degree" next?'

'Yes, it's his turn to be grilled,' Alec said, with a grin. Let her think he believed her. Of one thing he was tolerably certain: she expected Cedric Norville to meet her at the chapel tonight.

CHAPTER 11

The night was clear. The air had a frosty feel when Alec and Miles took up their positions on either side of the chapel by the river. As Alec had expected, Miles was quite willing to assist in the apprehension of Cedric Norville. After all, if his sister's young man turned out to be the murderer, the Brockdene Norvilles would be freed from suspicion.

Alec had managed a brief, preliminary interview with each of them in the course of the evening. Now, waiting in the cold, unable to walk about for fear of alerting his quarry, he had plenty of time to think over those interviews.

Miles had provided more information about the Helstone Norvilles. The Mr Norville of that branch of the family was Lord Westmoor's second cousin, the grandson of the fifth earl's younger brother. He had another son besides Cedric, and two or three daughters. They lived on a small estate belonging to the earl, just across the river from Brockdene, in Devon.

'Under other circumstances,' Miles had said wryly, 'we might have been good neighbours and even friends. As it is, I've seen them occasionally in Calstock and received a distant nod – never the cut direct, I'll give them that but there was no closer communication. Until Flick "took up with" Cedric. I suppose they met last summer. I wish she hadn't been meeting him secretly, especially at night, but I can't blame her for not telling the parents.'

'They would have forbidden the association?'

'I don't know about that. It seems to me it's jolly difficult nowadays to stop girls doing exactly as they please. But they would have been upset. After all, the Helstone lot have been gently snubbing us for decades. We're not quite respectable, you know.'

'So Cedric's parents would have been even more upset?' Alec hazarded.

'Indubitably,' Miles confirmed. 'I say, suppose his father discovered they were meeting at the chapel, came over, found a clergyman there, assumed he was going to marry them secretly, and killed the messenger, so to speak?'

'A nice theory, if a little far-fetched.' At that moment, Alec had caught Daisy's eye – she was still taking notes – which had reminded him of his occasionally unwarranted dismissal of her wilder conjectures. 'Mind you,' he said hurriedly to Miles, 'I've seen too many far-fetched theories turn out to be the truth to dismiss it outright. I'll keep it in mind. By the way, why didn't you tell your parents about young Lord Norville's death?'

'Partly because by the time the medicos finished with me I simply didn't want to think, let alone talk, about the war. Mostly because it could only upset everyone, make a long-standing grievance more grievous, if you will. I mean, it was one thing as long as we had little to gain by proof of Gran's marriage, but if Uncle Victor should have been Westmoor's heir . . .'

'Yes, I see what you mean.'

'I'm all for a quiet life, though I don't seem to be having much luck that way.'

'No. I have to ask, where were you between eleven thirty and five last night?'

'Sleeping the sleep of the just. My grandfather had my bed, and Flick helped me set up a camp bed in the room for myself.'

'I take it you and he can't give each other alibis?' Alec said resignedly.

''Fraid not. Grandfather takes some mixture for the rheumatics which puts him out like a light, and I learnt in France to sleep like a log absolutely anywhere – except when I'm having nightmares, which I didn't last night. And I'm afraid it's even more unlikely that anyone "crept into my room and gazed entranced upon my sleeping form" than it was with my sister. Dash it, sir, how is it one can go on cracking asinine jokes when a man was murdered just a few hours ago?'

'It's a defensive mechanism. I was in the Flying Corps, not the trenches, but from all I've heard . . .'

'Yes, we went on joking in the teeth of hell. You're right, how else would one come through? The fact is, no, I have no alibi. I doubt you'll find many for that time of night.'

'I know.' Alec had sighed, and then proposed the expedition upon which they were now engaged.

Having secured Miles's assent, he saw the old lady next. Not that he thought her physically capable of trotting down to the chapel and stabbing a man in the back. However, as Daisy pointed out, her history was fundamental to the murder, and all they knew of it was a mixture of gossip, hints and speculation. Alec needed to hear it from her own lips.

She had come in quietly, as was her wont, giving Daisy a shy smile, not commenting on her presence. Alec settled her in a chair with her inevitable handwork, and asked for her full name for the record.

'My childhood name was Surata, but when I went to the mission school they called me Susannah, and that was the name on my marriage certificate. I am Mrs Albert Norville.'

She spoke with a gentle steadfastness. It seemed to Alec that, faced with that unassuming moral courage, the sixth Lord Westmoor must have found it difficult to deny her.

'Tell me about your marriage, Mrs Norville.'

'We were young. We fell in love,' she said simply. 'The Reverend Calloway married us secretly. He was not then so . . . uncompromising. Albert believed that the English in India were far more prejudiced against mixed marriages than those at home. He was sure his family would accept me when his tour in India was over and he brought me here. Then Victor was born. Albert's father found out and sent for him.'

'Why did you not go with your husband?' Alec asked, wondering how things might have been different if the couple had arrived together.

'By then I was expecting our second child. Albert would not let me travel. He would go ahead and prepare the way. Once his parents understood that we were married, not . . . cohabiting, all would be well. He was an optimist, my Albert. He was going to write to me when all was settled, and when the baby was old enough to travel, I would join him.'

'I see. It sounds like a sensible plan, but it was hard on you, waiting.'

'I had faith in Albert, but it seemed a long wait. At last the letter came. He had not yet seen his parents, but his eldest brother, who he had hoped would be sympathetic, was dead set against us and had tried to take and destroy the marriage certificate. Albert had it safe. I was to come at once. Once his parents met me, he was quite sure they must love me as he did. Love is blind, Mr Fletcher.'

'Very often.' But he was perfectly aware of Daisy's '"satiable curtiosity", and her penchant for meddling, and though she drove him mad sometimes, he loved her anyway. Still, Albert's refusal to see his wife's dark skin as an insuperable bar to his parents' acceptance was in its way admirable. 'So you set out,' Alec prompted.

'Yes. Godfrey was scarcely a month old, my poor boy. Albert had told me to go to his family's solicitor in London, who would tell me where to find him. But all he could tell me was that Albert was dead.'

Her tone had remained so soft and even that Alec was startled as well as dismayed to see slow tears rolling down her cheeks. After half a century, the memory still hurt. The reminder of his grief when Joan died shot a pang of anguish through him which left him feeling somehow disloyal to both his first wife and Daisy.

Though he usually had a spare handkerchief on him when he was interviewing suspects, he hadn't expected to need one today. Fortunately Daisy came to the rescue. Mrs Norville dabbed her eyes and continued her story.

'Our marriage certificate had disappeared. I don't know whether Lord Norville took it, or it was lost when Albert drowned, or if someone destroyed it when his body was found. Of course, without proof Lord Westmoor could not accept me as his son's wife, but he was generous. He gave me a home here and an annuity from the estate which continues even since he died, and he paid for Victor and Godfrey's schooling. If prices had not risen so since the war . . . but it is the same for everyone, isn't it?'

Agreeing, Alec noticed that Daisy was about to say something. He gave her a 'not now' look and said to Mrs Norville, 'Then Captain Norville turned up with Mr Calloway.'

'Such an unhappy man.' The old lady sighed. 'It was very dear of Victor to go to such trouble to find him for my sake, but though I would not tell him so for the world, I'm not sure it wouldn't have been better to let bygones be bygones. Such turmoil, even before this terrible business!' She sighed again. 'Still, Victor found himself in India with time on his hands, and he never was one to let sleeping dogs lie, dear boy.'

'Speaking of sleeping, ma'am, I have to ask where you were between eleven thirty and five last night, and whether you saw or heard anything out of the ordinary.'

Mrs Norville had nothing to report. Alec escorted her back to the library and returned with Dora Norville and Jemima.

The younger Mrs Norville had been so upset, she said, by Calloway's disastrous effect on her plans for a traditional jolly Christmas that she had had to take a powder to help her sleep. She had been dead to the world ('Oh dear, what a dreadful thing to say!') the moment her head touched the pillow and had not woken till broad daylight.

Jemima truculently proclaimed that Felicity's boyfriend had killed Calloway, with Felicity's help, and she didn't blame him a bit. Naturally this led to an immediate outcry from her mother, wanting to know what she was talking about.

Alec managed to extract an admission from Jemima that no, of course she hadn't seen him do it. Since playing the ghost, she had been strictly forbidden to set foot outside the bedroom after lights out. Pressed, she conceded that she hadn't actually observed Felicity leaving their shared room during the night. With Dora Norville wringing her hands and demanding explanations, it was impossible to continue questioning the two. Alec had let them go.

He had been following them to select his next victim when Daisy said, 'Darling, before you go any further, I should tell you . . .'

'Not now, Daisy. I still have three to see before dinner, not counting your mother, who just might have seen or heard something. I can't even attempt the servants till Tom and Ernie arrive. And I have to ask Bel and Derek if they moved the knife from the hall table.'

'I'll do that, if you like,' she offered. 'They'll be more likely to think it's just a matter of whether they've been naughty, not connected to Calloway's death.'

'Yes, please, love. Why don't you see if you can find them now, and I'll speak to Lady Dalrymple.'

'Good idea. Mother is bound to be obstreperous if she sees me helping you.'

They had grinned at each other and parted company.

Assured that she was a possible witness, not a suspect, Lady Dalrymple was comparatively cooperative, if having nothing to report could be described as cooperation. She did wonder aloud what was the advantage of having a chief inspector from Scotland Yard on the case if he had not yet managed to make an arrest. Alec forebore to point out that he'd only been on the case for a few hours.

Daisy returned. 'The children are over in the old house,' she reported, 'hunting for another treasure map. Godfrey's there. He doesn't seem to mind them messing about with his precious cabinets.'

'He has other things to worry about. What about the knife?'

'Derek admitted to taking it out of its sheath for another look, on his way up to bed last night. They both swear, cross their hearts and hope to die, that they left it on the hall table.'

'That doesn't get us any further then. Whereabouts in the old house is Godfrey? Not conveniently in the hall, I suppose.'

'No, up in the drawing room, in the tower. He seems to use it as a den, or office. Did you want him next?'

'Yes, before he hears of Felicity's misdeeds and gets distracted. It'll waste less time if I go to him, I suppose. How do I get to the drawing room?'

'I'll show you, darling. You haven't explored the old house yet, have you?'

'No,' he grumbled, 'and I'm not likely to have a chance now. But I'd rather you stayed here and headed off any attempt to tell Godfrey about Felicity's misdeeds. I don't need a note-taker for the amount of information I'm getting from these interviews. Tell me how to find Godfrey.'

She gave him directions. 'If the children are still there,' she said, 'you'd better send them to me. It's nearly time for their supper, anyway.'

Crossing the hall, Alec had scanned the display of weapons on the walls, looking for a gap. Polished blades glinted in the wavering lamplight. Nothing was obviously missing, but it was hard to be sure. He wondered whether there were – or had been – any seaman's knives on show. The maids who polished them would surely know. It was something for Tom to ask about tomorrow. He had a way with female servants, in spite of his deep devotion to Mrs Tring.

But Derek's knife was gone from the hall table. It was almost certainly the murder weapon.

Would that rule out the man Alec and Miles were now lying in wait for, or might Felicity have taken it to show him, perhaps to illustrate the amusing tale of the children's adventure? Or might she have taken it with every intention of his using it to kill Calloway? Or might she have killed Calloway herself?

If she was in love with Cedric Norville, she might have wanted the clergyman out of the way for Cedric's sake. But if she expected to marry him, she might have murdered for her own sake. It was infinitely preferable, Alec supposed, to be a countess than to be merely the sister of an earl, to find herself once again and forever a poor relation.

At this point in his musing, Alec had reached the drawing room. There was no sign of the children, but Godfrey was there, seated at a small Queen Anne writing-desk on a mahogany stand.

Apologizing for disturbing him, Alec noticed that the sheet of writing paper in front of him was blank. 'I hope Belinda and Derek haven't been a nuisance. Where have they got to?'

Godfrey gave him a vague look. 'Got to? Belinda and Derek? Oh, they wanted to know about secret drawers. I told them to try the walnut escritoire in the south room. Mrs Fletcher was asking them about the seaman's knife they found. It's really of no value, of no importance whatsoever. It doesn't matter if they have lost it. There is no need to search for it.'

Alec didn't tell him the knife had already been found, in Calloway's back. It had been a mistake to disclose that titbit to Miles and Felicity. Still, with any luck they'd keep it under their hats for the children's sake. If the murderer was the only other suspect who knew, he just might say something which would give him away.

Coming to the question of alibis, Godfrey Norville had no more than anyone else, since his wife had taken a sleeping powder. No sounds of doors or footsteps in the night had roused him from his slumbers. He expressed indifference towards Calloway's diatribes, seeming far more upset by his son having withheld his knowledge of the death of Westmoor's heir.

'I take no newspapers because I am in general uninterested in news of the modern world,' he said, 'but Miles should have known that that would interest me. The earl is my first cousin, after all. I can scarcely believe that Miles was so inconsiderate, so secretive. To think that Victor could have been Lord Westmoor's heir, and I after him!'

The fuss Godfrey Norville was making now quite

justified Miles's reticence, Alec thought. He thanked the
man, returned to the east wing and asked Tremayne to join
him in the dining room.

The old man was clearly upset by the mess his daughter's
family had got themselves into, but he remained a canny
lawyer. Though he obviously would have liked to claim to
have lain awake all night and thus to be certain Miles had
not left the room, he forbore. He refused to give his
opinion of Calloway or to say whether he had been told of
the clergyman's purpose in coming to Brockdene. He
would not even specify his reasons for not telling his
daughter about Lord Norville's death.

'Tomorrow,' he said, 'I shall walk into Calstock and
attempt to telephone a colleague in Plymouth who has
something of a criminal practice. I fear I may not reach him
because of the holiday, but I must insist that you take no
formal statements until Butterwick is able to be present.'

'I cannot compel anyone to give me a statement, sir,'
Alec pointed out.

'I fear I ought to have forbidden everyone to give you
any information at all until then, but my position is
invidious. I am a servant of the law and must not obstruct
the police. I am also under suspicion, as are all members of
my family. Yet I cannot believe any of them committed this
horrible crime! Why should they?'

And he had no more motive than the rest for that
horrible crime. Alec had let him go and called in the
captain. Of all the family, he seemed the most likely to
have murdered Calloway.

Captain Norville had slept like a baby, confident that the
good Lord would tell the reverend gentleman to do what

was right, which was, obviously, to swear to the marriage
he had performed.

'Aye, I would have been cross as a bear with a sore head
if he'd told me he'd changed his mind, but not a cross word
would I have said, for there was always a chance he'd
change it back. You learn patience at sea, Fletcher,
especially in the sailing ships where I learnt my trade. The
wind and waves are fickle, but I've always got where I was
going in the end.'

'Until now.'

'Until now,' he sighed. 'There's no fetching a man back
from heaven.'

He didn't sound like a murderer, but Alec again recalled
the ready fists when Tremayne had stopped him rushing
into the chapel.

And now Alec was back at the chapel, awaiting the arrival
of the suspect with by far the best motive for murdering
Calloway. The stars shone down through the leafless
branches. Somewhere in the distance an owl hooted. The
nip of frost in the still air made Alec long to stamp his feet
and beat his hands together, but the slightest sound would
carry far on a night like this, with no breeze to rustle the
bushes.

Longing for his overcoat, left off so as not to hamper his
movements, he hoped they would not have long to wait,
less for his own sake than for Miles's. Cold could trigger
excruciating pain in the phantom limb of an amputee.

No breeze, but a rustle came from the carpet of autumn
leaves on the far side of the path. Alec stared, straining to

see by the faint starlight. No figure appeared. Had Cedric Norville spotted them? If he stood behind a tree he'd be quite safe as long as he kept still. The carefully laid trap would turn into a test of endurance.

Another rustle. A badger strolled across the path, its black-and-white striped face obvious once it had left the striped shadows under the trees. Alec almost laughed aloud: Mr Brock of Brockdene, come to see what was going on in his domain.

The badger raised its long muzzle, sniffed the air and scuttered off among the trees. The waiting recommenced.

It seemed an age, but the manor's chapel clock had chimed no more than two quarters when Alec heard the regular crunch of footsteps approaching along the path from the quay. A dark figure in a trench coat and golf cap passed Alec and turned towards the chapel.

'Felicity?'

Miles stepped out from behind the chapel, his electric torch beam playing on the newcomer. 'Norville? You're Cedric Norville, aren't you?'

Cedric flicked on his own torch, shining it on Miles's face. Alec, approaching stealthily from behind, saw his shoulders slump. 'And you're Miles Norville. I suppose Felicity sent you to tell me she's givin' me the bird. Funny, I'd have expected her to have the guts to do her own dirty work.'

Gripping the young man's arms from behind, Alec enquired, 'Does that go for murder, too?'

CHAPTER 12

Alec had a bloody nose, which took his own, Miles's and Cedric's handkerchiefs to staunch. It was entirely his own fault for not immediately announcing himself as 'Police', he assured the apologetic Cedric.

At least he had managed to hang on to the young man while being assaulted. Cedric had quieted down as soon as the magic word was pronounced and, pending explanations, they all went into the chapel to apply first aid. Miles was not happy about entering the place, but Cedric showed no reluctance whatever. A clear conscience or no conscience?

If he knew of the murder, even if he had not taken an active part, surely some consciousness would be apparent in his voice. Alec, lying flat on his back on a pew with the chief suspect's handkerchief pressed to his nose, wished he had daylight to see Cedric's expression.

Apologies over, his tone was indignant now. 'What the deuce is a policeman doin' here? I don't need a copper to warn me off if Flick's handin' me my hat.'

'I gather you wouldn't be particularly surprised to hear Biss Dorville does't wa't to see you agaid.' Alec felt ridiculous interrogating a suspect when he couldn't speak properly, nor look the man in the eye.

'No.' Cedric sighed and sat down on the pew, at Alec's feet. 'That is, she ... she said there wasn't much point in marryin' me because I wasn't goin' to be an earl after all. I didn't believe she really meant it. Girls say these things, you know, just to tease. I thought she was actually quite fond of me.'

'Why were you dot to be ad earl after all?'

'Oh, because her uncle brought home a missionary chap from India who could prove her grandmother ... I say, old chap, this isn't quite the thing. I mean, discussin' a lady's – er – misfortunes, don't you know. And what's between me and Miss Norville is, frankly, none of your affair.'

Cautiously Alec sat up and lowered the handkerchief. 'I'm afraid it is my affair, Mr Norville,' he said.

'Look here, dash it, I can see that Norville here might have somethin' sharpish to say to me on the subject, but ...'

'Miss Norville claims she didn't tell you about the Reverend Calloway, the missionary from India.'

'Flick said that?' Cedric's voice was full of astonishment. 'But why the deuce would she say anythin' at all? That's what I don't quite get. Dash it, I never will understand women.'

'Mr Norville, I am Detective Chief Inspector Fletcher of the Metropolitan CID. I have a number of questions to put to you, which can more easily be accomplished up at the house. I must request that you accompany me thither.'

'Chief Inspector from Scotland Yard? I say, what's goin' on here? Righty-ho, I'll come along quietly, if only to find out what's up!'

Miles, who had admirably obeyed Alec's instructions to

keep his mouth shut, led the way. Alec appropriated Cedric's torch and took the rear, keeping the light shining on his captive's back. If Cedric was aware of the murder, he was a very cool customer indeed. He had not only returned to the chapel the next night but had volunteered the admission that he knew Calloway's purpose in coming to Brockdene.

He had the motive; the means was not impossible; opportunity had yet to be delved into. Yet his manner made it difficult to see him as the murderer, or even accessory to murder.

As they turned through the gate into the valley garden, Alec saw a lantern bobbing down the path towards them. So much for his hope that they would get back to the house before Felicity came out, or that her parents would stop her leaving. All the same, he hoped it was Felicity and not her father, come to wreak vengeance on his daughter's secret lover.

A moment later, the lantern-bearer spotted Miles's torch. 'Ceddie? Darling, you simply mustn't come up to the house, tonight of all nights! You can't imagine what's . . .' Felicity's voice trailed off. She must have seen two men's figures silhouetted against the light of Alec's torch and realized that a third person had to be carrying the torch. 'Who's there?' she called sharply.

'Alec Fletcher, Miss Norville, and your brother, and a friend of yours.'

'Sorry, Flick, they bagged me neatly. What's all the . . . ?'

'You haven't arrested Cedric, have you, Mr Fletcher?' The bobbing lantern started to move faster, Felicity dimly visible behind it. 'I told you, he wasn't here last night!'

'You also told me he wasn't coming tonight,' Alec
pointed out dryly. 'Miles, please escort your sister back to
the house.'

'No! I want to know . . . Oh!'

The lantern described an arc, followed almost simultan-
eously by a crash and a splash. Flickering flames showed a
pool of paraffin spreading from the broken glass towards
the tumbling streamlet where Felicity floundered.

Cedric dashed forward, ripping off his trench coat. He
almost slipped and fell, but recovered his balance and ran
on to smother the flames with his coat and his gloved
hands. More cautiously, Miles hurried after him, his torch
pointed towards his sister. Upper half bedraggled, lower
half sodden, she crawled out of the stream, aided by Cedric
once he was sure the fire was out.

'I think I've sprained my ankle,' she said. 'Oh hell!' And
she burst into tears.

Alec was old fashioned enough to disapprove of women
swearing as much as he disapproved of men swearing in the
presence of women (though he had long since ceased to
wince at Daisy's occasional 'Blast!' and had been known to
utter the odd 'Damn!' within her hearing). However,
Felicity had ample cause for her language and her tears. As
a modern young woman, she would probably regret the
latter more come morning.

Alec couldn't even offer her a handkerchief. The three
he had on him were all bloodstained.

Shivering, dripping, sniffling, in pain, her lie exposed,
her lover – for all she knew – arrested for murder, she
hopped up to the house supported on either side by Cedric
and Miles. Alec followed close behind, close enough to

hear that the only words exchanged were, 'Watch out for the steps!' and the like. He bore the trench coat, which stank of paraffin and scorched wool.

Not his most successful operation ever. Fortunately, as he had not actually made an arrest, he could leave the details out of his report.

As Alec closed the front door behind them, Daisy came out of the library, looking sleepy. She took one look at them, opened her mouth, closed it again, took a closer look at Alec's face, opened her mouth, closed it again, and then said, 'There's a thermos flask of cocoa in the library, darling. Let's get you into a hot bath quickly, Felicity. Miles, will you help her upstairs, please?'

Blessing her, Alec ushered Cedric into the library. In the looking glass over the hall table he had seen the daubs of dried blood on his upper lip. Now he hastily wiped them off with a spot of spit on the least bloody handkerchief.

Meanwhile, Cedric stooped to put a couple of logs on the dying fire.

He politely waited until Alec had finished his ablution before asking plaintively, 'Look here, sir, what exactly is the matter? I can't believe I'm about to be arrested by Scotland Yard for meetin' Miss Norville secretly.'

'Did you meet her last night?' Alec waved him to a chair by the fire, poured cocoa for each of them, and sat down opposite.

'No.' He perched on the edge of the chair, leaning forward, all anxious attention, a lock of fair hair flopping over his forehead. His face was too round to be called handsome, but its ingenuousness might well appeal to a strong-willed young woman such as Felicity. 'I couldn't make it.'

'Where were you?'

'Oh, just a family party,' Cedric said airily, his manly frankness suddenly turned to shiftiness. He leaned back in an attempt at nonchalance. 'Christmas Eve and all that, don't you know.'

Alec did know. The children had woken him at dawn with their Christmas stockings. It was now after midnight. His Christmas holiday had been ruined. He was fed up.

'Where?' he snapped.

'Er . . . at home.' Cedric was lying. Could he be at once a brilliant actor and a rotten liar?

'Who was there?'

'Oh, just family.' Under Alec's stare, he elaborated: 'The parents, my brother, my youngest sister.'

'That's all?'

'Er . . . yes.'

'No guests to keep you up late, then. You could easily have slipped out unseen after everyone retired and rowed across the river, as you did tonight.'

'No, dash it, I bally well couldn't!'

'How many of your family had you told about the Reverend Calloway?'

'None. I'd have had to say how I found out, and that would have set the cat among the pigeons, I can tell you! The pater would have hit the ceiling if he'd found out I was keen on Miss Norville.' Now he was telling the truth, Alec judged.

'So you were the only one who knew you were about to be disinherited,' he said.

'Yes, and that's another thing that would have made the pater hit the . . . I say, has somethin' happened to the Reverend? Is that what all this is about?'

'Mr Calloway was murdered last night.'

Cedric Norville looked stunned, unprepared for this blunt statement despite his dawning surmise. 'Murdered! Oh, lord, you did say somethin' about murder when you grabbed me. You think I had somethin' to do with it?'

'You and your family had the only apparent motive for preventing his testifying to Mrs Albert Norville's marriage.' Alec saw Miles come in. He stopped quietly by the door and Cedric didn't appear to notice his arrival. Alec went on, 'You have admitted to knowing that such was his purpose in coming to Brockdene.'

'Yes, but . . . I say, didn't you say Flick denied tellin' me about this clergyman chappie? By Jove, she was tryin' to protect me! I knew she didn't mean all that bosh about not marryin' me because I wasn't goin' to be an earl.'

'But now you are going to be an earl,' Alec pointed out.

'Oh. Yes, I suppose I am. Calloway's dead?' He shook his head in bewilderment. 'Dashed if I can keep up with the fellow. He only just arrived and now he's . . . murdered. You're not suggestin' Flick – Miss Norville – did him in, are you?' he added belligerently.

'I'm not suggesting anything. Where were you last night?'

'It's no good goin' on askin', I'm not tellin' you. In fact, I don't think I'd better say anythin' more without a solicitor.'

'That is your right, Mr Norville. However, you will understand that I cannot let you go home to concoct an alibi with your family. Unfortunately there is no bedroom to spare so I'm afraid you'll be spending the night in the wine cellar.'

'No, I say!'

'We've made up a camp bed for you,' Miles assured him with an ill-suppressed grin, as Alec went over to open the small door between the bookshelves. 'You've plenty of blankets and an oil lamp. And I've put a pair of my pyjamas out for you,' he added, casting a doubtful look at Cedric's shorter but sturdy figure. 'I hope they'll fit.'

'I'll manage. No, but dammit, it's a ruddy dungeon!' Cedric expostulated, stooping to peer into his chill and gloomy chamber. 'Suppose I give you my word not to escape and doss on the sofa?'

'Sorry, I can't risk it.' Alec was adamant. 'Unless you want to tell me where you were last night.'

'No go. Oh well, righty-ho, then,' said Cedric glumly, stepping into his prison. 'I'm generally a late riser, but you can wake me for breakfast as early as you like.'

Locking the door behind him, Alec glanced at the clock on the mantel but didn't reply. He'd have to be up by the time Tring and Piper arrived, and he wanted to cross the river to Helstone as early as possible. If that family were late risers, so much the better. He'd be able to question the servants without interference.

He took the key from the keyhole and pocketed it. 'I can't decide,' he said morosely, 'whether Cedric Norville is rather stupid or extremely clever, or just plain innocent.'

'If you ask me, he's a damn fool,' said Miles, and they went up to bed.

When Alec entered their bedroom, Daisy knew from one look at his face that it was not a good time to ask questions or expound her own views. She was sleepy enough not to mind. She didn't object, though, when lying on his back beside her with his hands beneath his head, he described the nearly botched capture of Cedric Norville. He was in the middle of telling her what the young man had said when he fell asleep. She leant over to drop a butterfly kiss on his poor nose.

He had sounded puzzled. To Daisy it seemed probable that Cedric had killed Calloway. He had a compelling motive, after all. The fact that he was asinine enough to return to the scene and to admit to knowing about Calloway was beside the point. Being heir to an earldom didn't require brains.

Or if Cedric Norville hadn't done it, maybe his father had. Drifting into sleep, Daisy tried to work out how that Mr Norville could have come by Derek's knife. She dreamt of crowds of shadowy Mr Norvilles rowing across the Tamar. Their oars were seaman's knives which flashed in the sun. Ahead of them, Mr Calloway strode across the water, a wreath of mistletoe on his head.

Not an illuminating dream, Daisy thought, recalling it on awaking. Some of the elements of the mystery were there, but they didn't lead to anything, as far as she could see.

What had wakened her was a tapping on the door. Alec, alert as always first thing in the morning, called, 'Who's there?'

'Daddy, it's me. Derek and I. And Nana. Can we come in?'

Alec looked at Daisy, who groaned but nodded. 'Come in!'

After punctilious 'Good mornings' – well brought up children both – and in Daisy's case a kiss on the nose from the puppy which made her sit up in a hurry, Bel burst out, 'Daddy, guess who's here? Uncle Tom and Mr Piper!'

'Detective Sergeant Tring and Detective Constable Piper,' Derek confirmed, hopping from foot to foot in his excitement. 'We think, Bel and I, it must mean Mr Calloway was murdered and they've come to help Uncle Alec find out who did it. And we wondered, Bel and I, whether you need a bloodhound to track down the murderer, because we've been teaching Nana to follow our tracks and find things and she's frightfully good at it.'

'Not at present, thank you, but I'll bear it in mind,' Alec promised, kindly stuffing his pillow behind Daisy's back before swinging his legs out of bed. 'In the meantime, I want you two – you three,' he corrected himself as Belinda wrested one of his slippers from Nana's jaws, 'to keep well out of our way. This isn't a game; it's serious business.'

'All right, Daddy, but you'll have to tell us where you're going to be or we can't stay out of the way.'

'This morning, Tom will be interviewing the servants here at Brockdene, and Piper and I are going across the river to do some investigating over there. Where are they now?'

'In the kitchen, having breakfast,' said Belinda.

'How do you know?' Daisy asked suspiciously.

'We were there, Mummy.'

'We get *hungry*, Aunt Daisy. We can't wait for proper breakfast. Detective Sergeant Tring stuck his head round the door and said was this the servants' entrance, and he could smell manna from heaven, and if that was Cornish bacon he was going to move to Cornwall. And Bel told Cook and Mrs Pardon he really was a Scotland Yard detective and your right-hand man, so they gave him and

Detective Constable Piper bacon and eggs and bread right from the oven. That's what we had, hot bread and butter and honey from their own bees. And bramble jelly, too. Ripping!'

'Granny always says hot bread's in-di-gestible,' Bel said anxiously, 'but I didn't get a tummy ache, honestly, Mummy.'

'Good,' said Daisy. 'I suppose I'd better get up. Off you go now.'

Alec was already at the hand basin, shaving. Daisy lay for a moment pondering whether, if she had to choose, she'd prefer to do without hot water on tap or gas or electric light. Actually, she could remember when the electric plant had been put in at Fairacres, but she couldn't really remember what it had been like before that. On the other hand, she had stayed in plenty of houses where a can of hot water for washing had been brought by a maid – and grown tepid by the time one got to it.

'I vote for hot water,' she said, reaching for her dressing-gown. 'I'm going to take a bath.'

Alec turned, half his face white with shaving soap, his safety razor poised for the next stroke. 'Daisy, I think you'd better take the children back to town.'

'Darling, no! For one thing, your mother gave Dobson leave till tomorrow. For another, my mother would undoubtedly leave with us, and I really don't think I can cope with her and the children and the dog and all the luggage by myself.'

'I did,' Alec said smugly.

'Thirdly, the boat's coming to fetch us tomorrow morning and it's impossible to get hold of the boatman. So that's that. And anyway, I've got simply heaps to tell you, though I suppose if Cedric Norville killed Calloway, it's all irrelevant,' she ended disconsolately.

'I don't know that Cedric Norville did kill Calloway.' Alec sighed. 'If he didn't, I daresay your information may prove useful, and I haven't time to listen now or I may be facing a suit for false imprisonment. Very well, then, stay, but keep the children out of my hair, please; don't ask the suspects leading questions; and you're going home tomorrow whether I've made an arrest or not.'

'Right-oh, darling.' Daisy kissed the soapless side of his face, wiped a blob of foam off the tip of her nose, collected her sponge bag and towel, and went to see if the bathroom was free.

Alec dressed and went down to the kitchen. The vast Tudor hearth was occupied by Victorian ranges, but the old iron dogs for holding spits, and hooks and chimney crane for hanging pots and kettles, were still in evidence. Another wall contained within it an enormous, primitive bread oven, seven feet across.

At the well-scrubbed table sat Detective Sergeant Tring and Detective Constable Piper. Young Ernie Piper, his breakfast finished, stood up when Alec came in. Tom was still busy with the remains of a heaped plateful. There was a lot of him to fill, a massive man whose bottle-green-and-maroon-check suit did nothing to mitigate his size.

'Morning, Chief,' he said, nodding a head as smooth and pink as a rose petal. His splendid moustache twitching with amusement, he asked, 'Like it?'

'Very smart, Tom. And quite subdued, compared to the yellow and tan.'

'Ah.' He grinned. 'It's a Christmas present from me old trouble and strife. She thinks at my age I ought to consider my dignity.'

'How is Mrs Tring? Furious with me, no doubt. I'm sorry to call the two of you out at Christmas.'

'What's going on, Chief?' Piper asked eagerly.

Alec persuaded a reluctant Mrs Pardon to lend the housekeeper's room for their confab. There, between bites of the bacon sandwich Cook had pressed upon him, he explained the situation to his men, as quickly as was consonant with thoroughness – and avoidance of choking. To tell the truth, he was a bit worried about having confined Cedric to the dungeon overnight, which was not at all according to Hoyle.

When he and Miles had prepared the prison, he had expected the threat of a night in the dank hole to persuade the young man to bare his soul. In spite of Cedric's recalcitrance, if it hadn't been for Alec's still tender nose he might have locked him in Miles's room for the night. Miles could have joined Tremayne in Calloway's room. If Cedric chose to report his mistreatment, it wouldn't do Alec's career any good.

Having put his men in the picture, Alec handed Tring the murder weapon, wrapped in brown paper. 'Here's the knife, Tom. Check it for dabs. Then you'll take the staff, indoor and out. I doubt they'll be much help – as I explained, it's not the usual situation where the servants know the family's every move.'

'It's surprising what people find they know when you make 'em think about it, Chief,' Tom rumbled.

'When you're done with them, go over to the chapel and fingerprint everything in sight. Piper, you and I will go and release the prisoner, feed him, and take him across the river. Let's hope he comes quietly.'

To Alec's relief, Cedric Norville was at least not beating on the undersized door of his cell and yelling for release. Neither the click of the key turning in the lock nor the creak of the hinges brought him rushing forth uttering all too justified complaints. The oil lamp had gone out. Alec took out his electric torch as he ducked through the doorway.

Cedric was sprawled on his back on the camp bed, mouth open, snoring gently. The torch beam gleamed on two bottles standing neatly by the head of the bed.

Piper picked them up. 'Empty, Chief. Both of 'em.'

Neither Piper's voice nor the light on his eyelids roused the sleeper. In response to a vigorous shaking, he opened red eyes at last, only to close them again with a grimace.

'Time to go, Norville. I thought you'd be keen to get out of here.'

At that, Cedric sat up, groaning as he swung his feet to the floor. He buried his unshaven face in his hands. 'Devil take it, if you lock a chap in a wine cellar, you must expect him to make the best of it. You might give a chap more choice, though. Sherry's not really my tipple. I've got an awful head this mornin'.'

'There's a thermos flask of coffee and a sandwich waiting for you in the library.'

'Sandwich, ugh! I could do with the coffee, though.'

'Come along, then.'

Cedric brightened somewhat as he drank the coffee,

though he still could not face the sandwich. Feeling his chin, he said, 'I don't suppose you could lend a chap a razor, my dear fellow? I can't see Felicity like this.'

'I'm afraid you won't be seeing Miss Norville this morning,' said Alec.

'But I must! Dash it all, when a girl does her very best to protect one from being had up for murder . . . I mean, doesn't it look as if she's got a soft spot for one after all? Changed her mind about givin' one the old heave-ho? At the very least one ought to thank her and enquire after her injuries!'

Alec kindly refrained from reminding him that, being once again in line to succeed to the earldom, he had therefore returned to his status as an object of interest to the girl. 'Not now,' he said. 'I want to get over to Helstone as soon as possible. You can write to Miss Norville from there, and I'll bring your letter back with me.'

'Oh, righty-ho, then.' Cedric sighed. 'You'd better tell her father I'll replace the sherry. After all, it's not his fault you forced me to accept his hospitality, and I can't help hopin' he's goin' to be my father-in-law some day. Let's get goin'.'

As they crossed the hall to the front door, Alec said, 'It will save a great deal of trouble if you will just tell me where you were on the night of Christmas Eve.'

Behind them footsteps sounded, descending the stairs. Cedric glanced back, then hurried forward through the door which Piper had opened. Outside, a gardener was raking the gravel path.

'No,' Cedric said vehemently, 'I'm not tellin'.'

CHAPTER 13

After her bath, Daisy wanted to talk to Felicity. The poor girl had been too distraught last night to make much sense, but by now she was probably dying for someone sympathetic to talk to. She might be ready to spill all sorts of beans. Unless, of course, she had had a hand in the killing of Calloway, in which case Daisy could not decently count herself as a sympathetic listener.

Either way, Felicity was quite likely still asleep. Daisy didn't want to wake her, especially when she remembered that Jemima was sharing her room. Jemima was not the person she would choose as an audience for a heart-to-heart.

Breakfast first, Daisy decided. With luck Miles would be there and could tell her more about what had happened last night than Alec had managed before falling asleep. She went downstairs. Godfrey and Dora and Jemima were in the dining room.

'Good morning, Mrs Fletcher,' Dora greeted Daisy. She looked as if she had slept on pins and needles, if at all. 'Jemima says you helped Felicity to bed last night . . .'

'She ricked her ankle rather nastily, but not a serious sprain, I'm sure.'

'Oh, I see. Thank you so much for taking care of her. Can you tell me,' she went on apprehensively, 'is it true Mr Fletcher has made an arrest already? And locked the murderer in the wine cellar?'

'I'm afraid I haven't had a chance to ask Alec exactly what's going on,' Daisy prevaricated, 'but you may be sure he would not put the household in danger.'

'No, of course not. I didn't for a minute . . . Jemima says it's the man Felicity has been seeing on the sly!'

'I'm afraid my husband will not be very happy to hear Miss Jemima has been spreading rumours,' Daisy said severely.

'Obviously, the only people with a motive for murder are the Helstone Norvilles,' Godfrey snapped, standing up. He looked no more rested than his wife. 'And if Felicity has been carrying on with one of them, she is utterly lacking in loyalty to her own family. Excuse me, Mrs Fletcher, I must get to work. No Bank Holidays for those of us whose work is measured in decades.' He stalked out, retreating to the comfort of the antiquities he loved.

'*I* know two more detectives have come,' said Jemima, uncowed by Daisy's stricture, 'and that's not a rumour 'cause it's true?'

'Jemima, take a cup of tea up to your grandmother and see what she'd like to eat.' Dora turned back to Daisy as Jemima left, pouting. 'My mother-in-law is such a frail little thing, we take the best care of her we can.'

Daisy murmured polite agreement, wishing she had the sort of mother-in-law she could take pleasure in cosseting. 'I hope Mrs Norville isn't too upset by what has happened,' she said.

'Naturally she's distressed, but at her age I believe the sorrows of the past have more weight than those of the present. Besides, as Godfrey said, all of us here had nothing to gain and everything to lose by this horrible crime, so the Helstone boy is clearly the culprit. My one prayer is that my poor Felicity is not desperately in love with the brute.' She ended on a sad, questioning note, as if she suspected her daughter had taken Daisy into her confidence in preference to herself.

'I've no idea of her feelings,' Daisy assured her, not adding that she meant to do her best to find out. Felicity would need support if, as seemed probable, her father was right and Cedric Norville was the murderer.

'Good morning, good morning!' The captain came in, a trifle heavy-eyed but with much of his jaunty bearing restored. 'I hear Fletcher has nabbed the villain already. Now that's quick work, if you like! Dora, my dear, since the police have sewn up the case, and the other business is sunk too deep for salvage – no use crying over spilt milk! – I'll be off back to my ship tomorrow. She's in the yard, but things will move along faster if I'm there to chivvy them along.'

'We'll be sorry to lose you, Victor. Especially Mother.'

'Never fear, I'll come back for a day or two before we sail. Well, now, Mrs Fletcher, I'm sorry to say you haven't had quite the merry Christmas we would have liked to give you.'

'The children are enjoying themselves no end,' said Daisy, 'and that's what really matters, isn't it? Besides, from your perspective we've been uninvited guests. We're very appreciative of everything you've done.'

'I'm afraid her ladyship is quite put out,' Dora said, and gave her lower lip an anxious, rabbity nibble.

Daisy could have told them that the Dowager Lady Dalrymple was never so happy as when she had good cause to be put out. A murder in the house where she was staying would give her fuel for months, if not years, of complaints. Refraining from saying so, Daisy murmured, not quite truthfully, 'I'm sure Mother doesn't hold you to blame for what happened.'

'It was our young cousin from over the river, of course,' the captain agreed, adding with fervour, 'but I wish I'd never found Calloway! The poor fellow would be living today in contented retirement in India, and the family's peace would not have been all cut up for nothing.'

'You meant it for the best,' his sister-in-law consoled him.

'For Mother's sake. And if he hadn't gone back on his word and shilly-shallied so, he wouldn't have been at the chapel in the wood in the middle of the night. Then that young wretch would have had no opportunity to harm him. Is my niece greatly distressed about Fletcher arresting him?'

'I haven't had a chance to talk to Felicity.' Dora turned a reproachful gaze on Daisy. 'No one informed me last night that anything had happened, and she was still sleeping when Jemima got up this morning.'

'She may be awake by now,' said Daisy. 'Shall I take her up a cup of tea and some toast?'

'That would be very kind.' Apparently Dora was not as keen to confront her erring and possibly heartbroken daughter as her previous words had suggested. 'I'm afraid

Godfrey is quite angry with her. She's been very naughty. Girls are so difficult!' she lamented helplessly. 'How could I ever have guessed that she'd take up with a murderer, and behind my back?'

Daisy had no answer she cared to pronounce. Leaving the utterance of soothing platitudes to the captain, she departed with tea and toast for the miscreant.

Cedric Norville was a convenient scapegoat, she thought, as she negotiated the passage and the glass-paned door to the entrance hall. Naturally the Brockdene Norvilles were eager to believe him guilty. Perhaps they were right. He and his father had an undeniable motive for wanting Calloway out of the way, and thanks to Felicity he knew it.

When Daisy came to the foot of the stairs, Jemima was halfway down. She obviously had no intention of standing to the side to let Daisy get by on the not-very-wide flight, so Daisy waited at the bottom.

As Jemima reached the last two steps, she turned on Daisy a glare of startling malignity and hissed, 'I wish you'd never come to Brockdene!'

Daisy stared after her. In her ears rang the echo of what Jemima had said of Calloway: 'I wish he'd never come . . . I wish he was dead!'

And Calloway was dead.

In the young girl's mind, the present trouble the clergyman had been causing might well have outweighed the possibility of future, ill-understood gain. She was in the habit of wandering the woods at night, spying on her sister. Well-grown, sturdy, she was physically quite capable of driving a knife home into the back of an unsuspecting man.

Physically ... but mentally? Daisy shuddered. Jemima was odd, but surely not so disturbed mentally as to murder a man who was, after all, no worse than a wet blanket.

No, the Reverend Calloway had posed a threat to no one but Cedric Norville and his family. Cedric must have killed him.

Daisy stopped at the top of the stairs, which she had climbed mechanically. She remembered her dream. It had seemed so unhelpful: crowds of Mr Norvilles rowing across the river with knives instead of oars – could it have been a warning rather than her brain's attempt to solve the mystery? Not that she believed a dream could foretell the future, but perhaps her unconscious mind had put two and two together and tried to tell her that Alec should not embark in a small boat with a murderer.

A tussle in a boat had begun this whole train of events, a tussle in which both participants had drowned.

Alec was a good swimmer, Daisy reminded herself. Ernie Piper was with him, and anyway it was too late to stop him. Perhaps, without asking leading questions, she could find out from Felicity enough about Cedric to reassure herself as to Alec's safety.

And now Felicity was coming from the lavatory, in an old brown flannel dressing-gown, limping slightly and making an unhappy attempt to smile at Daisy.

'How are you feeling this morning?'

'My ankle's much better, thanks.'

'I've brought you this. No, I'll carry it to your room. You're still a bit wobbly.'

'Thanks, Daisy.'

Jemima's camp bed, neatly turned back to air, took up

most of the floor space in the small bedroom. Without waiting to be invited, Daisy perched on the foot of Felicity's bed. The furniture was good and well cared for, probably the earl's property and therefore regularly polished by the servants. In contrast, what Daisy could see of the bedding was patched, darned and sides-to-middled.

A couple of paperbacked novels lay on the bedside table beside the lamp. On the whitewashed walls hung a couple of paintings obscured by sketches tucked into the frames, views of the exterior of the house. Drawing-pins supported more sketches, of elegant frocks and hats.

'Did you do those? Are they your own designs? They look rather good to me.'

'Honestly?'

'Yes, but I'm no fashion expert. Still, have you ever thought of going into the trade?'

Felicity shrugged. 'There's no money for training, or to set up in business.'

'I should think there must be apprenticeships or something similar. My friend Lucy would know. I could ask her, if you like. Though if you're going to marry the future Earl of Westmoor, I suppose you wouldn't be interested.'

'I shan't be marrying Cedric if he's hanged for murder!'

'So you think he might be?'

'Oh, Daisy, I just don't know,' Felicity said wretchedly. 'I simply can't imagine him stabbing someone in the back. He's always seemed such a perfect gentleman, so much so that I've often teased him about it.'

'Any kind of murder isn't exactly the correct, gentlemanly thing to do,' Daisy pointed out.

'No, but if – oh, say some rotter was blackmailing his

sister, or something like that, Cedric might confront him and shoot him, face-to-face. Do you see what I mean? There would be something gallant, at least, about risking being hanged for that, not like stabbing an elderly clergyman in the back because he threatened one's inheritance. No, I *can't* believe Ceddie did that!'

'But you can believe he was there, up at the chapel, on Christmas Eve?' A matter of opinion, so not a leading question, Daisy hoped. She was a bit vague about what exactly constituted a leading question.

'I wasn't expecting him. When I saw him on Saturday night, I told him about Calloway and said I didn't think I'd marry him after all, so he needn't come the next night. He said he probably wouldn't have anyway because the weather forecast was for high winds. And on Christmas Eve he couldn't come, though he wouldn't tell me why. I thought either he just said it because I'd told him I didn't want to see him again, or maybe he was going to a party with Bella Sidlow and some of that crowd. He used to be quite keen on Bella, before we met.'

'I see.'

'So when he said he'd be there on Christmas night, I said, well, I wouldn't. But he came then anyway, so he might have come the night before, mightn't he?'

Daisy absorbed the gist of this, not bothering to sort out which night was which. 'Are you in love with him?' she asked bluntly (a leading question, no doubt, but not directly concerned with the murder).

'I don't know!' Felicity wailed. 'I want to get away from here, and the only way seems to be to get married, and I don't meet many men. And after being a poor relation all my life, the prospect of becoming Countess of Westmoor doesn't exactly disgust me. But how can I tell if that's what attracts me to Ceddie, or if I've found my soul mate?'

'Did you really mean it when you told him you wouldn't marry him because he wasn't heir to the earldom after all?'

'I don't *know*! I was teasing him, of course, partly. But I wouldn't even have thought of such a thing if I wasn't a horrible mercenary person, would I?'

'It's something one has to consider,' Daisy said judiciously, 'the sort of life the future will hold. It would be – would have been – no good marrying Cedric if you were going to spend the rest of your life resenting the fact that you were still a poor relation, your uncle's, your father's, your brother's. I would have been an ass to marry Alec if I hadn't been pretty sure I could put up with being a policeman's wife.'

'Because you love him. But do I love Ceddie? Enough?' Felicity sighed. 'Never mind, it's all water under the bridge, now. Either he is going to be an earl, in which case I may as well marry him and find out whether I love him, if he still wants to marry me after I was so beastly. Or else he'll be arrested for murder, and that's the end of that.'

'Ye-es. You don't seem very upset to think he might be a murderer.'

'I suppose that really, at the back of my mind, I find it absolutely impossible to believe he killed Calloway. Daisy, your husband wouldn't make a mistake about it, would he? He wouldn't arrest Ceddie if he didn't do it?'

'Certainly not,' said the loyal wife, wishing she had met Cedric Norville to judge him for herself. Could Felicity's perfect gentleman actually be an utter rotter who would stab an innocent, if irritating, clergyman in the back? And if so, could Felicity herself be his accomplice, and her talk of confused emotions no more than a smokescreen?

All in all, Daisy had learnt nothing to reassure her that Cedric would not attempt to escape justice by drowning the detective who was on his trail.

CHAPTER 14

The walk down the steep drive to Brockdene Quay revived Cedric. He was almost jaunty as he led Alec and Piper across the cobbles to a small fishing dory moored to the wharf.

'A bit primitive,' he apologized, as Alec climbed down into the boat, whose accommodation consisted of two rowing benches. 'Belongs to a man I know. Hope he didn't want to go fishin' this mornin'. I keep a sailin' dinghy on the river in the summer, but this is actually better for just buzzin' across now and then.'

He followed Alec, and held the boat to a ring on the wall with the boathook while Piper cast off and joined them. Alec and Piper squeezed on to one bench. Cedric sat down facing them on the other and pushed off. As he fitted his oars into the rowlocks, it crossed Alec's mind that with one good swipe of an oar in the middle of the river Cedric might be able to dispose of both his captors at once.

Piper had quietly possessed himself of the boathook, Alec noted with approval. He himself watched Cedric's expression, alert for any sign of increasing tension which might prelude an attack.

The effort of rowing the heavy-laden boat showed, yet the young man's expression grew more relaxed as they drew out into the stream. The river was still as brown as when Alec had looked down on it yesterday from the site of the murder, but it was less turbulent. There was less debris, too, he thought, sparing a mite of his attention from Cedric's face.

The odd branch still floated by, though, including one large enough and close enough for Piper to shove it away with the boathook.

'Wasn't it rather dangerous rowing across on your own in the dark last night?' Alec asked.

'This old tub's strongly built, and for these waters.' Cedric grinned. 'But you're right, I was probably a bally ass to do it so soon after the storm. Still, when a fellow's keen on a girl, you know . . .'

'Swimming the Hellespont,' said Piper unexpectedly.

'That's the ticket,' Cedric agreed with approval, glancing over his shoulder to check his course. 'Those old Greeks knew a thing or two. Wasn't that the one with the hero called Henley?'

'Leander.' Piper sounded uncertain, whether about his facts or about contradicting a gentleman.

'I believe the Henley rowing club was named after him,' Alec put in, fascinated by the contrasting results of Piper's board school and Cedric's public school education.

Or was Cedric deliberately trying to appear a fool? 'Ah yes, knew it was somethin' to do with rowin'. So this hero chappy rowed across the Hellespont, whatever that may be, but I gather it was a longish trip, to see his girl, who had a funny sort of name, if I've got the right one.'

'Hero,' said Piper.

'The hero was Leander; we've got that straightened out.'

'And the heroine was Hero,' Piper insisted.

Cedric stared, rowing rhythmically the while. 'No, you don't say so? Dashed funny name for a girl. I expect you know what the Hellespont was, too, eh?'

Piper blushed. 'It's part of the Dardanelles, where we fought the Turks. But Leander didn't row, he swam across.'

'Well, you jolly well wouldn't catch me swimmin' the Tamar in December, even for Miss Norville, especially after a storm. Come to that, I don't know that I'd have risked rowin' it on Christmas Eve, right after the gale, even if I'd been able to get away. Which I couldn't, and now I can tell you why, Mr Fletcher.'

'Why you couldn't get away, and why you couldn't tell me, and why you can tell me now, I trust?' Alec said dryly.

'You can blame that dashed brat, Flick's sister. Little sneak, always listenin' at doors, Flick says, and tellin' tales, too. I daresay that's how you got on to me, isn't it? I'd swear Flick never told, even if she is givin' me the boot.'

'I can't reveal my sources of information.' An automatic response, not only rather pompous, Alec thought, but in this case futile since Felicity would tell him Jemima had given them away, assuming they got back together. 'What did you not care for Jemima to hear?' he asked irritably.

'It wasn't so much that I didn't want Jemima to hear, but she was bound to tell Flick and the rest of the family and I didn't – don't want them to know. You'll keep it under your hat, my dear chap, won't you? Oh, hold on a mo'. Here we are. Grab that rope, would you, old man?'

As he shipped his oars, Piper grabbed the rope. It was tied to a stake stuck in the riverbed on the edge of the reeds. A narrow channel cut through the shoulder-high

reeds, which rustled and creaked in the breeze. Pulling on
the rope, Cedric hauled the boat along the channel until
they came to a rickety wooden landing stage.

Cautiously, Alec stepped out and moved quickly on to
firm ground. At the end of his patience, he turned and
asked, 'Just what do you want me to keep under my hat,
Mr Norville?'

'Where I was on Christmas Eve and Christmas Day, of
course,' said Cedric, surprised. 'Where we all were, come
to that. All the family. It would hurt Flick to know because
she and her family weren't invited. Never are.'

'Invited where?' Alec bellowed. The sight of Piper
suppressing a snicker did not improve his temper.

Piper also whipped out his notebook and one of the
well-sharpened pencils always present in his breast pocket.
He apparently believed the moment of revelation was at
last at hand.

'To Tavy Bridge.' Cedric straightened after securing the
painter. 'My uncle's place. Or, at least, not really my
uncle of course. He's my second cousin once removed, or
somethin' of the sort, don't you know. Lord Westmoor.
We go every Christmas, and stay the night on Christmas
Eve. It's over beyond Tavistock, on the edge of Dartmoor.
Too far to stroll back in the hopes of seein' Flick, who
wasn't expectin' me, even if I could have sneaked out
amid all the song and dance and general merry-makin'.
Which I couldn't. And didn't,' he ended on a triumphant
note.

Alec groaned, foreseeing the possibility of having to
send someone to Tavy Bridge to check Cedric's alibi.

'I say, now that I've told you, you don't need to talk to

the parents, do you? Never fear, I'll row you back across.'
He crouched to untie the painter again.

'Not so fast! I most certainly must see Mr and Mrs
Norville, and anyone else who went with you to Lord
Westmoor's.'

'Dash it, can't you accept a man's word ... ? No, I
suppose you can't. But there's no need to tell them why
you're askin', is there?'

Alec considered, keeping Cedric on tenterhooks for a
change. 'No, for my purposes it's probably better if they
don't know exactly what's going on. You want to keep
them in the dark?'

'No point upsettin' the old dears over Flick and me if
she's not goin' to marry me.'

'If I don't explain why I want to know about your
movements, they'll surely ask you.'

'True,' Cedric said gloomily. 'Oh well, I expect I'll think
up something to tell them that doesn't bring her into it,
without actually lyin', of course. Righty-ho, let's get on with
it. If 'twere done when 'twere done, then 'twere well 'twere
done quickly, or words to that effect. All those 'tweres,
but he had it dead to rights often as not, old Shakespeare,
didn't he? Dashed clever chap. Like the Greeks.'

On that cheerful thought, Cedric set out to conduct Alec
and Piper across a soggy meadow towards the lane which
led to his home. He seemed very sure of himself. Alec
sighed. 'Too far' was a relative term in these days of
motorcars and motor-bicycles. Proving – or disproving –
the young man's alibi was liable to be a hell of a job.

* * *

Leaving Felicity distastefully sipping her now cold tea, Daisy paused on the landing. She wanted to go and look for Sergeant Tring, a great friend of hers. He would tell her not to worry, Alec knew how to look after himself. Or if there really was good reason to worry, he'd do something about it.

No, if there was any danger, Tom wouldn't have let Alec go off without him. Besides, he must be in the middle of interviewing the servants; an interruption could throw him off his stride. What Daisy ought to do next was check the whereabouts of Belinda and Derek. Obsessed as they were with secret drawers and passages, they might be pestering Godfrey, who had left the breakfast table in no mood to be troubled by children.

Daisy headed for the old house, through the dining room. Dora had left and Miles had joined his uncle. The two men were so deep in earnest conversation that they didn't notice Daisy's arrival until she shut the door behind her. Then they looked up, both with glum expressions, and gave her strained smiles. She wished she'd heard what they were discussing so unhappily. Or rather, what they were saying about it, for the subject was surely the murder.

'Good morning, Daisy,' said Miles, beginning to stand.

'Good morning. Don't get up. I'm just passing through, looking for the children. I didn't mean to disturb you.'

'Not at all. Won't you sit down a minute and have another cup of coffee? Uncle Vic says you went to talk to my sister.'

Though she sat down, Daisy said firmly, 'I can't tell you what Felicity said.'

'Of course not, dear lady,' said the captain. 'Wouldn't dream of asking you. The thing is, with her young man arrested for doing in the Reverend, she's going to need some distraction. She has a dull enough time of it down here as it is, poor thing. It's all very well for a child, but a young lady needs to see a bit of life.'

'My uncle has very generously offered to give Flick an allowance to keep her in London for a few months and buy some pretty dresses.'

'Pooh, pooh! I've got a nice little nest-egg tucked away for when I retire, but present need, you know! What comfort is there for a man if his family's unhappy?'

'The trouble being,' said Miles, 'as you'll realize of course, Daisy, that if Flick's to meet the right sort of people, she'll need someone to introduce her about a bit. Mother has no friends in town, even if she could be persuaded to leave Father, which I doubt. And he'll never agree to leave Brockdene for weeks on end.'

'Damn fool!' the captain exploded.

'Sir, I can't let . . .'

'Keep your hair on, lad. If a man can't damn his own brother, who can he . . . ? Beg your pardon, Mrs Fletcher! But if God had just bestirred himself to get about a bit, kept up with fellows from school and got to know people other than his stuffy historians, we wouldn't be stymied now.'

'I'm in touch with friends from school and the army,' Miles said ruefully, 'but they're not much use to Flick if she has no one to chaperone her. I hope you don't think I'm hinting that you should take her on, Daisy. You have your career, and Belinda, to cope with. We just hoped you might have some idea of how to go about this.'

'I haven't the foggiest,' said Daisy, rising, 'but I'll put my mind to it and maybe I'll come up with something.'

Crossing the hall, she wondered whether her mother might enjoy sponsoring a girl for a few months in London. She had made a huge fuss when Daisy refused to take advantage of what travesty of the social season survived during the war. However, the sort of society the Dowager Viscountess frequented was probably higher than Felicity could hope to fly. In any case, in the unlikely – considering the circumstances – event that Lady Dalrymple let herself be persuaded, Daisy wasn't sure she wanted to subject anyone to weeks of her mother's company.

What had sprung to her mind, as soon as she realized what the captain proposed, was that he should instead support Felicity while she worked her way into the fashion business. Daisy couldn't suggest that, though, without consulting Felicity.

The problem would not arise if Cedric was innocent and still wanted to marry Felicity, and she decided to marry him.

It worried Daisy that all the Brockdene Norvilles complacently assumed his guilt. If he proved an alibi, suspicion would come squarely back here to rest, and it would come as a nasty shock. Still, in all probability they were right; Cedric had killed Calloway. Alec would arrest him and that would be the end of that, so there was no point in Daisy bothering her head about it. Where were the children?

She glanced into the drawing room. No sign of Bel and Derek investigating the Italian cabinet, but Godfrey was there, sitting at the Queen Anne desk. He appeared to be having trouble answering a letter which lay before him, for the one he was writing hadn't progressed beyond the salutation. Or else he was understandably lost in unhappy reflection on the events of the past few days. He didn't raise his bowed head when Daisy looked in, so she didn't disturb him.

Remembering that the desk in the south room was supposed to have hidden drawers, she crossed through the red room to check whether Bel and Derek were investigating it. No sign of them, but she was reminded that she had never seen the squint to the hall, because of meeting Jemima there. She pulled back the tapestry in the corner, stepped into the alcove behind, and looked down on the hall.

The sun coming in through the south-facing windows shone on the gleaming rows of weapons hanging on the walls. From here they were even more impressive than from below, where most were hung above Daisy's eye-level, so that she had to crane her neck to study them. They were a vicious-looking lot. Really, given the availability of instruments of death, it was quite surprising that murders weren't a regular occurrence at Brockdene.

She was about to turn back, when Tremayne and Miles came through the door at the far end of the hall.

Miles was saying vehemently, 'No, I don't believe for a moment that she would have helped the blackguard, except inadvertently, by telling him about Calloway.'

'You don't think she might have taken the knife to show him?' Tremayne was obviously worried. 'Because if so, she's in serious trouble, whatever her intent.'

'Why should she? It isn't – wasn't of any particular

interest. I shouldn't have thought it was at all the sort of thing a girl would take to a rendezvous with her lover, though admittedly I haven't much experience in that line.'

With one arm missing, he probably assumed no woman would look at him twice, Daisy thought. She doubted he was correct. He was intelligent, charming, quite good-looking, gentlemanly. He would have a respectable and generally well-remunerated profession. Equally to the point, the slaughter in Flanders had left England with a huge imbalance between young men and women, so that bachelors were in high demand. Miles had no need to despair.

While these thoughts crossed Daisy's mind, Tremayne was saying, 'I expect you're right, my boy, if canoodling is anything like it was in my day. Felicity wouldn't have taken the knife with her unless she wanted to use it on him . . . or wanted him to use it.'

'Which, I repeat, I do not credit for a moment.' Miles stopped as they separated to walk on either side of the central table. He turned to face his grandfather, his back to Daisy. 'What really troubles me, sir, is that if no obvious murderer had turned up, it would not have surprised me in the least to discover that Jemima killed Calloway.'

'Jemima!' The elderly man leaned heavily with both hands on the table. His expression was deeply distressed but not startled. 'She's a child still! But one need not specialize in criminal law to know that such things happen. Do you think she's . . . unbalanced?'

'I confess I've sometimes wondered. Mother seems to consider her merely normally awkward for that age, and she must be a better judge than I . . . mustn't she?'

'Yes, yes, of course. Dora knows best.' Tremayne straightened, relieved.

'All the same, sir,' Miles went on, 'I don't think it's healthy for Jemima to go on living here as if nothing has happened ... after what has happened. After all, she wished Calloway dead, and he is dead, nastily. We can't brush that under the carpet. It seems to me she ought to go away to school, to learn how other girls behave. If you can see your way to coming up with school fees, I shall of, course, reimburse you as soon as I'm able.'

'Bosh, as Felicity would say. Jemima's my grand-daughter as well as your sister. I don't say I approve of education for women, but I daresay there are schools which concentrate on teaching conduct and manners, and Jemima could certainly profit from lessons in both.' Tremayne started walking again. 'To tell the truth, I wish now I'd sent Felicity to school for a year or two. She'd have made friends, been invited about no doubt. She wouldn't have taken up with that unspeakable bounder and ...' He and Miles passed through the doorway to the stairs, beyond Daisy's sight and hearing.

For an alarmed moment she wondered whether they had spotted her and were coming to ask just what she thought she was doing. No, they must have come into the old house for a purpose, which was surely to speak to Godfrey. Daisy wished she could hear what they said, but deliberately creeping up to eavesdrop was rather different from happening to overhear – and happening to stay put and overhear more than she need.

Oh dear, perhaps she too needed a few lessons in manners and conduct! But if she hadn't profited sufficiently already, for her school had definitely concentrated on both, then it was probably too late, she decided. Jemima, on the other hand, really needed most the company of normal girls her age, as Miles suggested.

So Miles had suspected Jemima of murder, and Mr Tremayne had suspected Felicity of complicity in murder. The worst of murder, Daisy thought, was less the death itself than the shadows it cast on the living.

CHAPTER 15

When Daisy, still hunting the children, stepped out through the front door, she saw Jemima standing a few yards away, gazing down the terraces.

'Jemima, have you seen Derek and Belinda?'

Jemima gave her a blank, inimical glance, shrugged and turned away.

If they were outside, Nana would be with them, her hearing probably the sharpest of the three. Daisy let loose the piercing whistle Gervaise had taught her, seldom employed because thoroughly unladylike. 'Nana!' she called.

A yip answered her. From the top of the long flight of steps at the far end of the terrace the puppy bounded towards her. She had something in her mouth, which she laid at Daisy's feet, looking up with eyes bright in the expectation of praise. When Daisy declined to accept the well-chewed, disgustingly sodden wad of blueish-grey rag, Nana picked it up, unoffended, and pranced ahead back towards the steps.

As she approached, Daisy spotted Belinda's ginger and Derek's tow head near the bottom of the flight. They were sitting on the bottom step, so absorbed in sorting through a heap of rubbish on the ground before them that they didn't notice Daisy's arrival. A couple of empty potato sacks lay beside the heap.

Daisy paused at the top, wondering what on earth they were up to. Behind her the gravel crunched. She looked round to find Jemima had followed her.

Once again she had that nervous feeling that she didn't want to be at the top of anything while the girl was behind her. She started down the steps, enquiring, 'What have you got there?'

Two animated faces turned up to her.

'Clues!' said Derek portentously.

'We wanted to help Daddy,' Bel explained. 'We didn't get in the way, honestly. Daddy and Mr Piper went across the Tamar to Devon, and Uncle Tom's in the house. We were in the woods.'

Daisy could only wish she had repeated yesterday's prohibition against going into the woods and made it clear it was separate from the instructions not to get in the way.

'We borrowed a sack, Aunt Daisy, and went to look for clues. Nana's a ripping bloodhound. She found this.' Derek presented for Daisy's inspection an ancient boot, laceless, the sole dangling from the upper by one or two remaining nails. 'It's our best clue. We think an escaped convict, or maybe a deserter, was living in the woods and Mr Calloway saw him and he was afraid he'd give him away so he killed him.'

'And then he started to run away, but the sole of his boot came off so he couldn't run.'

'So he took it off and Nana found it,' Derek concluded triumphantly. 'She found this, too.' A sardine tin. 'And we found a couple more tins. Where did you put them, Bel? Oh, here they are. Look, the labels are all gone and this one's rusted right through the bottom, so the man must have been living there for simply ages. And a broken beer bottle.'

'We buried that so no animal would cut itself,' Bel said, 'but Derek marked the place in case Daddy wants to dig it up for fingerprints.'

'D'you think Uncle Alec'll want this, Aunt Daisy?' Gingerly, by one corner, Derek held up a filthy, stained cloth, ragged and so faded its original colour could have been anything. 'It's pretty foul.'

Nana disagreed. She dropped one rag in favour of the other, which she seized and ran off with. Derek and Belinda gave chase, tally-hoing and view-hallooing as they galloped along the terraces.

Jemima clumped down the steps from the top, where she had been watching and listening. 'What rubbish!' she said scornfully, poking the boot with her toe.

Ignoring her, Daisy cheered on the pursuers and the pursued. Nana headed back towards her. Dropping the revolting object at her feet, the pup turned to sniff at the boot, then went to sniff around the as yet unsorted heap of junk. Belinda and Derek arrived, panting. Derek reached down to retrieve the rag, but Nana grabbed it first and dashed off again.

Derek groaned. 'She'll prob'ly bury it.'

'Never mind, let her have it,' Daisy advised. 'I doubt if it's a vital clue. What else have you got?'

'Rubbish,' Jemima said again. She went off back up the steps.

'Why doesn't she like us, Mummy?' Belinda asked anxiously.

'I don't think she likes anyone much, darling. Don't let it worry you. Is that a pair of eye-glasses I see?'

'Yes.' Derek abstracted a celluloid spectacle frame, minus lenses, from the pile and balanced it on his nose. One earpiece was missing. 'Bel found it. I don't think it's a clue, though.'

'Why not? Perhaps the escaped convict was short-sighted.'

'These wouldn't have been much use to him then. He couldn't have seen well enough to kill Mr Calloway or run away or anything.'

'I think we ought to keep them for Daddy,' said Belinda stubbornly.

'All right, we will. But look at this cigarette packet, Aunt Daisy. It'll tell Uncle Alec what brand of cigarettes the murderer smokes.'

The packet looked as if it had been in the woods for several weeks, at least. The Woodbine label was almost indistinguishable, and Woodbines were the most popular cheap cigarette. But Daisy said, 'Yes, keep that for him,' and she sat on a step and watched while they went through the rest of the heap. Not only did she not want to be a wet blanket, it was always possible they really had found something useful. Alec was always saying one never could tell what might be significant.

Nothing turned up, though, that looked to her in the least useful. Spreading out one sack, the children laid out on it the oddments they had decided to keep. The rest they put back into the other sack to take round to the kitchen court to the dustbin. Derek had just heaved it on to his shoulder when they were hailed from the top of the steps.

'Good morning, Mrs Fletcher!' Tom Tring doffed his hat, his bald dome gleaming in the fitful sunshine. He came down, with the peculiarly light tread which accorded so ill with his bulk. 'Hello again, Miss Belinda, Master Derek. What have we here?'

Eagerly the children explained their hunt and showed him the bits and pieces. He examined each, his small brown eyes twinkling. Nana rushed up to greet him, muddy feet and muzzle mute evidence of the burial of her rag. Belinda grasped her collar before she could besmirch the sergeant's splendid green-and-maroon suit.

'Sit,' she said severely. 'You're going to have to have *another* bath before you can go in the house.'

'I expect it'll wear off if she runs around a bit,' said Tom. 'You've a fine collection here. Put them somewhere safe for the Chief to see, won't you?'

'Don't take them into the house!' said Daisy.

'We'll put them in Nana's scullery. Come on, Bel.' They bundled their clues into the second sack and raced off, Nana lolloping alongside.

'Wash your hands!' Daisy called after them.

Tom winked at Daisy. 'Don't do no harm,' he said, stroking his moustache. 'I daresay we'll have young Derek joining us in the CID before too long.'

'Don't tell his father! Maybe by the time Belinda's old enough, they'll see the sense in having a few women detectives,' Daisy retorted.

'Ah.' That was Tom's multi-purpose monosyllable. 'I'm off to the chapel to try for dabs. That way, is it?'

'I'll show you. You've been talking to the servants, haven't you? Did you find out anything useful?'

'Not from that lot. They knew Miss Norville was carrying on with Mr Cedric Norville right enough, but none of 'em could say whether he came over on Christmas Eve. Someone down at the quay might know, they said. I'll leave questioning them till I hear from the Chief, though. Now, there's one interesting thing I did find . . .'

'What's that?'

Tom waited until he had followed Daisy through the tunnel under the lane before he answered. Emerging beside her, he said, 'Dabs on the murder weapon. There's a couple of little 'uns, could be a small woman but more likely a child.'

'Derek! It was his knife.'

'Could be. I'll have to fingerprint him to be sure.'

'He'll be thrilled to death,' Daisy said dryly. 'Could you possibly fingerprint Belinda too, to be fair?'

Tom's moustache twitched as he grinned. 'For sure. The prints could be hers, after all. But that'd better wait for the Chief, too.'

'Yes. You'll have to check Jemima's, too.'

'The younger daughter? She's known to have handled the knife?'

'No,' said Daisy, troubled. 'Not as far as I know, though she may have when the children showed it to Godfrey. Mr Godfrey Norville. You'd have to ask them, or rather the Chief will.'

'Mr Godfrey Norville touched it?'

'Probably. He examined it. As did Captain Norville, though I can't recall whether he handled it. I expect the Chief will remember.'

'There's what looks like a man's prints on the haft, but blurred and not in the right position for stabbing, whichever way . . . Here, hold on, Mrs Fletcher!'

'I'm all right,' Daisy said, but rather faintly. His words had summoned up the picture she had hitherto managed to hold at bay: the knife raised, then plunging down into the unsuspecting man's back. Feeling sick, she sat down on the bench Tom had steered her to, under the arbour by the carp pond.

He stood looking down at her. 'The Chief'll give me a flea in the ear for upsetting you,' he growled, 'and quite right, too.'

'Bosh!' said Daisy, perking up. 'I shan't tell him, and you're not to. He'd give me a flea in the ear for meddling. I'm quite all right, truly. It was just a momentary vision . . .' She concentrated on the vigorous check of his jacket. 'Is that a new suit? I don't recall seeing it before.'

'Christmas present from the wife.'

'It's spectacular,' she said sincerely, remembering the equally mountainous Mrs Tring, whom she had met at her wedding.

He grinned again. 'Takes the bad lads' minds off who's inside it, at least for a moment. Long enough, sometimes. Now you sit here, Mrs Fletcher, till you feel well enough to go back to the house.'

'I'm perfectly all right now. I'll walk a bit farther with you. You know,' Daisy continued as they passed the dovecote, 'if the fingerprints on the knife do turn out to be Derek's, then the question arises again: How did Cedric Norville get hold of it?'

'Ah,' said Tom.

'Won't the Chief have to prove how he got it?'

'It'd help the case, but all that's absolutely necessary is to prove that he could have, that it wasn't impossible. Young Derek left it on the hall table?'

'Not exactly. That is, it wasn't exactly his. Alec didn't explain?'

'He didn't have time to go into details. Why don't you tell me about it, Mrs Fletcher?'

The sergeant was hugely entertained by the story of the children's discovery of the knife. He regarded it as further evidence that Derek was cut out for a detective's life.

'So you see,' Daisy finished, 'it really belongs to the house, but Godfrey Norville didn't think much of it. He told Derek to leave it on the hall table.'

'And no one knows when it disappeared. I asked the servants, of course, but it seems none of 'em even knew it was there in the first place. They gave the table and the stuff on it a once-over with a feather duster before her ladyship arrived, but it's not their place to tidy the family's belongings. 'Specially as they didn't reckon Lady Dalrymple'd have much cause to hang about in the hall. A pretty state of affairs!'

'It's an odd household, though normally it seems to run quite smoothly.'

'The Chief said the staff don't have hardly anything to do with the family?'

'They're Lord Westmoor's servants, employed to take care of his house and possessions. The family have to pretty much fend for themselves. I'd better tell you all about it.' Starting with the Indian marriage, Daisy worked her way via the sixth earl's will – leaving old Mrs Norville with a home and now-insufficient allowance – to a thumbnail sketch of each family member. She and Tom Tring reached the chapel just as she finished describing Jemima. 'And then there's Mr Tremayne, Mrs Godfrey's father.'

'The solicitor?'

'Yes. Don't tell me Alec already told you all this!'

'No, no, he just warned me there's a lawyer about. That's a great help, Mrs Fletcher. I've got a much better idea of what's going on.'

'Not that it'll be much use to you if Alec arrests Cedric Norville, as seems probable.'

'Ah,' said Tom, 'there's many a twist between handcuff and wrist.'

Daisy laughed. 'Don't count your villains until they're catched,' she said. 'I'll leave you to your fingerprints. Shall I tell the children you'll want theirs?'

'Better not. I shan't take 'em without the Chief's say-so, so best wait till he gets back.'

'Right-oh,' said Daisy.

As she turned away, she saw Captain Norville approaching along the path from Brockdene Quay.

'I've been down to the pub for a pint and some 'baccy,' he said, 'and came back the long way to stretch my legs. I always take a morning constitutional around the deck at sea.' He looked enquiringly at Tom.

'This is Detective Sergeant Tring, Captain, my husband's assistant. Captain Norville, Sergeant.'

The two big men gave each other assessing stares, wary as a pair of strange dogs. Then the captain offered his hand and Tom, after a barely perceptible hesitation, shook it.

'Happy to make your acquaintance, Sergeant. This is a nasty business, whichever way you look at it. I hope you and Mr Fletcher are going to find enough evidence to hang the young wretch.'

'If there's evidence, we'll find it, sir, never you fear,' said Tom, a trifle ambiguously. 'I'm after fingerprints right now.'

'He'll surely have been wearing gloves on a December night. The lack of prints won't spoil the case, will it?'

'Not at all, sir, but finding them would help no end.'

'Yes, of course. Well, carry on. Are you returning to the house, Mrs Fletcher? If you don't mind, I'll walk along with you.'

'Do,' Daisy invited, and they set off.

Glancing back she saw Tom gazing after them with a frown on his boundless forehead. Doubtless he was concerned about her going off with a man who must remain a suspect until Cedric Norville was arrested. Daisy was not at all fearful. Victor Norville was no homicidal maniac. Though he might conceivably have killed Calloway in a fury if the clergyman had refused to give his testimony, he hadn't any reason to be angry with Daisy.

She waved to Tom and he raised a hand in acknowledgement.

'I'm glad I met you, Mrs Fletcher,' said the captain. 'Have you any notions as to how I can help my niece?'

'Felicity? Yes, actually, but I must make sure she likes the idea before I broach it to anyone else. And I'm not at all sure her father would approve.'

'God's an obstinate fool!'

'I'm not at all sure you'd approve, either, or her mother

or grandfather, or grandmother, come to that. Or Miles, even.'

'Well, well, we'll have to see about that,' said the captain, taken aback. 'But if it's just Godfrey who stands in the way, I won't let him spoil Felicity's chances. I've been trying for years to make him accept enough to make the family comfortable.'

'That's very generous of you.'

'Not a bit of it. When I mentioned a nice little nest-egg – well, it's not so little after all these years. I've done pretty well for myself, and I've no rent to pay nor wife and kiddies of my own to keep. There was a girl once, but a seafaring man's seldom home and whether it was that or the doubt about my birth . . . But never mind that. What it comes down to is God's family is my family, and old Tremayne and I between us are quite able to keep them, not to mention young Miles's help in a year or two. But it was a fight to persuade God to let Tremayne pay for Miles's schooling, so he's bound to kick against the pricks whatever's proposed for Felicity.'

'I see,' said Daisy. She understood Godfrey's position, having been in much the same situation herself. After all, she had refused to let herself be beholden to Cousin Edgar, though he was perfectly willing and able to support her in a comfortable life of leisure. She wondered if Godfrey's pride was the cause of the brothers' quarrel in the hall, overheard by Jemima.

'So don't hesitate to propose whatever you think is best for Felicity, Mrs Fletcher,' said the captain earnestly. 'Leave God to me.'

They were nearly at the tunnel under the lane when

Alec, followed by Piper, emerged. 'Daisy, is Tring at the chapel?'

'Yes, darling, we left him fingerprinting away like mad.'

'I hope he's finding something,' Alec said grimly. 'Cedric Norville has an excellent alibi for Christmas Eve. We're going to have to start over from the beginning.'

'What?' cried the captain, going very red in the face. 'Felicity's young man didn't kill the Reverend? That means, I take it, we're all under suspicion again!'

CHAPTER 16

'That's right, someone at Brockdene murdered Calloway.' Alec's appraising scrutiny of Captain Norville's face told him only that the man was angry. If he felt any guilt or fear, it was well hidden. 'Piper, go on to the chapel and tell Sergeant Tring to come back to the house directly he's finished with the fingerprinting.'

'Yes, sir! Er . . .'

Daisy took Piper's arm and pointed out the way to him, leaving Alec to concentrate on the captain, who burst out, 'An alibi! Aren't alibis made to be broken?'

'I'm afraid you read too much detective fiction, Captain. Mr Cedric Norville has sound corroboration for his presence elsewhere at the time of the murder.'

'Where was the young whippersnapper then, dammit, and who says so?' Obviously the captain was not going to cooperate without the whole story.

Alec had warned Cedric that his secret would probably have to come out. 'He and his family were guests of Lord Westmoor at Tavy Bridge from late afternoon on Christmas Eve until the evening of Christmas Day.'

'Near Tavistock? He could easily have motored back to murder the Reverend!'

'He didn't know Mr Calloway would be in the chapel,' Daisy pointed out.

'Obviously he came to see my niece and met the Reverend by chance.'

Alec shook his head. 'A tree weakened by the gale fell across Lord Westmoor's drive that evening. Several dinner guests were unable to leave and had to stay the night. The obstruction wasn't cleared until the following morning. I telephoned from Helstone and spoke to Lord Westmoor myself . . .'

'He's protecting Cedric,' the captain roared. 'Doesn't want another scandal in the family. Don't tell me you believe him just because he's an earl!'

Alec shook his head, frowning at Daisy, who showed signs of springing to his defence. 'Lord Westmoor is going to have another scandal in the family whether the murderer is a Helstone Norville or a Brockdene Norville. It's only thanks to your isolation here that we haven't already suffered a reporter or two sniffing around. But I also rang up a couple of the dinner guests – the earl's butler gave me the names – who confirmed everything, as did the butler. Believe me, Cedric Norville did not kill Calloway. And the same applies to the rest of the Helstone Norvilles.'

The captain deflated. 'A tramp?' he offered half-heartedly.

'Most unlikely. The knife was a stumbling-block where Cedric was concerned, unless Miss Norville was involved . . .'

'She wasn't!'

'But the chances of a tramp getting hold of it verge on nil – assuming it's proved to be the one the children found.'

'Sergeant Tring found their fingerprints,' Daisy said. 'At least, he's pretty sure they're children's. He wants to take Derek's and Bel's fingerprints to match up, darling, but he wouldn't do it until you got back.'

'Well, I'm back, and I'd better get cracking. I've wasted a whole morning thanks to that young fool's notions of chivalry.'

Alec returned through the tunnel, followed by Daisy and Captain Norville. Though he was glad to have had a chance to assess the captain's unguarded reaction to the news of Cedric's innocence, he wanted the same opportunity with the rest of the family. How could he prevent the captain warning them? He suspected that Victor Norville, if not himself the murderer, would prefer not to find out who was.

Emerging into daylight, the captain appeared to be brooding. 'Fletcher,' he said abruptly, as they started up the terrace garden, 'I don't like this business one little bit, but I suppose if it's not cleared up pretty quick, before it gets into the papers, the cloud will hang over us forever. The young people have enough reefs in the offing already. Count on me to give you whatever help I can.'

'You realize that it's highly unlikely to be one of the servants? That the murderer is a member of your family?'

'I know. But not only is killing a defenceless man a horrible crime, whoever did this was betraying Mother, betraying the whole the family.' His brow furrowed. 'I don't understand it. I don't understand it at all.'

Alec wished he did. 'Very well,' he said. 'All I ask at the moment is that you don't reveal to anyone that Cedric is proven innocent. I'll get everyone together and make an announcement.'

'After lunch, darling,' said Daisy. 'Let them fortify themselves for the shock.'

He didn't want his suspects fortified for the shock, but on the other hand, they would be more relaxed after lunch and the shock would be the greater for the delay. The children's presence at table should deter the others from pressing him for information.

'I'd better let Belinda and Derek know Tring wants their fingerprints,' he said. 'Where are they?'

'Upstairs washing, I hope. It's nearly lunchtime, they're bound to be starving, and they're filthy, as usual, having been out all morning searching the woods for clues for you. We didn't tell them not to go to the woods this morning.'

Alec grimaced. 'I ought to have searched the woods myself, if I'd had the time and the men. Apart from the difficulty of rounding up a horde of village bobbies, their tramping all over the place would be as likely to destroy evidence as to discover it.'

'The children found the most amazing assortment of stuff. You will be nice, darling, and not tell them it's all rubbish, won't you?'

'Who knows,' said Alec, 'they may actually have come up with something useful.'

'I think you're about to find out,' said the captain. 'Here they come.'

'Still filthy,' Daisy sighed.

Derek, Belinda and, needless to say, Nana raced towards them along the top terrace.

'Daddy, Uncle Miles told us you'd come back. We were waiting for you.'

'Uncle Alec, will you please come and see our clues, *please*? Now. They're in Nana's scullery. It won't take a minute. We'll still have time to wash before lunch, Aunt Daisy, *promise*.'

The captain consulted his pocket chronometer. 'Twenty-one minutes,' he announced. 'May I come, too?'

Alec shot him a swift look, but agreed, and the children were eager to show off their finds to anyone at all. They all went off together. Daisy went into the house and upstairs. At the top, she was startled to hear her mother's carrying voice coming from old Mrs Norville's sitting room.

'I do sympathize, Mrs Norville, I assure you,' the Dowager Viscountess said condescendingly. 'Girls have no idea of duty to the family these days, no consideration for their parents. I'm sure I would never in a thousand years have contemplated such disgraceful behaviour.'

Mrs Norville's soft voice said something Daisy could not make out.

'Yes,' said Lady Dalrymple, 'your granddaughter has been isolated here with few opportunities to meet eligible young men. But one can hardly regard that as an adequate excuse for secret meetings with a murderer. I can quite understand your feelings, and those of your daughter-in-law. I myself was utterly distraught when I discovered my own daughter was – in the vulgar phrase – keeping company with a policeman.'

'Mother!' Daisy burst into the room. 'You can't compare Alec to a murderer. Really, you mustn't! I'm sorry to interrupt, Mrs Norville. I was passing and I simply couldn't let it pass.'

'Of course not, my dear.' Mrs Norville gave Daisy a sad smile. 'We must remember that Felicity, however wrong her actions, had no way of knowing the young man was going to commit so dreadful a crime.'

'True,' said the dowager judicially. 'Indeed, had it not been for the secrecy, Miss Norville's behaviour was infinitely to be preferred to Daisy's. After all, Miss Norville had the sense and discrimination to pursue the next heir to an earldom.'

'I hope that was not her first consideration,' Mrs Norville said with quiet dignity. 'I hope she loved him, and I hope that discovering his true character will not break her heart.'

Daisy was frightfully tempted to tell her that Cedric was not the murderer after all, but Alec had been adamant on the point. Not that Mrs Norville was a suspect, but she'd be bound to tell someone else. Besides, the news would be cold comfort. While relieved for Felicity's sake, she could only be aghast at the return of suspicion to her family.

Daisy could, however, and did relieve her by removing the dowager. 'Mother, could I have a word with you, please?'

'I shall see you at luncheon, no doubt, Mrs Norville,' said Lady Dalrymple with a regal nod, and followed Daisy out. 'What is it, Daisy?' she asked testily, as Daisy shut the door firmly behind them.

'I wondered if you'd mind reading my article this afternoon,' Daisy invented rapidly, 'to make sure I haven't said anything that might offend Lord Westmoor. It's such a delicate situation.' Not that she had mentioned the current residents.

'By all means. I never expected such a proper sentiment of you.'

'And I never expected to find you chatting with Mrs Norville.'

Her mother gave her an impertinent-depressing stare, but said, 'She may be black, but it would appear that at least she was properly married to Albert Norville. Eva was quite wrong. I can hardly wait to set her right.'

'Ah, I see!' All was now plain. 'Well, I'd better go and get ready for lunch.'

'Where is my grandson?'

Daisy waited.

'And my granddaughter,' her mother added grudgingly. 'Where are they?'

'Helping the police with their enquiries,' said Daisy, and she bolted into her room and closed the door.

Alec joined her a few minutes later. 'Bel and Derek are washing and changing,' he reported. 'Little ragamuffins.'

'Belinda's always clean and neat at home. I don't suppose anything they found seemed significant?'

'Not at first sight. I told them to keep it all, you never can tell.'

'Bless you, darling!'

'I gather they're planning to resume the hunt this afternoon. They can't do much damage, and it will keep them out of the way.'

'You're getting everyone together after lunch to tell them about Cedric?'

'Yes, immediately after. In the library, I think. What

about Felicity?' he asked. 'Is she fit – physically fit, I mean, not emotionally – to come down?'

'I don't know if she's coming down to lunch, but I expect she could make it, with help. Only I'm not sure you ought to trust her reaction to the news. She is pretty fragile, and confused, emotionally.'

'I'm not surprised. You've taken her under your wing, haven't you? There's always someone.'

'What about you and Miles?' Daisy demanded indignantly. 'If having him help you catch Cedric isn't taking him under your wing, I don't know what is!'

'Don't you like Miles?'

'Yes, I like him very well, and Felicity, and the captain, and Godfrey's been extremely helpful, and old Mrs Norville's a sweetie. And Dora's done her best for us, and I've nothing against Mr Tremayne. But Miles could have killed Calloway, even with only one arm.'

'I don't deny it, love,' Alec soothed her. 'At the time I asked his help, it seemed obvious that the heir about to be dispossessed must be our villain. I still can't see what motive Miles could have had.'

'Nor can I,' Daisy admitted. 'But none of the others had either, except ... Blast, there's the gong. I hope the children are ready.'

'I deputed Miles to chivvy them,' Alec confessed, laughing. He straightened his tie and ran a brush over the dark, crisp hair which never seemed to get disarranged.

'Darling, you won't try to keep me away when you tell them about Cedric, will you?' Daisy asked urgently. 'Another pair of eyes might pick up someone's reaction you'd otherwise miss.'

'Yes, I think you'd better be there,' he said, to her surprise and delight. 'Are you ready? Let's go.'

When they reached the landing, Derek and Belinda were already halfway down the stairs, Miles about to start down. Turning to Daisy, he said, 'You'd better not mention the possibility of going to London to Flick. My father's dead against it.'

'Because he won't accept any favours from Captain Norville?'

'In part, but he sees it as rewarding her for consorting with the enemy. As a matter of fact, he's still furious with both of us for not telling him about Lord Norville's death.'

'Oh, dear! I won't say anything then. Is Felicity coming down for lunch?'

'I just asked her. She says she simply can't face either food or the family. I don't blame her, poor girl. It's not just Father. The whole situation with regard to Cedric is perfectly beastly for her, even if he hasn't actually been arrested yet.' Miles looked enquiringly at Alec.

With the wooden expression perfected by all detectives, Alec said, 'I'll bring everyone up to date with the investigation after lunch. I'll want Miss Norville there, in the library.'

'I'll see that she comes down,' Miles promised.

Lunch was an extremely uncomfortable occasion. As soon as Mrs Pardon and the maid left, Godfrey turned on his brother. 'What's this nonsense Miles tells me about sending Felicity to London?' he demanded angrily.

'A change of scene seems . . .' the captain started in a placatory tone, then he glanced at Alec and went on, '*seemed* a good notion.' Not so urgent since her lover was not a murderer after all, Daisy interpreted.

'I'm not surprised she doesn't care to face her family after letting us down like that,' Godfrey snapped. 'I only wonder that Miles doesn't feel the same sense of shame! To keep his father in the dark about so important a matter . . .'

'Father!' Miles protested.

'Miles acted as he thought best.' The captain's face was beginning to redden.

'An admirably lawyerly sense of discretion,' Tremayne put in.

'Miles may have his excuses.' Godfrey's scowl at his son belied his words. 'Felicity has none. She kept quiet in order to conceal her own misbehaviour, and why you want to—'

'The sky has clouded over,' observed the Dowager Lady Dalrymple loudly. 'I fear we are in for more rain. This seems to be an extraordinarily damp part of the country.'

'Oh, surely not!' Dora was obviously torn between relief at the enforced change of subject and anxiety over the criticism.

Tremayne kept the ball rolling with comments on the weather of the British Isles as gleaned from reports on his wireless set. The captain, overcoming his rising temper with a visible effort, came through splendidly with tales of typhoons in the China Seas, fogs in the North Atlantic, and hurricanes in the Caribbean.

Godfrey was silenced, though hardly calmed. Lips pursed, he ate hardly a thing, but his agitation was betrayed by his nervous fidgeting with knife and fork. His elder daughter's misconduct had hit him hard. Daisy wondered whether he was as adamantly opposed to shipping his younger daughter off to school. Jemima, who had worn an unpleasantly gloating smile when her sister was being castigated, had lapsed into her usual sullenness. Miles, preoccupied rather than sullen, was also taciturn.

Derek and Belinda's quietness was good manners: permitted to join the adults at table, they knew better than to speak unless spoken to. Daisy was proud of them, especially as the initial discord had alarmed Bel, while Derek was fascinated by the stories of storms at sea.

Those same stories dismayed Mrs Norville, who said tremulously, 'Must you go to sea again, Victor?'

'I'm not ready to retire for a few years yet, Mother. No harm's going to come to an old sea dog like me, don't you fret.'

'The sea is a respectable profession,' Lady Dalrymple stated, with a disparaging glance at Alec. 'My uncle was a rear admiral.'

And throughout, Alec watched and weighed and measured his suspects.

As the last bite of jam roly-poly disappeared into the captain's mouth, Alec rose. 'I should like everyone except the children to gather in the library,' he announced. 'I have news for you. You need not be present, Lady Dalrymple.' He wondered whether he'd ever dare call her Mother.

'Please make use of my sitting room, if you wish, Lady Dalrymple,' Mrs Norville offered.

'Thank you,' said the dowager, rather sniffily, 'but if news is to be imparted, I have no desire to be excluded.'

Her son-in-law would have preferred her elsewhere, but if he insisted on excluding her, the others might begin to guess what he had to tell them.

'I'll see if Mrs Pardon will serve coffee in the library,' Dora said brightly.

'I'll go and roust Flick out and give her a hand down the stairs,' said Miles.

Alec thanked him. 'I'll join you in a minute or two. Belinda and Derek, come with me, please.'

'Have we done something naughty, Daddy?' Bel asked, as he led the way through to the old house.

'Not that I know of, my pet. I want Sergeant Tring to take your fingerprints, both of you, just so that we don't get them mixed up with other people's.'

'Crikey!' said Derek, eyes glowing. 'Ripping! Wait till I tell the fellows at school.'

Tring and Piper had just finished their lunch in the kitchen. They all went to Nana's scullery, where Tom Tring fingerprinted the children. Bel and Derek then went off cheerfully with the puppy.

It only took Tom a minute to report, 'Young Master Derek's dabs on the knife, Chief. Looks like it's the one they found.'

'Which virtually eliminates escaped convicts and lunatics, deserters and common or garden tramps,' Alec said, as they crossed the kitchen court. 'It's got to be one of the family. They're waiting for us in the library now. I want you to watch them like hawks when I tell them Cedric Norville's out of the picture. Two of them won't be surprised: the captain and the murderer – or one, if the captain *is* the murderer.'

'Him being top of the list, Chief?' asked Piper. 'Along with Miss Norville and Miss Jemima?'

'That's right,' Alec confirmed. 'Unfortunately, they're also the three we're least likely to get straightforward reactions from. The captain already knows; Miss Jemima is too young to necessarily behave as one would expect of an adult . . .'

'Besides being more than a little odd,' said Tom. 'I've heard some tales from the servants.'

'I'll want to hear them later, Tom. Then there's Miss Norville, whose relationship with Cedric complicates matters. She may be overjoyed to hear he's been cleared despite the effect on her own family.'

'Cor!' said Piper. 'I bet Mrs Fletcher knows what's what with Miss Norville, though.'

'She can hardly help knowing more than I do,' Alec admitted, silently deploring Ernie Piper's determination to believe Daisy infallible.

He entered the library, Tring and Piper on his heels. As the murmur of voices died, he saw Godfrey glaring at Felicity. The errant daughter put on a good show of indifference, all but her clenched hands.

Before Alec could speak, Tremayne stood up and came towards him. 'Mr Fletcher, presumably you would have told us at luncheon had you arrested Cedric Norville, so we can assume you have found insufficient evidence to do so. I assure you we shall do all in our power to assist you in gathering the necessary information.'

Damn all lawyers, Alec thought. He had forgotten he had to deal with someone accustomed to drawing conclusions from a few facts – though this time he had got it wrong.

'You're right, I haven't arrested Cedric Norville,' he said. 'However, there is no prospect of my ever doing so. He has proved conclusively that he could not have killed Calloway.'

Felicity fainted.

CHAPTER 17

Felicity slumped against Daisy. For a few moments Daisy had her hands full preventing the girl from sliding off the sofa. By the time Daisy was able to look around, everyone was reacting to Felicity's faint, not Alec's announcement.

Dora started forward anxiously with a cry, 'Oh, my poor child!'

'Trust her,' Jemima muttered venomously. 'She's just trying to be interesting.'

'Brandy!' exclaimed the captain, heading for the wine cellar. Daisy was afraid he'd get stuck in the little doorway. 'Or rather sherry, I suppose.'

'Sal volatile,' murmured Mrs Norville. 'I used to have some somewhere.'

Meanwhile Miles, the third on the sofa, had jumped to his feet. He tried with his one arm to raise his sister's legs on to the sofa, but he was off balance. Ernie Piper sprang forward to assist. Tom Tring was diligently scanning faces. Daisy guessed his moustache hid mild amusement. Alec stood by the door, his thick, dark eyebrows raised in a sardonic appeal to heaven. The door opened behind him, and Mrs Pardon brought in the coffee.

By this time, Felicity was lying back uncomfortably

against Daisy's thighs. She started to rouse, one hand going to her forehead in the best cinema-heroine style. Daisy expected her to mumble, 'Where am I?'

'I feel sick,' she croaked.

'Don't say anything!' That was Tremayne being lawyerly, not Dora being motherly. 'I knew I should have gone to telephone Butterwick, even with Cedric Norville in custody.'

'I'm going to be . . .'

In a couple of strides Alec reached her with the slop-basin from the coffee tray, as she leant forward retching. Mrs Pardon gave one disgusted look at the scene and departed, nose in air.

'In my day,' observed Lady Dalrymple impartially, 'one loosened a gal's corsets. But these days, I gather, they don't wear anything worthy of the name.'

'She didn't come down to breakfast or lunch.' Dora wrung her hands. 'No wonder she fainted, my poor child.'

'Sherry.' The captain's large hand, holding a glass of amber liquid, thrust between the surrounding bodies.

'Not on an empty stomach,' said Daisy. 'Nor coffee, I should think. Hot milk might help.'

Tom Tring had already poured a cup. He passed it through, but Felicity said, 'No, please, all I want is peace and quiet and to lie down with my eyes closed.'

'I'll carry you up to your room, my dear,' said her uncle, tossing down the sherry so as not to waste it. He lifted Felicity in his arms and started towards the door.

'Daisy?' Alec nodded towards them.

So Daisy followed them upstairs, taking the milk with her just in case.

The captain set Felicity down on her bed and patted her hand. 'Don't you fret, child. It'll all come out in the wash, you'll see.'

He left. Daisy managed to persuade Felicity to drink the milk, which brought a tinge of colour to her pale cheeks.

'Thanks, Daisy. That does make me feel a bit better. I just couldn't bear to have everyone looking at me, when I've utterly humiliated myself. First falling in the blasted stream, then bursting into tears, then fainting! Isn't it all too, too Victorian?'

'Too Victorian for words,' Daisy candidly agreed. 'What made you faint?'

Felicity reflected. 'Do you know, I think it was a shock of relief! I mean, obviously we're all in trouble again, but all I could think of was that Ceddie's safe. He's not a murderer after all. I suppose that must mean I really love him, doesn't it?' Her eyes turned dreamy and a small smile played on her lips.

'It sounds like the real thing.'

The dreamy look vanished and Felicity said soberly, 'Unfortunately, the reality is that not only did I let him down by believing he had killed Calloway, but it seems there's a murderer in my family, to add to all the other disadvantages. Even if he still wants to, his parents will never in a million years let him marry me.'

'This is 1923,' said Daisy. 'What's more, his father can't disinherit him because they both depend on Lord Westmoor. It's the earl Cedric's going to have to talk round. I shouldn't give up yet, if I were you.'

'But Lord Westmoor . . . Oh, come in!' she called as someone tapped on the door.

Jemima flounced in. 'Mummy said I had to bring you these,' she said, depositing a plate of digestive biscuits on the bedside table. And she flounced out again, pulling the door to behind her.

'Horrid little brat,' said Felicity irritably. 'Make sure the door's closed, would you, Daisy?'

It wasn't. Daisy shut it with a click. When she turned, Felicity was already nibbling a biscuit. 'Mother knows best,' Daisy observed with a smile, though it was a maxim nothing could persuade her to believe, at least in her own case.

Felicity took a big bite, crunched twice, swallowed the crumbs, and said, avoiding Daisy's eyes, 'Do you think Mother knows who killed Calloway?'

'Do you think she might?'

'She might guess, I suppose. She wouldn't give him away, though.'

'Who do you think did it?'

'It's my family, too! If I knew I wouldn't tell. But as it happens, I haven't the faintest idea.'

Daisy believed her.

'You believed her?' Alec asked.

Daisy had joined him and Tom and Ernie Piper in the dining room. Tom had reported on his interviews with the servants, who had seen and heard nothing useful. When Daisy arrived, Alec had just begun to review the notes on his first interviews with the suspects. That morning he had only had time to give Tom and Ernie a brief sketch of the situation and the people involved. With more detail, he hoped, they might pick up something he'd missed. Also he was refreshing his memory before tackling them all again.

Felicity had been the first, with her confession of her secret lover – forced from her because Jemima had let the cat out of the bag.

'Yes, I believed her,' Daisy said. 'She's a rotten liar. It was perfectly obvious, remember, when she lied about whether Cedric was coming over last night.'

'True,' Alec agreed, 'though she did manage to deceive her family for quite some time.'

Daisy frowned. 'Yes, I'd overlooked that. I told her you'd want to speak to her anyway, that even if she hadn't the foggiest who did it, she might be able to give you a piece of the puzzle. She was all set to be sticky about helping you to pin the deed on one of the family. I pointed out that if the culprit wasn't found, all the family would be under suspicion for the rest of their lives.'

'Well done. That's a line I can take with anyone else who has qualms.'

'I take it, Mrs Fletcher,' Tom rumbled, 'you don't think Miss Norville did it herself.'

'No. I know she had a sort of motive – making sure Cedric would inherit the title – but she's been so confused about her feelings for him, I simply can't see her doing anything so drastic.'

'Cedric is equally confused about her feelings for him,' Alec said. 'He's by no means counting on her agreeing to marry him. And he's an even less competent liar than she is.'

'Though he did manage to deceive his family about knowing Felicity,' Daisy said dryly.

Alec grinned at her. 'Your point. Still, I agree that her motive is thin.'

'But, Chief,' Piper protested, 'most of 'em haven't got even that much motive for doing the old chap in, have they? Seems more like they'd do just about anything to keep him alive. I mean, seeing he could prove they're not born the wrong side of the blanket.'

'Exactly, Ernie. Don't worry, Miss Norville's still high on the list. I'll have to see if I can squeeze anything more out of Jemima, who's sharing her room.'

'If Jemima knows anything to Felicity's detriment,' said Daisy, 'you won't have to do much squeezing.'

'Unless she's holding it in reserve, which seems to be another unpleasant little habit of hers. But we'll come to her in a moment.' He looked down at the notes Daisy had taken for him and typed out from her incomprehensible shorthand. 'Miles next. He shared his room with his grandfather.'

'That's Mr Tremayne, right, Chief?' Tom queried. 'He give Mr Miles an alibi?'

'No. Apparently he takes a draught for his rheumatism which makes him sleep heavily. Though come to think of it, he seems spry enough and doesn't think twice about walking to and from Calstock.'

'It's prob'ly lying still makes him stiff and achy,' said Tom. 'Moving about helps. That's the way it strikes me old dutch, anyway.'

'I expect that's it, then. Which begs the question, did Tremayne perhaps not take his medicine that night and wake up feeling the need to move about? To walk over to the chapel, for instance.'

'Miles can't give him an alibi, either?' Daisy asked.

'No, he says he generally sleeps soundly. So it could be either of them. Miles has the stronger motive for keeping Calloway alive, since it's his father who is otherwise the bastard. Tremayne might feel almost as strongly about his daughter's husband, but he did, after all, let her marry him.'

'And they both knew of George Norville's death,' Daisy said, 'so they knew legitimation meant Victor inheriting the earldom, and thereafter probably Godfrey and then Miles.'

'Which gives neither the slightest hint of a motive for murdering Calloway.'

'Now wait a minute, Chief,' said Tom, 'does this mean not everyone knew Lord Westmoor's son died? You didn't tell us that.'

'Didn't I? Sorry! Tremayne and Miles knew, and Miss Norville, and Lady Dalrymple, who was the one to break the news to the rest, including me.'

'Miss Norville knew her uncle, then her dad, then her brother would be earl?' Tom shook his head. 'Then I can't see her bumping off Calloway so's Mr Cedric'd get the title instead. Mind you, I've known blokes bump off other blokes for some pretty silly reasons, but that doesn't make any kind of sense.'

Daisy nodded agreement. 'Especially as she had already told Cedric she didn't want to see him again, so she couldn't count on marrying him.'

'All right,' said Alec, 'we've already said that Felicity is unlikely, though not quite as unlikely as Miles or Tremayne. Who did I see after Miles?'

'Darling,' Daisy said tentatively, 'it's fearfully confusing the way everyone's all mixed up with everyone else, if you see what I mean. We've only covered your interviews with Felicity and Miles, yet practically everyone else has popped in. I think it would be easier to consider means, motive, and opportunity in turn, rather than go through the list person by person. I'd say we'd be less likely to miss something important.'

Predictably, Piper seconded her. 'I'm getting confused all right, Chief.' He displayed a page of his notebook, the rows of neat shorthand symbols defaced with circles and arrows.

Alec sighed. 'You may be right, Daisy. We'll try it that way.' He scowled at Tom, whose moustache had given the telltale twitch which meant he was amused. 'Means is easy, now that Cedric's out of the picture. Anyone in the house could have taken the knife from the hall table.'

MEANS, Piper wrote across the top of a fresh page. ANYONE, he wrote below it, and turned the page. MOTIVE was his next heading.

'We'll tackle motive last,' said Alec, 'as that seems to me the most complex of the three. Opportunity next.'

Piper diligently crossed out MOTIVE and substituted OPPORTUNITY. Tom's moustache twitched again.

'Let's consider the precise time of the murder,' Alec continued. 'We haven't got the medical evidence yet, and the time that passed before the body was discovered makes off-the-cuff estimates nearly worthless. Calloway said he was going to pray at the hour of Christ's birth, generally assumed, for no reason that I'm aware of, to be midnight. Anyone planning murder would not leave it too much later, in case he had already returned to his bed.'

'That's pretty early, Chief,' said Tom, ''specially for a holiday.'

'Not for Brockdene. Lady Dalrymple yawned at twenty to eleven, in the middle of a game of bridge, and by quarter past everyone had turned in. No one has an alibi. There are a few other factors to consider. Felicity, for instance – if she had left the room, Jemima would probably have said so, unless she was sleeping too soundly to notice.'

'Jemima was in the habit of following Felicity to the chapel,' Daisy pointed out. 'She must often have lain awake waiting for Felicity to go.'

Alec turned back to the notes of that interview. 'Felicity seemed pretty sure Jemima was fast asleep when she went up.'

'Oh yes, I'd forgotten.'

Piper paused in his scribbling to ask, 'Miss Jemima went to bed earlier then?'

'Yes,' said Daisy. 'She's always sent to bed at half past nine.'

'Anyway, neither has an alibi,' Alec said impatiently. 'Nor do Miles and Tremayne, though they shared a room. I would judge all four to be robust enough for the effort involved.'

'Mr and Mrs Godfrey?' asked Tom. 'Do they have separate rooms?'

'No, they're together, but she claims she took a sleeping powder and he confirms it. So either she's out of it, or he's lying to protect her. Would you say she's physically capable, Daisy?'

'I should think so. I don't know if he'd lie for her, though. He's pretty self-centred.'

'You're telling me!' Piper exclaimed. 'The way he took himself off when everyone else was fussing over Miss Norville!'

'Did he?'

'Yes, soon as the Chief moved away from the door, he sloped off. I would've stopped him, but I reckoned he wouldn't go far.'

'Back to his antiques, no doubt,' Daisy said tartly. 'Anyway, he vouches for Dora, but she can't return the compliment. Who else?'

'The captain,' said Alec. 'He had a room of his own. And the old lady.'

'Mrs Norville doesn't look strong enough to walk that far,' Piper objected, 'let alone stab a man when she got there.'

'She's not as frail as she looks,' Daisy said, 'but that would be a bit much for her, don't you think, Chief? In the dark, on those slippery paths?'

'I'm prepared to write off Mrs Norville,' Alec conceded. 'That's the lot for alibis, or lack thereof, Ernie. Got it all down? Let's get on to motive. We've already covered Miss Norville. Can anyone think of a motive for Miles strong enough to overcome his obvious interest in having Calloway testify to his grandmother's marriage?'

Daisy shook her head, her shingled curls bobbing like a bronze chrysanthemum in a breeze. 'He's not so dedicated to his profession as to kill rather than give it up to be an earl. And he appeared to be mildly amused by Calloway's diatribes, not particularly resentful, let alone furiously angry.'

'The servants say he's a good-tempered chap,' Tom

reported, 'though he's got some pretty funny ideas about Germans. But I gather that's on the lines of "Forgive them that trespass against you", not shell shock and thinking he's surrounded by enemies.'

'I've seen no signs of shell shock,' Alec agreed. He remembered the German carol Miles had sung so earnestly, and his forbearance with Cedric, whom he had every reason to abhor. 'And he's not the vengeful sort. To continue with the young people, what did the servants have to say about Miss Jemima, Tom?'

'Spiteful. Cantankerous. Holds a grudge. Sneaky – she's been seen listening at doors.'

'She makes a habit of it,' said Daisy, her cheeks rather pink. Alec guessed she'd done a spot of eavesdropping herself, all in a good cause, of course. 'I caught her at the squint in the south room listening to Godfrey and Victor squabbling in the hall.'

'Squint?' Piper's busy pencil paused.

Daisy explained the medieval peepholes, which Alec hadn't got around to viewing. He was more interested in the squabble.

'You haven't mentioned a quarrel before. What were they arguing about?'

'Sorry, darling, I kept meaning to tell you, but other things got in the way. It didn't seem vital because I didn't hear what they were saying. Or rather, shouting. Jemima wouldn't tell me. I daresay it hadn't anything to do with Calloway. The captain told me Godfrey refuses to accept any funds to help the family make ends meet, so it was probably about that.'

'Possibly, but I'd like to be sure. If I can't get a straight tale from Jemima, I'll try the combatants themselves. Remind me, Ernie.'

'Right, Chief.'

'Where were we? Jemima and motive. She felt Calloway was spoiling Christmas, and she tried to drive him away with a stupid trick. He won that encounter and got her into trouble with her parents, so she then had a double grudge against him.'

'She hated him,' said Daisy bluntly, 'and she has a temper, though I doubt she could sustain it through a cold, dark walk in the woods. And I'm not convinced the idea of cold-blooded murder would cross her mind as a way to get rid of Calloway. She's very naive and childish. She'd be more likely to tie a string across the stairs, hoping he'd break a leg, not even thinking it could be his neck. Besides, she must have been aware that he had come to Brockdene to benefit her family, including her father, who seems to be the only person she's at all fond of.'

'Objections noted,' Alec said, 'but Jemima had the motive, and in my opinion lacks the sense and maturity to foresee the consequences. What about her mother? That's Mrs Godfrey Norville, Ernie. Tom?'

'Well meaning but useless, Chief. By which I take it they mean ineffectual.'

'Take care, your superior vocabulary is showing through.'

Tom grinned. He was superb at questioning servants but quite capable of coping with the gentry if necessary. Like his taste in clothes, his usually plebeian speech tended to make people underestimate him. 'Mrs Godfrey's never been able to control her children,' he continued, 'and she's had no help from Mr Godfrey.'

'Why does that not surprise me.' Daisy asked rhetori-
cally, with what might have been a snort if she had not
been too much a lady to make any such sound. 'Dora
would have been sorry to leave Brockdene, but she'd
hardly . . .'

'What?' Alec snapped.

'She told me that as a girl she'd always admired
Brockdene from afar, and she considers it a privilege to live
here. I've wondered if that's why she married Godfrey. But
she'd hardly go so far as murdering a clergyman so as to
stay here, especially as . . .'

'But why should she leave?'

'Oh dear,' Daisy said guiltily, 'I've only just thought of
it. It's the sixth earl's will. Mrs Norville has life tenancy of
Brockdene, but only as long as she doesn't kick up a dust
trying to prove she really was married to Albert.'

'Which is exactly what Victor, with Calloway's aid, was
about to do.'

'I wouldn't have thought the present earl would be so
beastly as to throw them out – noblesse oblige, after all –
if it wasn't for how he treated Mother. But if what I've
been told is correct, he'd have had the right to evict them
all as soon as the captain started the ball rolling. Of course,
when Mrs Norville dies the rest will have to leave anyway.
They'll go and live with Tremayne, I suppose.'

'From what I've heard,' said Tom, 'Mr Tremayne's often
here, and they all get on pretty well with him. It don't
sound to me like Mrs Godfrey would kill to avoid going
back to live with her pa, 'specially if she's going to have to
in the end, come what may. And the same goes for the rest
of 'em.'

'Tremayne may not care to have to support them any sooner than absolutely necessary,' Alec mused, 'but again, it's hardly a motive for murder.'

'The captain told me he and Tremayne are quite ready and able to keep them in comfort,' Daisy recalled. 'Also, Miles will soon start earning his living. Godfrey won't like having to depend on them, but as Tom said, it's going to happen in the end, come what may.'

'That's a washout as a motive then,' said Alec. 'I can't conceive of any other motive for Tremayne. He didn't seem particularly upset by Calloway's zealotry, would you say, Daisy?'

'Mmm? Sorry, I was thinking.'

'Calloway's maunderings didn't incense Tremayne?'

'Oh, no, not particularly. It was Jemima and the captain who got really upset.'

'Yes,' Alec agreed, 'and what upset the captain was the possibility that Calloway's disapproval was strong enough to persuade him to refuse to testify to the wedding after all.'

'Ah.' Tom ruminated for a moment. 'You said that's what he went to pray about, Chief? Seems to me likely what happened is Captain Norville went after him to find out what he'd decided to do. The captain has a temper? Quick to heat and quick to cool, they say.'

'He does.'

'So the reverend gentleman says, "Sorry, mate, it's off" – doesn't even bother to turn around to speak to him, to add insult to injury – and the captain blows up and sticks the knife in him.'

'The question here, Tom, is that if the captain killed

Calloway on the spur of the moment, in a fit of temper, what was he doing with the knife?'

'That's easy, Chief. It's a seaman's knife, right? Captain Victor Norville's a seaman. Here he is off out into the woods in the dark, prob'ly scarier to him than being on deck in a hurricane. His eye lights on the knife as he goes through the hall. He's used to carrying one just like it. So he picks it up just in case he meets any of those escaped convicts or lunatics, or deserters, or just plain tramps. When he loses his temper, there's the knife to hand – and quick as winking, there's Calloway dying.'

CHAPTER 18

Belinda was getting just a bit tired of being a detective. She walked along rustling her feet through the dead leaves, wondering if Daddy really liked being a detective all the time. Not that he spent much time searching the woods for rags and bones, as far as she could see.

So far on their second hunt, she and Derek and Nana hadn't found anything except two empty beer bottles. Nana kept finding sticks she thought were interesting and bringing them to Bel or Derek to throw. Here she came now, dragging a bit of branch so big she couldn't pick it up and had to pull backwards. Derek started a tug of war with her. Belinda thought he was getting rather bored with being a detective, too, though he wouldn't admit it.

She watched them. That was when she saw, where Nana's feet scuffed up the leaves, something gleaming.

'Stop! Look!' she cried, running forward to pick it up. When she turned it back and forth in her hand, it sparkled, even though the sun had gone in. It looked like a shoe buckle, all covered with glittering stones.

'Crikey,' breathed Derek, awed, 'diamonds! It must be pirate treasure?'

'They had smugglers here, not pirates,' Bel objected.

'I bet they had pirates, too. I bet they were friends with the smugglers. Anyway, I bet the smugglers got rich enough to put diamonds on their shoes, just to show off.'

'Do you think they're really diamonds? If someone lost that many diamonds they'd search and search till they found it.'

Derek took it from her and twisted it back and forth. 'They must be diamonds. Look how they shine, and they're not coloured like rubies and emeralds.'

'They could be imitations, you know, like the diamonds we saw in the Natural History Museum. My gran has a hat brooch that's all sparkly like this, but she says it's diamanté, not real diamonds.'

'Oh well,' Derek sighed, 'maybe. But it could be real and anyway I bet it's an important clue. We'd better keep it safe. Here, you can keep it in your pocket,' he said generously. 'But if Uncle Alec doesn't need it for evidence, we can use it for pirate treasure. Let's play pirates after we've finished looking for clues. I'll tell you what, I'd like to make Jemima walk the plank.'

From behind a nearby tree came a screech. Jemima jumped out, shouting, 'I heard what you said! That's murder! I bet you murdered Mr Calloway, too! I'm going to tell.' She ran away towards the garden gate.

'Crikey!' said Derek, looking a bit scared. 'I didn't really mean it.'

'Never mind, Daddy won't believe her. Come on, let's find some more ... Look, Nana's got something. Nana, come!'

Nana wouldn't come. When Belinda tried her newly learnt whistle no sound came out of her lips, however hard she blew, but anyway, the puppy took no notice of Derek's ear-splitting whistle. She bounded off with something long and dirty white dangling from her mouth. The children ran after her. When she got far enough ahead to feel safe, she lay down for a good chew. Derek crept up on her and pounced. She gave up the object without a struggle, rolling over on her back for a tummy rub.

Derek held up her find: white artificial silk with lace trimmings. 'What is it?' he asked blankly.

Belinda giggled. 'Cami-knickers! However did they get here?' Then she had a sudden awful, terrible thought. 'Oh, Derek, you don't think the murderer killed a lady too and buried her in the woods?'

''Course not. No ladies are missing, are they?' He glanced behind him, but not as if he thought a murderer was creeping up behind him; more as if he wanted to make sure no one was listening. 'There are bad women,' he whispered, 'who go into the woods with a man and *get naked*. I heard them talking about it at school.'

'Why?' Belinda asked sceptically.

'I 'spect they dance. Men like to watch ladies dancing with not much clothes on,' Derek said, in a very superior voice. 'Gosh, Bel, you don't think this is Aunt Felicity's?'

The idea sent them both into whoops.

Meanwhile Nana, deprived of the cami-knickers, had wandered off sniffing. Now she came bouncing back and deposited yet another treasure at their feet. Bel picked it up.

'It's the other glove of that pair.'

'What pair?'

'The pair we found the other one of before, 'member?'

'Oh, the mitten.' Derek frowned. 'Yes, but it wasn't in the stuff we showed your father. We didn't stick it in the dustbin, did we?'

'I don't think so. I don't think we would've. Nana prob'ly ran off with it and buried it.'

'Stupid dog. Let's see.' He took the dampish mitten and examined it. It was striped blue and grey, with a brown stain along the side of the hand. 'Blood!' he said ghoulishly.

'It's not red.'

'No, but it wouldn't be. Remember when you get a cut or a graze and they put a sticking-plaster on you, and when they take it off it's bloody inside and it's brown.'

'I don't look,' said Belinda.

'Well it is,' Derek insisted. 'And look, the rest isn't dirty at all, so it hasn't been here very long. We'd better take this to Uncle Alec right away. And the cami-whatsit just in case no one's noticed she's missing yet. You can carry that. And the shoe buckle in case it's hers and she was murdered by a robber. Come on!'

'So you think Captain Norville is our man, Tom?' Alec asked.

'Aye, Chief, and I'm sorry for it. He seems like a nice enough chap, good to his ma and all. Given time enough to think, I daresay he'd have remembered there was nothing to stop him trying to change Calloway's mind. After all, he didn't gain anything by killing him. I'd say he must've regretted it at once.'

'Too late. One way or another, I'm afraid the

accessibility of that knife was probably a deciding factor. What do you think, Daisy?'

'Uh?'

'Haven't you been listening?' Alec was rather peeved. Daisy insisted on involving herself. Admittedly she was occasionally helpful, but surely the least she could do was listen!

'No, sorry, darling, I was thinking.'

'About Captain Norville?'

'The captain?' she asked, astonished. 'Good heavens, no.'

'Tom has just presented a very convincing case against him.'

'Oh no. Sorry, Tom, but it wasn't him. That is, I've been thinking, and I'm fairly certain . . .'

'Daddy!' Belinda burst in, excitedly interrupting with no trace of her usual well-behaved diffidence. (Was Daisy having a bad influence on her, as Alec's mother kept insinuating?) She was waving a soiled white object – great Scott, an intimate garment! Piper blushed.

Derek followed Bel, no less precipitately. 'We've found a Real Clue!' he announced. 'Look!' He dropped a woollen mitten on the table in front of Alec.

'It's another one like the other one we found. Derek thinks it's got blood on it.'

'And it's quite clean otherwise so someone dropped it not very long ago. We had the other one, too, Uncle Alec, but we're awfully afraid Nana must have buried it, or chewed it up, or something. Is it blood, d'you think?'

Alec examined the rusty brown patch. 'It could be,' he admitted cautiously and passed the glove to Tom.

Tom took out his magnifying glass, at once awing and delighting Derek, who held his breath, waiting for the verdict.

'I'd say so, Chief. It'd have to go to the lab boys to make sure, of course.'

'Where did you find it?'

'We were near the path, Daddy, the one that goes to the chapel.'

'Not far from the chapel, but actually we didn't find it ourselves. Nana brought it to us, but I don't think she'd gone very far, so it was quite near where we were. We could show you where we were, couldn't we, Bel? Bel said we must notice the trees and remember exactly.'

'Well done, Belinda.'

His daughter's freckles vanished in a tide of red. 'Is it a real clue, Daddy?'

'It very well may be.'

'It is,' Daisy said positively. 'Darling, I rather think it would be a good idea if the children took Mr Piper to see whereabouts Nana found it.'

Alec assumed she wanted the children out of the way while she expounded her theory. It wouldn't hurt to have Ernie go and make a note of the spot, just in case the mitten turned out to be significant. The possible bloodstain was along the little-finger edge of the hand, away from the thumb, in exactly the right place, assuming the murderer had held the knife in his fist to strike downward.

'Detective Constable Piper, proceed to the woods near the scene of the crime with our two witnesses to mark and make a note of the area they point out to you as the vicinity where the evidence was discovered.'

'Yessir!'

'Gosh!' breathed Derek blissfully.

'May Nana come too, Daddy? We left her in the scullery 'cause we didn't know where you were.'

'No, pet, better leave her behind this time. This is official police business.'

'Gosh!' said Derek again, and he and Belinda went off with Ernie Piper.

'I suppose they *are* witnesses,' Daisy said, frowning. 'Will they have to give evidence in court?'

'Not if I have any say in the matter,' Alec assured her. 'A sworn deposition should do. But we're getting ahead of ourselves. What makes you think this dog-bedrooled object is important?'

Daisy answered him with another question. 'Do you recall seeing its mate among the debris Bel and Derek showed you before?'

'No. Did they invent it?'

'Tom, you looked before they threw the least promising rubbish away. Did you see the other mitten?'

'No, Mrs Fletcher,' Tom said positively.

'Well, I did. Nana was carrying it, and she laid it at my feet as she did this one with the children.'

'And then she took it away and buried it,' Alec presumed.

'I don't believe so. She ran off with some other rag which appealed to her more. And I think – I'm pretty sure – the mitten disappeared while Bel and Derek were chasing her.'

'Pouf, into thin air!'

'Sarcasm does not become you, darling, as my old Nanny used to say. No, as it happens, Jemima was lurking nearby at the time, pouring cold water – scorn, that is – on the children's clues. I was watching them, not her. I believe she recognized the mitten, which she herself had knitted, and pinched it.'

'You think Jemima killed Calloway?'

'It's possible of course,' Daisy said slowly, 'but no, I don't think so. She made the mittens for her father. I think she was protecting him.'

'Very well,' said Alec, his scepticism slipping, 'let's hear your theory.'

'Right-oh,' said Daisy, pleased with her attentive audience. 'It all goes back to when I arrived at Brockdene. Gosh, it feels like months ago, but it's less than a week. Godfrey was actually the first of the Norvilles I met.'

She recalled following the boy with her bags under the entrance tower. When she had emerged into the hall court, he had disappeared and she had found herself faced with a plethora of doors.

'I went to the door of the old hall by mistake,' she said. 'Godfrey opened it. Even before he introduced himself, he told me he had devoted his life to studying the history of the house and its contents. He seemed to think it natural that Westmoor's staff should take care of the antiques while refusing to serve the residents. When he rang the bell for the housekeeper to come and look after me, he had no expectation of its being heeded. And when Mrs Pardon did come, his first thought was to complain of some tarnish he'd detected on the suit of armour.'

'Ah,' said Tom sagely. In Piper's absence, he was making notes.

Daisy realized that she was not merely propounding a

theory, she was giving direct evidence which might have to be given again in court. She didn't have to explain her conclusions. Both Tom and Alec were obviously drawing their own.

Alec, his brows knit, nodded to her to go on.

'The mittens come next. I decided to take some photos of the exterior while the sun was shining. Godfrey agreed to go with me to tell me what I was looking at, but before he would set foot out of doors, he sent Jemima to fetch his coat and hat and gloves and galoshes. It was a mild, dry day and he was already wearing a woolly waistcoat and muffler. I was quite warm enough in my costume, without my coat, let alone gloves and a hat, and Jemima just had a light cardigan over her blouse. In fact, it was warmer out than in. Before Mother arrived, the fires were positively miserly.'

'Daisy, is this relevant?'

'Yes, darling, I'm not just reminiscing. You'll see where it's leading in a moment. Where was I?'

'The miserly fires,' he said dryly.

'Yes, well, that was a slight digression,' she admitted. Tom, winking at her, ostentatiously ran a line through his last note. 'To resume: Jemima brought her father's outdoor clothes, among which were a hand-knitted woollen pom-pon hat, striped in grey and blue, and matching mittens. Felicity told me later that Jemima had knitted them for him, and his muffler, also grey and blue, and the waistcoat, which was green and clashed horribly.'

Ignoring the irrelevant waistcoat, Alec said, 'Yes, but anyone could have worn the mittens.'

'I'm aware of that,' Daisy retorted. 'They'd have got in

the way on most people though. Look at it.' They all
studied the mitten on the table in front of Alec. He placed
his hand beside it. It was half an inch longer. 'Godfrey has
hands almost as big as Victor's,' Daisy went on, 'only you
don't notice them so much because they're thin and sort of
etiolated.'

'My superior vocabulary doesn't stretch to "etiolated",'
Tom confessed.

'Nor does mine, really,' she assured him, 'but I
remember it from having to look it up when I read *Jane
Eyre* at school. It means pale and limp, doesn't it, darling?
Rather feeble-looking. Whereas the captain's hands are
brown and strong, and Miles's are quite a bit smaller.'

'So the captain might have borrowed them.'

'He might, but if he killed on unplanned impulse, why
should he wear gloves at all? Not to protect against leaving
fingerprints, and he's not the sort to worry about the cold.'

'That he's not,' Tom agreed. 'Seamen have a sight worse
to put up with than a winter's night in Cornwall. Come to
think of it, I doubt he'd care much for mittens. They need
the use of all their fingers aboard ship.'

'All right, Daisy, it's unlikely – but not impossible – that
Captain Norville borrowed his brother's mittens. What's
next?'

'I'll have to jump back a few hours now, because it was
the boatman who brought me up the Tamar who mentioned the chapel in the woods. While I was outside with
Godfrey, I asked about it and he told me the story of the
first baronet's escape.'

'What's that, Mrs Fletcher?' Tom asked.

'Didn't you notice the sign over the chapel door?'

'Can't say I did. Too high for dabs,' he pointed out.

'Nor did I,' said Alec.

Daisy glanced at him. 'It's not strictly relevant.'

'Never mind, let's have it,' he said resignedly.

She told them about the cap thrown into the river to make Sir Richard's enemies think he had drowned. 'He hid in the bushes nearby till they went off. Anyway, it's a good story and I decided to put it in my article, so I thought I might take a picture of the chapel. I asked Godfrey to show me the way, but he was absolutely horrified at the idea of walking in the woods in winter. He said it was damp and I'd catch my death of cold. He refused to go, said he never went near the place in the winter.'

'Sounds to me like that knocks him right out of the running,' said Tom.

'Yes, Daisy, that's evidence for the defence.'

'It may be, of course. But if you were to find leaf-mould on his shoes or galoshes . . .'

'He'll have cleaned them,' said Tom.

'I doubt it. He doesn't strike me as the sort to clean his own shoes. I bet Dora or Jemima usually does them. If he worried about the leaf-mould at all, he wouldn't want them to see it, so he'd probably just quietly put them away and try to forget them.'

'If he's hidden them in the old house,' said Alec grimly, 'we'd never find them.'

'But the servants would, and that would really set the cat among the pigeons. I'd try the back of the coat cupboard in the entrance hall or his wardrobe.'

'It's possible. Tom?' Alec gestured with his head towards the door. 'And keep your eyes open for the other mitten?'

'No search warrant, Chief. Mr Tremayne'll jump on it.'

'I took the precaution of asking Lord Westmoor's permission to make any necessary searches when I spoke to him on the telephone. It'll have to do. We haven't a hope of getting a warrant today.'

'Right, Chief. What about the second mitten?'

'That, if I'm not altogether mistaken,' said Daisy, 'you'll find under the mattress of Jemima's camp cot, in Felicity's room.'

'Right, Mrs Fletcher.' The sergeant went out.

Alec regarded Daisy in silence, shaking his head.

'What is it, darling?' she asked anxiously. 'Do you think I'm altogether mistaken?'

'No, love, or I wouldn't have wasted Tom's time. One factor we haven't gone into is that Godfrey has been the most fidgety of the lot of them since the murder.'

'He's really upset that Miles didn't tell him about Westmoor's heir being killed,' said Daisy, trying to be fair.

'Why?'

'Why? Because his son ... Oh, I see what you mean. Because if he was going to be earl some day, then even if he was chucked out now, some day Brockdene would actually belong to him. If he'd known, he would never have killed Calloway.'

'Exactly. Though it's all circumstantial, your theory makes more sense than most. Even if Tom finds the shoes, it's not proof, but it's more than enough to tackle Godfrey with some hard questions. The motive has always been the sticking point in this case, and you've provided one that's believable.' Alec stood up. 'I must try and get corroboration from the captain that that's what they quarrelled about.'

'*I* never told you that's what they quarrelled about,' Daisy said virtuously. 'It's pure speculation, which you're always exhorting me to avoid. But all the same, assuming your guess is the same as mine, I bet we're right. What are you going to do with the mitten? You can't leave it here for anyone to pinch.'

'Would you mind dealing with it, love? We don't want the servants speculating about it, so put it in Nana's scullery, out of her reach, while you get hold of some brown paper or whatever they use in the kitchen. Then make a parcel and lock it in one of our suitcases.'

'Ugh! It can go in your suitcase. Right-oh. What about the cami-knickers?'

'Those,' said Alec, 'can go in the dustbin.'

CHAPTER 19

Alec glanced into the library, where Miles was studying some legal papers. 'Do you know where the captain is?' he asked.

Miles jumped up and came towards him, saying in horror, 'You don't believe Uncle Victor murdered Calloway?'

'I don't know who murdered Calloway. I have a few questions for your uncle, that's all.'

'Oh, right-ho. He and my grandfather went outside for a pipe and a cigar, respectively.' He waved at the east-facing window.

Alec found the captain and Tremayne pacing the upper terrace, smoking in silent companionship, their boots crunching on the gravel.

'I'd like a word with you, Captain Norville,' he said.

'By all means,' said the captain guardedly.

Tremayne laid a hand on his arm. 'Victor, do you wish me to act for you?' he said, his face grave.

'It's good of you to offer, sir, but I don't reckon I need a lawyer, not having done anything wrong. Scotland Yard's got the best detectives in the world, and knowing the chief inspector here personally, it's my opinion he won't arrest an innocent man.'

'I'm not about to arrest you,' Alec affirmed. 'Just a question or two.'

'Be careful what you say,' Tremayne warned, 'and call me if you need me.' He went to stand with his back to them, gazing down over the gardens towards Calstock and the peace and quiet of his office.

Victor Norville faced Alec squarely. 'At your service, Fletcher.'

'It was very much in your interest to keep Calloway alive, as long as he was prepared to testify in your mother's favour. However, he was obviously having second thoughts. Did he give you a decision?'

'Why, no. It's what he went off to the chapel for, to pray for guidance, wasn't it?'

'You must have been very anxious to hear what he decided. Anxious enough to go after him.'

'That I did not!' the captain roared. 'And if I had, and he'd told me he'd decided against us, the last thing I'd do would be to kill him before I had a chance to change his mind!'

'Unless you lost your temper.'

Unexpectedly, the captain grinned. 'Yes, I've got a temper. Always have, since I was a child. If I'd had a father, I daresay it'd have been beaten out of me at an early age. As it was, my mother's tears were just as effective. As soon as I was old enough to realize how much I upset her, I stopped lashing out when I lost my temper. I've been in rough parts of the world, and there are times when a fist in the face is the only answer, but I haven't hit anyone in a fit of temper since I bloodied God's nose when I was six.'

Momentarily confused, Alec had a sudden, brief vision

of Blake's *Ancient of Days* being socked on the nose by
Captain Norville because he gave Calloway's prayers the
wrong response. But of course, 'God' was what the captain
irreverently called his brother. He had given Alec the
perfect opening for the questions he really wanted to ask.

'So you and your brother didn't come to blows when
you quarrelled the other day,' he commented dryly. 'What
was that all about?'

'Oh, God was furious that I'd brought Calloway. He's a
selfish, shortsighted fool. He never gave a thought to
Mother's feelings. All he cared about was that he'd have to
leave his precious Brockdene. He's been immured in this
museum too long. So have my mother and my nieces, and
I've a good mind to take them away anyway. I can afford
to keep the lot of them, and so I told him.'

'But all he cared about was that he'd have to leave
Brockdene,' Alec repeated.

'He's obsessed with . . .' The captain's voice trailed off
and he gave Alec a grim look. 'Well, I've said it. I suppose
you'll be asking me to make an official statement and to
give sworn evidence in court against my own brother.'

'Possibly. Will you?'

'Possibly. I'll have to think about it.'

'Just remember, Captain,' Alec said, 'that if we don't
catch Calloway's murderer, everyone in this house will be
regarded with suspicion for the rest of their lives. Think
about that.'

'This cursed house,' the captain muttered as Alec turned
away.

When Alec stepped through the front door into the
entrance hall, Dora Norville was staring with a puzzled

frown at something to his right. Following her gaze, he saw a vast maroon-and-green checked backside protruding from the coat cupboard. Tom moved back on his knees until he was clear of the coats, then turned as he rose to his feet. In one hand was a pair of galoshes.

Seeing Dora, he asked, 'Your husband's, madam?'

'Yes, those are Godfrey's. I wonder why he put them away dirty? I'd better clean them.' She held out her hand.

Tom shook his head. 'Sorry, madam, I can't let you have them just now.'

Alec took a pace forward. Tom turned the galoshes over to present the soles. Rich, dark brown leaf-mould clung in every groove of the patterned soles. Alec wished he had tried harder to find footprints near the chapel.

'Tucked in there right at the back,' said Tom.

Alec took out his handkerchief. 'Wrap them up, Sergeant.'

Fright crept into Dora's eyes. 'W-what . . . ?' She moistened her lips. 'Godfrey never goes into the woods. They must belong to someone else.'

'Who?' Alec asked gently.

'Not Miles! Miles always wears boots.' She glanced beyond Alec and moaned.

Captain Norville and Tremayne had both come in behind Alec. Their feet displayed, respectively, a pair of salt-stained sea-boots and a pair of sturdy countryman's boots.

Tremayne looked at Alec's face and moved to take his daughter's arm. 'Come with me, Dora.'

He led her away unresisting. Her tortured expression hurt Alec. Why did people never consider the effect on

their nearest and dearest when they took it into their heads
to commit murder?

'If it's all right with you, Fletcher,' said the captain
gruffly, 'I'll take Miles for a walk down to the quay.'

Alec nodded. 'Don't be too long though. I'll need
statements.'

The captain opened the library door and stuck his head
into the room. 'Miles, I do believe those wretches have sold
me dried kelp instead of tobacco. It's unsmokable. D'you
want to walk down to the quay with me to have it out with
'em?'

'Yes, I'll come, Uncle Vic. Half a tick.'

Before Miles appeared, Alec hustled Tom through the
glass door and along the passage towards the dining room.
'Daisy went to the kitchen to ask for some wrapping paper
for the mitten,' he said. 'I expect we'll find her in the
puppy's scullery.'

'The second mitten was just where she said, Chief. I've
got it in my pocket. No blood on it that I can see, but the
dog's chewed it up pretty thoroughly.'

'If the children can identify it as one of the items they
retrieved from the woods, it might be useful to be able to
prove that both of the pair were there. Was Miss Norville
in her room when you searched it?'

'No. I think she was in the lav.'

When they reached the scullery, Daisy looked round,
grinning as they fended off Nana's enthusiastic greetings.
'Sorry I've been so long, darling. First I found that Nana
had managed to pull the sack of "clues" off the draining
board and scattered them in bits and pieces all over the
place. Then when I'd cleared up the mess, I discovered I'd

forgotten to ask for string, so I had to go back and get some. I'm on the last knot.' She presented a neat brown-paper parcel. 'I took some extra paper just in case.'

'We have the other mitten and the galoshes,' said Alec, setting down the handkerchief-wrapped bundle on the draining board.

'Darling, your hankie!' she said reproachfully. 'Oh dear, it looks as if it's true, doesn't it? In a way it would be better if it had been the captain. Mrs Norville would have been hurt still, but at least he doesn't have a wife and children.'

'Dora's guessed.'

'Oh, poor thing!' Daisy hesitated. 'I wonder if I ought to go to her.'

'Tremayne is with her.' Alec metaphorically kicked himself as soon as the words were out. He could have got her out of the way without an argument.

'She won't need me, then. What's next? Did you talk to the captain, darling?'

'Yes. The quarrel was caused by Godfrey's objection to the captain's bringing Calloway to Brockdene, because his testimony would lead to the family's eviction.'

'Just as I guessed!' Daisy said triumphantly. 'Are you going to tackle Godfrey next?'

'Yes,' said Alec, 'and you're not coming.'

'But, darling . . .'

'Daisy, this isn't just a matter of interviewing a suspect. Godfrey is almost certainly the murderer, and it seems clear he murdered on impulse, certainly without careful planning. He may be dangerous. Your presence can only hinder us. At this point, you can best help by wrapping the galoshes and the second mitten and stowing them away safely, so that I don't have to waste time on it.'

'Right-oh, Chief,' she sighed, and took up a sheet of brown paper.

Alec and Tom went out into the kitchen court. 'Norville's probably up in the drawing room, as usual,' Alec said, leading the way to the door to the old house. Inside, though, he turned towards the hall, not the stairs.

'Want me to go fetch him, Chief?'

'Not yet. I think we'd better first work out exactly how we're going to tackle him.' He perched on a corner of the long refectory table. 'I want a confession if we can possibly extract one. Any lawyer worth his salt could easily persuade a jury to doubt everything we have so far. It's all . . .'

'Chief!' said Tom warningly.

Alec swung round. Jemima had just come through the archway at the far end of the hall. She stopped at the sight of them, arms akimbo.

'I heard you,' she crowed. 'I told Daddy you took his mittens and galoshes. He's gone away.' She glanced behind her. 'You'll never catch him now!'

Before she finished speaking, Alec was running, Tom on his heels. Jemima, in the doorway, spread her arms wide. Alec picked her up and set her aside. They dashed through the dining room, along the passage, across the hall, and out of the front door.

Felicity stood at the top of the terrace steps, gazing down. Hearing their footsteps, she turned, frowning. 'I say, what's going on? I was coming down the stairs and I saw Daddy putting on his coat and hat, and when I called to him he just waved and went out.'

'Did you see which way he went?' Alec demanded. 'Yes, he's just disappeared into the tunnel. Did you want . . . Oh lord, not Daddy?'

Her last words were addressed to their backs as Alec leapt and Tom trotted down the steps.

Emerging from the tunnel, Alec stopped by the carp pond to scan the valley garden. No sign of their quarry. Evergreen shrubbery hid parts of the maze of paths, and the massive medieval dovecote blocked the view of a great section. He pounded down towards it, Tom right behind him.

As they rounded the dovecote, he saw Derek and Belinda coming up the hill, nearing a nexus where one path went off to the left and another forked to the right. Piper, just beyond them, was looking back over his shoulder.

'Uncle Alec, we saw Mr Norville walking down the other path, that one over there, not the one we're on, and Mr Piper called to him and he started running . . .'

'Thought I'd better see the kiddies home safe, Chief.'

'Quite right, but after him now.'

Piper spun round and ran.

'What's happening, Daddy?' Belinda asked anxiously.

'Go back to the house, you two.' He gestured to the left-hand path. 'Tom, go that way, down to the northern gate, to cut him off in case he doubles back towards Calstock.'

Alec took the right-hand branch, which soon converged again with the path Piper was on. The detective constable in the lead, they sped on. Alec, who had run all the way from the house, began to fall behind.

'There he is, Chief! Just went through the gate. He's going towards the chapel.'

Towards the quay, Alec thought, gasping for breath. Was Norville hoping to steal a boat?

When Piper reached the chapel he stopped and gazed along the track, which here veered sharply to the right, parallel to the river. Alec, puffing along, saw him turn full circle, then try the chapel door.

'Lost him, Ernie?'

'If he's scarpered into the woods, Chief, it'll take a dozen men to roust him out.'

Alec thought aloud. 'He's not the sort to camp out in the woods, especially as it's coming on to rain. He'll make for either Calstock or the quay, though what he's intending to do there I can't imagine. He can't have much cash, if any. It was sheer panic made him run. He may even come straight back to the house. But I'd rather not wait, if possible. Just make sure he's not hiding behind the chapel.'

Piper went back along the side of the little structure, while Alec kept watch on the track. A moment later, Piper called in a queer voice, 'Chief, come and look at this!'

Alec hurried after him, and found him staring down the face of the cliff. The tide had ebbed, exposing a stretch of mud flat where synchronized sandpipers scurried to and fro.

Lying on the mud was a blue-and-grey striped pompom hat.

CHAPTER 20

Not bothering to be neat, Daisy hastily bundled up the galoshes and the well-chewed second mitten in brown paper and string. Alec could keep her from attending his interview with Godfrey Norville, but she was determined to be nearby to hear the result right away. With an apology to Nana for shutting her up alone again, she picked up her three parcels and returned to the east wing to lock the evidence in Alec's suitcase.

The key in her pocket, she made for the stairs. As she passed Mrs Norville's sitting room, she heard the Dowager Viscountess's voice. For a moment she was tempted to knock and go in, to make sure her mother wasn't bullying the old lady, but more urgent matters called for her attention. She pattered down the stairs.

In the entrance hall, Felicity was sitting on the chaise longue. Her back was as stiffly straight as any Victorian lady's, her hands clenched in her lap, a stunned look on her face.

'Daisy, tell me it's not true! I know it has to be one of us if it's not Ceddie, but . . . Daddy?'

'What makes you think . . . ?'

'Oh, don't try to throw dust in my eyes! I saw your

husband and the fat sergeant chasing him down the
garden.'

'The valley garden? Oh dear, I'd better go and see what's
going on.'

As Daisy headed for the front door, Tremayne came
down the stairs. 'Dora wishes me to stand by Godfrey,' he
said. 'Do you know where . . . ?'

'Come along with me,' Daisy advised and hurried on.

She soon outpaced the elderly solicitor. When she
reached the valley garden, an extraordinary sight met her
eyes: not Godfrey at bay, but Derek and Belinda walking
backwards up the slope with little tiny steps.

'What on earth are you two up to?'

'Daddy told us to go back to the house, Mummy. So
we're going, just not very quickly.'

'It's not fair, Aunt Daisy. Whenever something exciting
happens, we get sent away. Uncle Alec and Mr Piper and
Mr Tring all went off chasing Mr Norville, like hare-and-
hounds, like we do at school. I bet I could have caught him.
He's not much of a runner, but he had a good start, and all
because Mr Piper thought he ought to take us back to the
house, as if we were sissies, instead of chasing him.'

'Which way did they go?'

'Towards the chapel, except Uncle Tom. Daddy told him
to go to the other gate.'

'To cut Mr Norville off if he goes that way,' Derek
explained. 'Did he kill Mr Calloway?'

'Only a jury can decide that, darling. Now both of you
stop dawdling. Go straight up to the house and stay there.
Off you go now.'

As soon as she was certain they were obeying, Daisy set

off again, not waiting for Tremayne who had just hove in sight. A sudden breeze rustled the leaves around her and flung a flurry of raindrops. Hatless, her ruffled curls were no protection, but the breeze dropped as quickly as it had arisen. The brief shower was only a warning. To the west dark clouds loomed over the unhappy house.

When Daisy reached the gate, she vacillated. She wanted to see whatever was going on, but if Alec saw her he would undoubtedly send her back to the house, just like the children.

Of course, Norville and his pursuers might be halfway to Brockdene Quay by now, or the station. Listening, she heard nothing but Tremayne's footsteps and laboured breathing, catching up with her. Even the birds were silent, disturbed by all the unwonted activity, except a wood-pecker's tock-tock-tock somewhere in the wood.

'What are you waiting for, Mrs Fletcher? What's happened? The children told me Godfrey ran away and the detectives are after him.'

'I'm afraid so. I don't know what's up just now. We mustn't get in Alec's way.'

'Nonsense, it's my duty to be present if my client is about to be arrested, though I shall endeavour not to obstruct the police in the performance of their duty. Which way did they go?' Tremayne marched through the gate, which had been left open. Stopping in the middle of the path, he glanced up to the left, towards the hairpin bend. 'Ah, here comes Sergeant Tring.'

Joining him, Daisy waved to Tom. If he was coming down, presumably Godfrey had not turned that way. She looked the other way. Nothing to be seen. She set off towards the chapel, keeping to the near side of the track.

On the same side, Alec and Piper were standing just past the chapel, their heads together, facing her. As soon as he caught sight of her, Alec put his finger to his lips, then made a shooing motion. Daisy moved back a few paces around the bend and took cover behind a tree trunk. When Tremayne drew level with her, she hissed so urgently that he joined her, whatever his duty to his client. She put her hand on his arm to detain him.

'I reckon he threw his hat over to make us think he'd drowned,' Alec said loudly, 'so we'd give up the chase, as in the legend of Sir Richard Norville. Pity for him there's nothing but mud down there. He'll be halfway to the quay by now. We'd better hurry.'

'Right, Chief,' said Piper, and set off at an unnaturally heavy run, making as much noise as the crunchy leaves allowed. He only went thirty yards or so, though, then doubled back as quietly as possible through the trees, where the leaves were damp underfoot.

He and Alec converged on the laurels on the far side of the chapel.

Daisy hoped they had guessed right, and that Godfrey was not in fact halfway to the quay. From her position she had a better view than they did down the path because of the way it curved. She glanced that way. Two men were walking up the slope.

Tremayne took a step forward. Daisy clutched his sleeve and held him back as Alec and Piper dived into the thicket.

Godfrey Norville shot out of the bushes like a pea from a pea-shooter and set off at an ungainly gallop towards the quay. After a couple of strides he became aware of the approaching figures. Swinging round, he started back the other way. As Alec and Piper extricated themselves from the bushes and jumped at him, he ducked and dodged them with a surprisingly neat bit of footwork.

In the process he lost his glasses. He ran blindly on, straight into Tom Tring.

'Now, now, sir,' said Tom benevolently, clasping him to his massive green-and-maroon bosom, 'the chief inspector would like a word with you.'

'I have nothing to say!' Godfrey shrilled.

'That's your right, sir, but you'd better come along and tell Mr Fletcher to his face.' Tom's hand encircled Godfrey's wrist as if it were no thicker than a tin whistle. He gently urged his captive down the slope towards the chapel. 'I must warn you that anything you do choose to say will be taken down in writing and may be used in evidence.'

Alec and Piper advanced to meet them, Piper holding the fallen glasses. Daisy realized she was still clutching Tremayne's sleeve, as he emerged from his startlement and took a step forward. She quickly let go, deciding to stay back, out of Alec's line of sight. It was beginning to rain, and if she stood directly under a broad branch she was somewhat sheltered.

'Your glasses, sir,' said Piper, presenting the spectacles to Godfrey with one hand and, with the other, feeling in his own breast pocket for his pencils.

Tom released his wrist to let him put them on. Surrounded by the three detectives, he made no attempt to flee. He and Tremayne both started to speak at the same moment, just as pounding feet announced the arrival of the two men Daisy had seen coming up from the quay: Miles and, several paces behind him, Captain Norville.

'Father, was it you?' Miles cried. 'I can't believe you did it! But why?'

'Because you didn't tell me George Norville was dead!' Godfrey snarled. Miles recoiled. 'If I'd known Brockdene would be mine some day, I wouldn't have had to do away with Calloway. As for you ...!' He turned with a ferocious glare on the captain.

'Say no more, Godfrey!' Tremayne urged in dismay.

His son-in-law paid him no heed. 'Mother's pet had to interfere,' he raved, 'to rake over old coals, to wake sleeping dogs! *He* didn't care if the rest of us were thrown out on our ears. What should he care about Brockdene? If you hadn't brought that cursed clergyman here, he'd be alive today. What else could I do? With a lawyer in the house, I had to kill him quickly, before he could swear an affidavit.'

'Godfrey, as your legal adviser ...'

'All right, all right, I'll shut up. Just remember, it's not my fault, it's Victor's and Miles's!'

Rain was falling in earnest, a steady drizzle which had probably set in for days. Godfrey Norville, now hand-cuffed and apathetic, and Tom Tring would be soaked through long before they reached the police station in Calstock. Tremayne went with them, despairing but determined to do his duty to the last. The captain – muttering, 'Exactly what I'd hoped to avoid!' – had just set off, leading a stunned Miles back towards the house.

'I'm going to have to go straight to Calstock, love,' Alec told Daisy. His dark hair was still crisp, shedding water like a duck's back. 'With the Cornish force in disarray, my authority may be needed to get the necessary formalities under way.'

Daisy pushed aside one of the bedraggled locks plastered to her face. 'I doubt you'd be a welcome guest just now, darling,' she said wryly. 'I only hope they don't throw me out of the house, along with Mother and the children.'

Alec laughed. 'I'd back your mother against any number of Norvilles. You'll manage. I'll have to come back tomorrow to get statements signed, but you should have left by then. Piper will come up to the house with you now to collect the evidence. You did put the parcels away safe, didn't you?'

'Of course! I hope you have an electric torch, Mr Piper. It's going to be dark by the time you get to Calstock.'

The dark clouds had brought on an early twilight. Alec frowned and said, 'I don't want you – or the evidence – falling into the river, Ernie. Perhaps you'd better see if the housekeeper will give you a bed.'

'I'll doss with the puppy if need be, Chief,' said Piper with a grin.

He politely turned his back while Daisy and Alec bade each other a fond farewell. Then he and Daisy went through the gate, and Alec strode off after Tom Tring.

'You'd better put my coat over your head, Mrs Fletcher.'

'Too late, I'm sodden,' said Daisy, shivering as a cold stream flowed down her spine. 'Let's hurry.'

She was glad of Ernie's hand at her elbow at slippery spots in the path. They came to the tunnel and she led the way through. At the far end, she saw that they had nearly caught up with the captain and Miles, who were just starting up the steps. Miles's shoulders drooped and every step seemed to cost him a huge effort.

Daisy and Piper in their turn started up the steps, Piper staying one below Daisy in case she slipped on the slick stone. She was about to set foot safely on the top terrace when, with a piercing yell, Jemima charged out from the shelter of the shrubbery growing along the house wall.

'It's all your fault!' she howled. In her hands was a halberd, and it pointed unwaveringly at Daisy.

With a scream, Daisy recoiled. Piper caught her. They teetered together between the steep fall behind and the vicious spike bearing down upon them.

Then Miles was there, crashing into his frenzied sister and bringing her to the ground. The captain was there, reaching for Daisy's flailing hand, grasping her wrist, anchoring her and Piper with his solid weight.

Daisy found her balance. Piper's arms relaxed their painful grip on her waist and the captain released her wrist. Suddenly weak at the knees, she sat down on the top step. 'Gosh,' she gasped, rubbing her wrist, 'I thought I was well and truly sunk!'

The captain bent over her. 'You're not hurt, Mrs Fletcher?'

'No, not at all, thanks to you. And thanks to . . .'

Ernie Piper had leapt past her. Swivelling, she saw him kneeling beside Miles, who was writhing on the ground. His sister knelt on his other side.

'Miles, I didn't mean to hurt you,' Jemima wept. 'Oh, Miles! Is he going to die?'

'I think he's just winded, no thanks to you, miss! And you're under arrest for . . .'

'Oh, no, Ernie! Mr Piper.' Daisy sprang to her feet. 'You mustn't arrest her. She's been having a perfectly dreadful time and she's utterly miserable and she's simply not thinking straight.'

'She's not in her right mind,' said Captain Norville grimly. 'I take it kindly of you, Mrs Fletcher, to stand up for my niece, and I'd rather not see her arrested, but I've seen enough of her tricks. You can be sure I'll be sending her to some sort of sanatorium for treatment of nervous troubles, and if they can cure her, she'll be going to a school that'll teach her to behave herself.'

'What's going on?' Felicity arrived on the scene, with Cedric in tow. 'We heard screams. Oh hell, Miles!'

'I'm . . . all . . . right . . . Flick. Just . . .'

'Winded, miss,' Piper pronounced again. 'I reckon Miss Jemima's elbow or knee must've caught Mr Miles in just the wrong spot.'

'She attacked Mrs Fletcher,' the captain explained, gesturing at the halberd which lay abandoned on the gravel, no doubt already beginning to rust under the persistent rain. 'Take her to her mother, will you, Felicity? Come on, Miles, old fellow. This young 'tec and I will give you a hand.'

'Let me, sir!' exclaimed Cedric.

So the captain helped Daisy up, and the sorry procession wended its dripping way into the house.

Felicity marched Jemima straight upstairs. The girl was sullen and whining, apparently oblivious of the gravity of her offence. All Daisy wanted was dry clothes and a cup of hot tea, but first she had to thank her rescuers. The captain and Miles met her gratitude with heartfelt apologies for Jemima's behaviour. However, Daisy was glad to note that Miles seemed to have been roused from his state of shock by the need for action. In spite of having been violently deprived of breath, he looked better than he had since his father's arrest.

In answer to Daisy's thanks, Piper said, 'My pleasure, Mrs Fletcher, but it wasn't no more than my duty. Now if you could hand over them parcels, ma'am, I'll go beg a place to doss and write up my notes.'

'Right-oh, come along then.' Turning towards the stairs, she heard Cedric begin an explanation of his presence. Much as she would have liked to hear, she was too wet and chilled to linger. As she reached the landing, she said to Piper, 'Would you like to borrow my typewriter for your notes?'

'That'd be a great help, ma'am.'

Felicity came along the passage towards them. 'Daisy, I'm so awfully sorry. Mother's putting Jemima to bed with a powder, for all the good that will do. Actually, if you don't mind my saying so, it's a bit of a blessing in disguise or a silver lining or something like that. Jemima's going for you has given Mother something to think about other than Daddy.'

'I'm awfully sorry about your father,' Daisy said.

'Thank you.' Felicity shrugged with a wry moue. 'Of course it's an awful shock, but . . . Well, there's nothing to be done about it now, is there? One has to carry on. I told Cedric Daddy was about to be arrested, and he wants to marry me anyway.'

'Have you accepted him this time?'

'Oh yes! Anything to get away from Brockdene.'

'Unless you'd prefer to go to London to study fashion. I'm sure your uncle would . . .'

'Daisy!' The Dowager Viscountess swept out of Mrs Norville's sitting room. Felicity ducked down the staircase and Piper effaced himself, though he was in any case invisible to her ladyship.

'What's up, Mother? You look like the cat that stole the cream.'

'Don't be vulgar, Daisy. I've been sitting with Mrs Norville. I consider her very hard done by. Since that wretched parson's death, there is no way to prove she was Albert Norville's wife. I have a great deal to tell Eva.'

'And the world! Lady Eva won't keep it to herself. Be careful you don't find yourself in contempt of court, if that's the right phrase. Godfrey was just arrested for murdering "that wretched parson".'

'Is that what all the fuss has been about? Then the poor woman needs my sympathy more than ever and, I daresay, my encouragement to keep a stiff upper lip. I must persuade her it is her duty to go down to tea just as if her son were not a criminal. After all, she is very nearly British.' Lady Dalrymple turned back towards the sitting room, pausing for a Parthian shot: 'One's children are so often unsatisfactory. I trust you mean to change before tea, Daisy?'

EPILOGUE

Daisy decided to forgo a hot bath in favour of a hot cup of tea. She met Captain Norville on the landing.

'My mother's already gone down,' he said. 'I expect you're good and ready for your tea.'

'More than ready,' Daisy agreed.

He followed her down the stairs to the hall. As he stepped ahead to open the library door for her, Belinda and Derek burst through the door from the passage to the dining room and the old house.

'Is it teatime, Aunt Daisy? I'm starving!'

'We've found something, Mummy.'

'Not a treasure map,' Derek sighed.

'We were searching for secret drawers in the old desk and we found this.' Belinda held out a folded piece of yellowing paper. 'Derek was going to put it back, because it's not a treasure map, but I thought it might be important.'

Daisy opened the paper. It was headed 'Certificate of Marriage', and below, amidst the official wording, were the names of the Honourable Albert Norville and Susannah Prasad, followed by Calloway's signature.

'Yes, darling, it's important!' Daisy handed the

certificate to the captain. 'I believe this belongs to your mother, Captain. You're the best person to give it to her.'

The captain took one look and turned white beneath his tan. Then his face bloomed ruddily and tears started to his eyes. 'Thank you,' he choked out, and rushed into the library.

'Is he happy, Mummy?' Belinda asked anxiously.

'Very happy, darling,' said Daisy, hugging her. *So much for Mother's grousing*, she thought. *My child is altogether satisfactory.*